Praise for Tricia T. LaRochelle

A slow-burn romance wrapped in memory, mystery, and emotional depth.
—Prairies Book Review

Let Me Go is a little emotional, very sweet, and most importantly, a book you won't be able to put down . . . because I know I couldn't.
—Book Blogger - Reading in the Red Room

You'll love the gorgeous prose, the skillful exploration of the emotional turmoil in the characters, and the psychological underpinnings of this gripping romance.
—Readers' Favorite

Let Me Go

A Gripping Second-Chance Contemporary Romance

Tricia T. LaRochelle

 Formatted with Vellum

I dedicate this book to my childhood dog, Laddie, and to Lily, my sister's beautiful German Shepherd, who are both now in doggie heaven.

I also dedicate this book to our grandpups, Maggie and Sadie, plus, the newest member of our family, Daisy.

Daisy and Sadie didn't make it into this story, but something tells me they will be back to star in one of my future books.

The last portion of my dedication honors the many pet owners out there. May all of your furry friends live long and healthy lives.

Let Me Go

Chapter One

JC

It was Saturday afternoon. I should have been studying the market index, more importantly, an order imbalance that could create volatility. Instead, I was driving down this sorry excuse for a road, stirring up dirt and creating a small dust storm in my SUV's wake. I grumbled to myself. A strip of grass ran down the middle, sweeping the undercarriage of my Lincoln Navigator as rocks popped beneath my feet like popcorn.

Dirt roads? Really, Gramps? And not just any dirt road; this one came with ruts so deep a car with a lower wheelbase heed its warning or lose its muffler due to the driver's ignorance.

At least I hadn't driven my 911 up here, which remained untouched beneath Charles Street in its own private parking space. I hoped Gramps had a hose, allowing me to clean the black paint, not a smart color for dust and dirt. Yeah, it wasn't *that* big of a deal, but I grew up near Boston. I now lived in Manhattan. Paved roads. This wasn't my neck of the woods.

Why the hell my grandpa had decided to purchase a vacation home located in the back corner of *Nowheresville*, Vermont, I would never know. (Buckingham, to be precise.) And why he had left me *said house* in his will—one I had never seen—remained another mystery. The sale of his home in rural Massachusetts, along with the rest of his belongings, would be split up between my father, my uncle Kenny, and the rest of the family. The Vermont place was all mine. Not that I wanted it. Gramps knew I was a city guy. Plant me in the middle of Wall Street, I was right at home.

Since he'd bought the place two years ago, he'd asked me to visit him several times. *It's the closest thing to heaven any man or woman could ever find on earth, JC.*

I was too busy. *Always too busy.*

I wasn't thrilled with myself for being so neglectful. My stiff neck from the drive started to throb, and my shoulders felt more like rocks. "Why did you have to up and die on me, Gramps?" I always assumed we'd have time. My throat ached from the loss of him, my eyes trying to produce tears. It wasn't happening. I hadn't cried much in over a decade. Not around people that was. When Gramps died, I let a few tears fall, but only when I was alone. I wasn't one to wallow. *No use in crying over spilled milk* my father would often say to me or my sisters when he didn't have the energy to deal with our drama. Mom wasn't much better. Dragging me and my siblings through many explosive years of an unhealthy marriage—eventually divorcing—my parents drudged up enough drama of their own. We didn't walk on eggshells; we avoided land mines.

Gramps would never be so callous. If we were upset, he'd want to hear about it. *No problem is so big we can't work it out. Together.* I never quite understood how my father could grow up around a man so compassionate yet lack any of those qualities for himself. Even my uncle Kenny emulated Gramps.

Then again, I wasn't one to talk. When it came to matters

of the heart, tying myself down to one woman was about as appealing to me as shooting a nail gun through each eye socket. Maybe if I hadn't spent so much time away from my grandfather, I'd be a better person too. I'd value relationships, not run from them. I was a chip off the old block.

A slow ache formed in my temples from wearing my sunglasses too long. It was a new pair, one that didn't quite fit my head. Given the high price tag, I'd have to have my assistant, Jen, return them. And I had another pair in my suitcase. All good. I pulled this pair off, placing them in the sunglass holder above my head, and flipped the visor down to shield my tired eyes. The Vermont sky seemed to be cooperating, boasting big puffy clouds today, some with darker edges, promising rain at some point, the sun barely making an appearance. Less glare. I'd been checking the weather in this region for weeks, long before this trip began, so I knew rain was not only common in Vermont but expected. That and cooler temperatures. The gauge on my dash flashed sixty-six degrees in the middle of June, no less. It was eighty-three when I had left Manhattan at 11:00 a.m. That was five-and-a-half hours ago.

I'd left clogged roads, hordes of human traffic, and an abundance of air pollution behind me. Noise, noise, noise. Planes flew overhead. Helicopters headed for one bigwig's launch pad or private hangar. But as I crossed the border into Vermont, it was like someone had flipped a switch. Vehicles ran sparse on the interstate, something I definitely wasn't accustomed to witnessing. The frenetic pace of NYC fueled and motivated me. What I'd draw from Vermont was yet to be determined, other than complete and utter boredom.

The farther I drove down this goat path to parts unknown, the more the weeds, bushes, and other vegetation encroached, some slapping against my side mirror. *And* I was down to one lane now. If another car came in the other direction, I'd have nowhere to go except backward, which would take some skill since the last pull-off was at least a mile back. I'd drive into the field if the need required. I had the wheels for it.

A large rock punched the undercarriage of my vehicle as annoyance ground my teeth together. I rubbed the back of my neck. "Jesus, Gramps. Where the hell is this place?" I wasn't sure how much more of a beating I'd allow this car to endure. I changed my satellite station from Bloomberg and cranked up some Red Hot Chili Peppers to placate my mood. But then I lost the station, my annoyance toward this place growing stronger.

If anyone else had asked this of me . . . And then I reminded myself who I was doing this for. *Gramps.* The man who had taught me to fish, work hard for what I wanted, and so much more. The man who always wore a smile, even when I *knew* his heart was wounded.

It's only a car, dipshit.

I could buy a fleet of SUVs. I'd made a killing in the stock market. Cars were replaceable. Gramps wasn't. He'd not only requested in his will that I visit this remote location of his, but he'd also required one month out of me. If I wanted to sell the place after that, I had his blessing. He'd spelled it all out in his will. After everything Gramps had done for me, I owed him this. The stock market *and* my sex life could wait. I just wished I'd made the trip sooner. When he was here to enjoy it with me. Especially when there hadn't been a whole lot for the man to celebrate over the past few years.

Losing Gram three-and-a-half years ago was the worst for him. We could all see it. The lost look in his eyes, searching for the woman who told him on a daily basis to take his boots off at the door and wash up for dinner. The woman who watched over him with her scrutinizing yet loving gaze. She fussed at

Gramps more than she complimented him, but somehow, they worked. Sixty-five years together. To this day, I had never seen two people more suited for each other. Or more devoted. Certainly not *my* parents, who presented my sisters and me with a very different reality.

At twenty-six, Alyssa was working on her second divorce, her latest relationship lasting eight months. *No thanks.* Grace, my other younger sister, who lived with a woman named Carrie, came out five years ago. So far, the two seemed to cohabitate just fine. "Don't get married," I'd told her, "and keep your assets separate."

Gramps and Gram were the exception. (My other set of grandparents had died many years ago. *Health issues and alcoholism.* I never really knew them.)

Every now and then, Gramps caught Gram staring at him with a twinkle in her eyes or a slight tilt to her grin. For him, it was a signal. Her guard was down. That was when he'd grab her around the waist and dance throughout their two-hundred-year-old farmhouse, most of the time without music, until she snapped out of her lovesick haze and shoved him away. "You old fool," she'd say, shaking her head and returning to whatever chore had required her attention.

During my visits, I'd witnessed it multiple times, a hand over my mouth to hide my smirk from her view. I knew if she spotted me, it would break their bubble all too soon. Coming from a house where a man and woman couldn't exist within the same room for more than half an hour before all hell broke loose, this was a refreshing change. I never wanted those tender moments between my grandparents to end.

And neither did Gramps, who would wink at my five-, six-, or twelve-year-old self (depending upon the year) and declare with the utmost certainty, "Poor thing, she can't keep her hands off me." Then he'd wave me over, saying with gusto,

"Come on, JC, let's feed the chickens" . . . or "clean out the barn" . . . or "fix the fence line along that lower pasture" . . . or my favorite, "let's take the johnboat out and see if the fish are bitin'."

JC. Short for Jacob Callum Sullivan. The middle name, Callum, came from my father, bestowed by his father (Gramps). The nickname JC derived from Gramps too. He started calling me that when I was little. Not sure why, other than it seemed to fit the initials of my full name. And since Gramps had thought of it, I prided myself on the moniker. There wasn't a lot that man could do to upset me. Except for making me drive down this fucking road!

As much as I loved him, this place was *not* what *I* would call heaven. (You blink, and you'd miss the entire town of Buckingham.) And was I on top of a mountain? The hill I climbed to get here would certainly suggest as much. Not this road, though, which remained flat.

Heaven would be my luxury apartment back in New York with a doorman and everything one could possibly need located within a few blocks. And that included the women. Some of the most beautiful in the world. The streets of New York had every restaurant, nightclub, theater, and shop known to man. They also acquired a certain smell, a pungent odor that rose up from the grates—old food, urine, and a few other unsavory ingredients. That had to be why the manure odor breaching the cabin of my SUV hadn't bothered me so much. (I'd passed a farm on the way here.) Although, I did roll the window down to clear the air.

One more mile.

A house appeared in the distance. Not Gramps's place, according to my GPS, which indicated I still had another three-quarters of a mile yet to go. "Someone else lives out here?" All I could imagine was a survivalist or a recluse. Who else would want to be so far away from civilization? Not me, that was for sure. One month, and I'd be out of here.

As my vehicle ventured closer, a mailbox peeked out from the overgrown vegetation, alone and sad on the side of the road, the black metal covered in rust, the post leaning unhealthily to one side. And next to it, a driveway cut through a field of tall grass, intermixed with an abundance of wildflowers (maybe they were weeds), all the way up to what appeared to be a small cottage, painted white with faded green shutters and a small red barn as its loyal companion on the right.

Large maple and oak trees surrounded all but the front, their leaves reaching far above a roof covered in streaks of black mold. I eased my foot off the gas pedal and focused my gaze. Chipped paint, cockeyed shutters, and a not-so-white picket fence sloping over like an old man about to collapse told me the place was probably abandoned. That made more sense. *Maybe the owner got sick of this shitty road and hightailed it out of here.*

I continued on my way until another house turned up, one with natural wood siding and a wraparound porch. It even had Adirondack chairs positioned just so, allowing any occupants a direct view of the driveway, more specifically, who might be approaching, which today was me. I could almost see Gramps sitting in one of them, waving me over. *I can't believe my eyes. My favorite grandson has finally come to visit.* If only. And to be fair, I was his only grandson (Uncle Kenny never had kids), but that was unimportant. When Gramps called me his favorite, I savored the moment.

I parked my SUV next to a familiar old brown pickup truck —a wide cream-colored stripe running down its sides—and climbed out.

How'd it get here? Uncle Kenny must've helped him. Or maybe it was Dad, but I suspected not.

I ran my hand along the hood. Gramps kept his GMC in

good condition. The tires wore thick treads, and the paint, although faded by decades of wear, showed few rust spots. That was Gramps all the way. He didn't have a lot, but what he did have, he took care of. He could also fix just about anything from lawn mowers to transmissions, putting most mechanics to shame. He'd taught me a thing or two as well, not that I'd ever needed such knowledge. What I wanted or needed, I hired or paid for, and that *didn't* include the women.

If the keys to the GMC were inside the house, I'd have to take it out for a spin. I just wished Gramps were here to go with me. I shook the thought from my mind. As my dad would say, *spilled milk.*

Before I turned fifteen and hormones controlled my life, I was my grandfather's sidekick every summer and holiday vacation my parents would allow. He had also paid me to help with chores, teaching me the value of a dollar and the power that came with having a nest egg, albeit a modest one at that age.

After I turned fifteen, I was a ghost in his world. In my defense, who knew Summer Davis was going to blossom and steal my heart at the beginning of my sophomore year? Once my romance with Summer Davis ended, Ericka Miller caught my eye. And so on. I kept myself busy with a new love interest every year. (I also worked part-time, played on the high school football team, and kept up with my studies.)

Not much had changed in the fifteen years since. I was a busy man with little time for love. The women in my life weren't all one-, two-, or three-night stands. Some stuck around a bit longer than that. Just not long enough to leave a toothbrush. Did it bother me that my thirty-first birthday would land on July 15th, the day I was planning to leave here—the end of my probation, so to speak? Not a chance. I'd give this time in the wilderness a fair shake, and then I'd return home. As I'd reasoned with myself on multiple occasions, it was the least I could do.

I climbed out of my SUV and stretched my legs, my lower back tight from lack of movement. Rolling my shoulders back, I appreciated the ability to loosen the knots. I'd have to go for a run later to finish the job, probably on the road I had just traversed.

A small garage stood before me. Or it could have been used as a shed. It wasn't large enough for a full-size vehicle (maybe a compact). The natural siding matched the house, with a single garage door offering entry but closed at the moment.

As the sounds of birds chirping all around me reached my ears, a few crickets making their own music from the tall grass, I walked around the shed/garage, peering through the window of a side door. There wasn't much to see aside from a few gardening tools leaning against the interior walls, a snow shovel —even though I was pretty sure Gramps only came here in the summertime—a small tool bench with tools either hanging on a pegboard above or stacked and organized on the bench itself.

In one corner, a lawn mower sat next to a Weedwacker, ready to tackle a lawn no one had touched in months. None of that gave me pause. The johnboat, sitting atop a trailer and centering the room, however, sent goose bumps up my arm. Evie (named after Grams) was my grandfather's pride and joy. This was a surprise. I hadn't realized he'd brought Evie here with him. That explained the need for the truck.

The boat is mine now?

Once again, my throat ached, the image of Gramps and my younger self whiling away our afternoons in Massachusetts with a fishing pole in our hands, a tackle box opened and primed, and the conversation as easy as a summer's breeze. I had enough money to purchase a speed boat, a yacht, and a series of jet skis, yet this rinky-dink boat with wooden oars and a patchwork of nicks and dents was more than I could ever ask for. Before my month was over, I'd have to find a water source and take the old girl out. And then, I'd make arrangements to bring Evie home and store her somewhere safe. My homage to the memories.

I returned to my SUV, where I grabbed a manila envelope from the back seat containing the house keys and a few other housing instructions (how the heat worked and how to turn on the water, etc.). They accompanied my copy of the will.

Inside that same packet of information, a white business-sized envelope remained sealed. Two letters scrolled across the front in my grandfather's hand: *JC*. His personal message to me. He'd given my father and my younger sisters one as well. They had opened theirs. I hadn't found the strength.

I should have been there for Gramps, especially after Gram had died. I should have taken a leave of absence from work. Money wasn't an issue for me anymore. Hell, I could have done my job in NYC, Massachusetts, or the Sahara Desert if I so chose. Stocks didn't care where you lived. All I needed was a laptop and Wi-Fi.

So why didn't you, asshole? Sometimes, I wanted nothing more than to kick the shit out of my inner voice. My conscience. That was a question I didn't have to answer—not for myself—or anyone else.

Leaving the packet (and the sealed envelope) on the back seat, I took the keys and approached the front porch, a scatter of dried leaves and small sticks left behind by the army of maple and oak trees crowding out the sun. A lone paper birch branched out by the porch steps, contributing to the constant shade cast over the house.

Thump, thump. I stepped onto the porch, admiring the somewhat fresh coat of stain protecting the floor, the railing, and the exposed wood beams. Gramps probably did it last year before his heart had decided to call it quits during the winter. The man always had a project up until his eighty-eighth year.

A solid-looking door, the color of a red barn and adorned with a brass handle, awaited my key, which I inserted a moment later, its hinges squeaking from the same problem my lower back had suffered. Inactivity. Gramps had been gone for just over six months now, and this place hadn't been touched since, so the musty smell permeating from the interior was no surprise as I stepped over the threshold.

The essence of Gramps came at me in all directions, from the antique hall tree standing proudly next to the door, its hooks still holding his favorite fishing hat and the thick canvas jacket he wore when the season required, to the dark-brown work boots lined up underneath the bench, ready for almost any occasion. Even his fishing pole had made the trip here, as well as his faded green, dented-up old tackle box loaded with hooks, extra fishing line, sinkers, bobbers, artificial lures, and a small knife—if memory served—all of it banked against the wall, right next to a small net for catching the things his trusty pole couldn't. A wicker basket took up the far end of the bench. A Father's Day gift from Grams many years ago. The basket was supposed to be for the day's winnings, but somehow, it never quite went that way, probably since my grandmother had always stocked it with plenty of sandwiches, cookies, and fruit to keep our bellies full when the hours demanded more of us. (Gramps used an old bucket for the fish.)

It was all there, a little dusty but in good condition, ready for that day when their owner would return—a day that would never come. I took a few more steps, the pine scent of the tongue-and-groove paneling overriding the stale odor, which was much more agreeable to my senses. Gramps had paneled a few rooms of his farmhouse in the same wood, a light-colored stain enhancing the natural shade, blemishes and all. *The knots are what make it special*, he'd say, *tells you it's real.*

Gramps loved nature in all its forms, evident from his place in Massachusetts, where he lived with Gram for over six decades, so it was no surprise he'd brought that same indispensable quality here.

With the ghost of Gram fussing at me, I removed my loafers and set them by the bench before I stepped off the slate entryway in my bare feet. A modest-sized living room opened before me with a large picture glass window looming ahead and two double-hung windows anchoring each end.

A small gallery of Norman Rockwell treasures embellished the walls. Two in-wall recessed bookcases (also pine) flanked a wood fireplace on my right, the faint scent of ash nearly indistinguishable. My grandfather's literary collection consisted of books about farming, fishing, and anything pertaining to nature, a few manuals for farm equipment mechanics, and even some classic fiction from authors such as Ernest Hemingway and Dickens.

Several framed photos were woven throughout his library, which included pictures of my siblings and me sliding down one of the hills on his property during the winter and swimming at a nearby lake in the summer. In a five-by-seven frame, I posed, grin from ear to ear, in my Boy Scout uniform, along with an eight-by-ten of me in my graduation gown, taken many years later. My sisters were also there in all their glory. He'd even brought a photo of all of us standing at the top of Mount Washington in New Hampshire. Both of my parents had tagged along on that trip—a rare occurrence. I could almost feel the wind, fierce and unrelenting, against my cheeks.

Facing the fireplace and a small TV on a lower shelf of the bookcase—a TV remote standing by—a soft leather easy chair still bore the indentations of my grandfather's body, a dark-brown metal TV stand positioned right by its side for what I assumed were some lonely meals. Angled toward the window, a small couch of the same leather provided a resting place for one of my grandmother's hand-knit afghans. I was pretty sure she had also made the braided multicolored rug that centered the room. Two small antique-looking end tables, each one hoisting brass lamps with an off-white shade, completed the furnishings.

Above the wood mantel, a portrait of my grandparents on their wedding day smiled down at me. Shot in black-and-white, an antique car in the background, a small white church off to the left, the couple looked so young and innocent, the sprouts of who they used to be before life and age had taken them away from this earth. The house was a trove of sentimental treasures. Why had he left it all to *me*?

I checked out the kitchen, which came equipped with old, white appliances—the kind that lasted longer than their warranty—and a small table with four chairs offering a place to enjoy meals for my month-long stay. A quick survey told me I also had two bedrooms, a laundry room, and an office, which surprised me. The tight space included a desk and an office chair for me to conduct business. That was, if I could get Internet.

I lugged my bags inside and plunked them down in the living room, causing dust particles to float, enhanced by rays of sunshine draping into the room. Not a suitable environment for anyone with allergies, which I suffered from every now and then.

The picture window didn't open, but the two small double-hung windows on each end did. I made my way there, ready to offer the room a breath of fresh air. However, before I could open the window, the view in front of me caused my jaw to drop. As it turned out, I wouldn't need to find a water source for a day of fishing after all. Gramps had one right behind his house. The trees out front had done a good job of shrouding my view from this magnificent spectacle. A large wooden deck reached out toward a small lake, or maybe it was a pond, I wasn't sure. A mountain range surrounded the lake, its arms reaching around all but one side, the side facing my cottage. Tall, robust evergreens, maples, oaks, and many other species of vegetation took root along the range, the lush greenery resembling fur coating the back of a large beast.

A door with a small window stood between the living room and the country-style kitchen, where I flipped the deadbolt and stepped out into a Vermont postcard. Birds continued their songs from the trees, frogs croaking from the water's edge. I lifted my face toward the sun as it peered out from behind a thick cloud. This *was* paradise. A few steps down, a rock path led to a small dock. The grass bordering the lake and the house was in dire need of a trim. With ticks in mind, I decided on my first landscaping task, after unpacking and turning on the utilities, of course. The packet said I had power and water. It didn't mention Internet, something else I had to address.

Before long, I was standing on the dock, water lapping up against its supports. The scent of windswept balsam, coupled with a miasma of fresh algae, stirred memories of Gramps and me spending our afternoons together. We'd have to get up early (like 4:00 a.m. early) to get the chores done first. Our reward: a couple of hours at the reservoir near his Massachusetts home. The warmth on my cheeks quickly spread to my heart as I reminisced about him teaching me how to hook bait and later, how to *unhook* a fish. But it was those moments when the fish weren't biting and the wind had stilled that I cherished the most. That was when Gramps would share his innermost thoughts.

"Nothing important in life comes without hard work, JC. It's the hard work that makes the reward all the better." He smiled. "It took me a full year to get Gram to go on a date with me. And let me tell ya *that* took some work."

"Really?" I said, thinking I would have given up much sooner. I was thirteen at the time. My view of girls was in flux—they weren't totally on my radar yet; but they were approaching fast.

"You betcha. She worked at the local library every summer. I knew this because I had seen her at Zayre's Department Store one day. She was picking out a scarf with a friend. When she glanced over at me with those amber eyes and beautiful full lips, long brown hair, I thought my heart was going to stop right there and then. I was smitten. It was love at first sight for me. I found out she worked at the local library through my friend Freddie, whose father was the postmaster in town. Anyhoo, I wasn't much of a reader back then, but I had to meet her, so I checked out a book every Sunday." His smile turned bashful. "I'll admit, I'd picked titles I thought would impress her—Hemingway, Dickens, Orwell." He shrugged. "Before long, Evie started asking me what I thought about each book. Well, imagine if I hadn't read them? I would have been dead in the water. Your gram didn't put up with any hogwash or lyin' either.' If I wasn't bein' genuine, she'd have called me out on it, and that would have been the end of it." He stared down at his pole, his voice soft as a rose petal. "We talked about Hemingway in particular, one of her favorite authors. And that was all fine and good. But she still hadn't agreed to go on a date with me. So, the next time she asked me about one of the books I was returning, I told her I would be more than happy to explore that topic with her . . . but over dinner." He chuckled. "I thought I was gonna sweat through my Sunday best that day."

Hearing about Gram in this manner had me riveted. "What did she say?"

Gramps rubbed his hand across his jawline, his eyes reflective. "Well, she thought about it, and then she said, as she tapped my book with her finger, 'Tell me one quote from this book, and I will go out with you.'"

A smirk spread across his face. "The book in question happened to be *The Old Man and the Sea*. I knew right then and there that if I didn't come up with what she had asked for, she would never have looked at me twice again." He paused, his bushy eyebrows raised. "Well, as I said, I wasn't much for books back then, and I will admit, I may have skimmed a page or two, but I also knew that I was facing, hands-down, one of the most important moments of my life." He paused again, probably for effect. The man loved to tell a tale.

"Well, don't leave me hanging, Gramps. What happened?"

"Oh, I tossed the words from that famous book around in my noggin until one quote finally came up for air. And so I said, 'But man is not made for defeat . . . A man can be destroyed but not defeated.'"

My eyes must've been the size of saucers as I awaited the rest. "Did it work?"

Gramps took his fishing hat off and whacked me over the shoulder with it. "You already know the answer to that one, JC."

He was right—sixty-five years of marriage said so. What Gramps spoke of was a simpler life, a time when you wanted something and went after it. No bullshit. You didn't play head games, and you didn't push yourself, only to get ahead of the next guy. It wasn't about that. It was about integrity. And Gramps had more integrity than anyone I had ever met, me included.

Why hadn't I come to see him? Why had I let my world become so complicated? I was in a constant power struggle to make more money and show my colleagues who they were dealing with. Hell, even my relationships were a competition of sorts. *Never let them see your underbelly.* If you did, you'd be yesterday's news.

All at once, an odd sound brought my mind back to the present. My skin prickled as though someone were watching me. I turned around and there, standing on the dock with me and blocking my path to the house, stood a large German shepherd, its eyes zeroed in on me.

Chapter Two

JC

This is not good.

How had I managed to put myself in danger and so soon? I'd only been here for less than an hour. Yes, I was a city boy, but I'd been in the country enough to appreciate its power and its danger, especially when faced with raw elements. Well, a raw element was staring me down at that moment. My heart ramped up, my body starting to sweat. *Has the temperature just climbed twenty degrees?*

I didn't have a dog growing up, but Gramps did. He had a few over the years that helped him usher cattle or provide companionship. The dog I remembered most was called Rex, a black Labrador retriever. Rex would lie underneath the table at breakfast, lunch, and dinner, ready to snatch any crumbs, a few I donated on purpose to his cause.

I'd always had a healthy fear of animals. And this shepherd had the eyes of a predator, the body of one too. At its full height, I guessed its ears reached close to three feet. If the animal came at me, I'd shove it into the lake. Readying myself, I imagined the scene playing out in my mind. That should give me all the time I needed to reach the house.

But it didn't come at me. It just stood there on all fours, staring me down. What was this? An alpha-male situation?

"Get out of here, dog!" I moved my legs apart and broadened my shoulders. This mutt wasn't going to take me down. "I said, go!" I thrust my hands out, trying to appear threatening and maybe even a tad crazy. "Go. Get!"

If I were on the path leading to the house, I'd grab a rock. But I wasn't. I was on a dock with nothing but weathered wood and water all around me.

The staring contest continued. No growling came from its mouth. Its hazel eyes were cold and calculated, trained to pounce or hunt or whatever the fuck this dog did for fun.

It took a couple of modest steps toward me, and I gulped.

How much danger am I in right now? German shepherds were used as police dogs. They were smart *and* fierce. My hands started to shake, and my breath became more like rapid and shallow pants. Maybe I was the one who should jump into the lake. Guessing the water was probably about seventy degrees, it would be a very cold bath. And that would piss me off. As intimidated as this dog made me, it was also quite beautiful. A patchwork of auburn-and-beige fur grew thick over most of its body, a large swath of black in the shape of a saddle across its back. Its ears pitched forward in a curious sort of way.

Don't be such a pussy. You just benched 320 pounds at the gym last week. *That's right, you mangy mutt, you're looking at six feet, two inches and 225 pounds of muscle. If anyone is going down here, it will be you!* I clenched my fists, ready to fight the dog off if I had to. Was it feral? Its coat grew full, no burdocks embedded or bald spots from malnutrition, things that a dog in the wild would encounter. It also didn't have a collar. And this was a pretty remote area. *Other than that rundown house on my way here.*

The shepherd took another step forward. Still, no growling. No teeth bared. Whenever Gramps's dog, Rex, had spotted a woodchuck in his lower pasture—the one bordering the woods—there was always a lot of growling and chasing, until the poor rodent would perish or dive into a burrow with lightning speed, barely escaping certain death.

This dog wasn't doing anything, other than staring. And then it lowered its head and approached. It was right in front of me now. What did it want? The dog looked up at me. Was it trying to make friends? Nah, that couldn't be true. Somehow, my hand lowered to its head and began stroking its fur. The dog seemed to settle into my gesture, and soon it was sitting at my feet.

"Well, what have we got here? You're not a predator at all, are you? You're just a big baby. Lookin' for some love." How my voice had taken on the tone meant for an infant was beyond me. When the dog lay on its side, I discovered it was a she. Before long, I was sitting with her, stroking her fur, enjoying that she was letting me. "Where'd you come from, girl?" I looked around for an owner who *had* to be looking for her—no one in sight. No sound of broken branches or footfalls reached my ears either. When she put her paw on my arm, my heart swelled. "Whatcha need, girl? I wish I had some food for you. But I gotta go to the store first." I scratched around her jaw line and then her rib area, finally settling behind her ears.

The dog relaxed against me, and my affection grew. Who knew German shepherds could be so calm and loving?

My stomach rumbled, and I realized the time. More specifically, it was getting past dinner time. I hadn't eaten lunch, so I was starving. I was too focused on making it here and putting the drive behind me. "Okay, girl." I moved to get up, the dog springing to her feet. "I don't have any food that I'm aware of, but I'm sure I can get you some water." I stroked the fur on her head. "Would you like that, girl? Are you thirsty?" There came that cooing voice of mine, the one I didn't know existed. "Let's go see what Gramps has inside." The dog followed, and I took comfort in having her near. I couldn't explain why. I'd only known her for five minutes.

My younger sisters had cats growing up, and one bunny that got out of its cage and ran away. (At least, that was what my mother had told us.) I wasn't that interested in owning pets. I enjoyed the animals on Gramps's farm, though.

I rationalized my affection for this dog because I was alone for the first time in a very long while. This would take some getting used to.

When I crossed the border into Vermont, I advised Jen to route all my business calls through her. "I need to set myself up before I can start doing business. I'm not even sure if there is Wi-Fi where I'm going. Field all my calls until further notice." I'd worked around the clock for weeks to make sure all was well in client-world. But that wouldn't guarantee a smooth transition. The market had a mind of its own.

"Not a problem, JC. It's as good as handled" was her response.

With a degree from UVA and a mind smart as a whip—pages of stellar references—Jen hadn't come cheap, but she was the best damn assistant I had ever had. The woman could almost finish my sentences for me. And she was always willing to learn. If she weren't fifteen years older, married, and happy to stay that way, I might have tried to whisk her away.

Truth be told, I grew to appreciate that I *didn't* harbor those types of feelings for her. Less complicated. I'd made that mistake with an assistant before . . . or two. Sex and business didn't mix well, not in my world. When you started fucking the help, it wouldn't be long before they wanted more. And I wasn't the kind of person who had more to give. Sex. I could do that . . . and do it well, but that was as far as my tender side would grant. I'd been called a selfish bastard, a cold-hearted prick, and a man who only wanted one thing from women. I was happy to allow it. Don't get me wrong. I respected the fairer sex. But once the actual *sex* started, I knew our time would be limited. And I didn't pretend I was any different. I was honest. I was generous in the bedroom (or wherever else we screwed the brains out of each other), but I was a closed book. I saw what bad marriages did to people and families. And I had no interest in driving off that cliff.

Distracting me from my thoughts, the dog nudged my hand with her nose, leaving a wet spot on my palm. "Okay, girl. Let's get you something to drink."

The same stone path that led me to the dock peeled off, snaking around the left side of the house to what I assumed was the parking area out front. I needed that packet of information about the house, which I retrieved a moment later, my furry friend close at hand.

Returning to the house, I read the necessary instructions before I successfully found the breaker box near that cramped laundry room off the kitchen, which also housed the water heater. I flipped the switch for power. *One down.* The water turn-off valve resided under the front deck. Before I turned on the valve for the hot water heater next, I made my way to the kitchen to ensure I did have water. Gramps had taught me that a hot water heater without incoming water could easily burn out the compressor. The faucet sputtered and spat air a few times—all of which made the dog jolt—before water flowed into the sink.

"Well, look at that?" I said with pride. "We have water, my friend."

The dog tilted her head this way and that. I was sure she was wondering what the hell I was talking about.

"Sorry, girl. But my cell phone is showing me zero bars right now, so you are all I've got at the moment."

More head tilts.

In a high cupboard, the cabinetry made of a similar pine as the rest of the house, I located a medium-sized plastic bowl in faded orange. I filled it with water and placed it on the ceramic-tiled floor next to an empty trash can near the entrance to the laundry room.

With the sound of a dog's tongue lapping up water, I remembered another thing Gramps had taught me about water heaters. Many years ago, I had helped him replace the one in his farmhouse. Check for leaks. No one had used this one for several months, so I gave it a full inspection. My motivation? Avoiding the need to locate a licensed plumber out here.

No leaks.

Now that I had power, water, and the promise of *hot* water at some point (I was sure I would have at least one cold shower in my future), I opened the white fridge with rounded edges, which looked like it weighed about as much as a small car, and turned that on as well. With only one door, I wondered where I'd freeze my food, until I found a small compartment with its own metal door hidden inside. I wouldn't be buying a lot of frozen dinners.

Good thing I liked my scotch neat. I might not have brought any food to speak of, but I had brought my scotch. And plenty of it.

The shepherd continued to hydrate while I surveyed the cupboards. Apple cider vinegar, salt, a sealed jar of sugar, a bag of brown rice, and a few jars of dried beans were all that remained of my grandfather's stock. Not enough to live by. I'd have to find a store.

I unpacked the rest of my SUV, wishing this dog could help. My stomach was hollow by now, and I was starting to get rather *hangry* about it.

"Okay, girl, you want to go for a ride?" I bent down as I said those words with enthusiasm, and then I clasped my hands together. Yeah, I was already losing it. Two hours in the boondocks, and I was channeling Gram. She might have been a tad stiff with Gramps, but when it came to us kids, she was a marshmallow. And she made the best chocolate birthday cake with chocolate frosting I had ever tasted.

I locked up and approached Gramps's pickup truck. Time to take it for a spin. I opened the passenger side door for GS (short for German shepherd) to hop inside. *JC and GS.* What a pair. Something about this dog made me feel less alone and even safer. I almost wished she could stay with me, but I knew there had to be an owner somewhere looking for her. And I could see why. This dog was a sweetheart.

I turned the key in the ignition, trying not to cringe. Would it start? Or explode? After several attempts, the engine turned over and grumbled to life.

I exhaled. *Phew.*

And then my gaze found the gas gauge. Full tank. Gramps never let a tank get below half. "Isn't this our lucky day?" I ruffled GS's fur atop her head.

The truck bumped along the same goat path I had come from, GS watching out the window as trees and nature blurred past. "You want some fresh air?" I leaned across the bench seat and manually rolled her window down, allowing GS to poke her head out and take in the sights and smells. More dust stirred up in my tailwind, the faint scent of manure coming from somewhere nearby. Probably the farm I had passed.

As I approached the dilapidated cottage, GS got antsy, first with whining noises and then with a full-on bark, her body almost pacing the passenger seat. "Is that your home, girl?" I stopped by the mailbox, contemplating whether or not to venture up the driveway.

As though performing for Best in Show, GS flew out the truck window and up the driveway without even a glance back. I was surprised her large body could fit through the window without injury. But it had.

And that was that. My loyal companion had left me.

I chose not to drive up to the house and let the owner know where his dog had been. The condition of the house *alone* gave me pause.

How had I become such a snob? I was used to luxury and convenience. This was anything but. And I didn't need some backwoods asshole accusing me of trying to steal his dog.

The truck forged forward, and I was on my way. When I finally hit the main road, my cell phone picked up two bars. I pulled over and used the Internet to pinpoint Rolling Creek Grocery. *Interesting name.* And then I called Jen to see if there was anything I needed to know.

"Are you really going to stay out there an entire month?" she asked, skeptical.

I released a heavy breath. "Not sure. But I'm gonna try. I've already touched base with all my clients, but make sure they know if they need anything urgent, I'll take care of it. I'm sure I can find a place to conduct business around here. Shouldn't be too hard." Backwoods or not, we were still in the twenty-first century.

"Oookay. Don't be a stranger for too long. You know how this market can get. You're in one day, and then you're out!"

"You and I spent the last month getting everything in order, Jen. I've got my book with me if anything comes up *and* three laptops."

Her tone softened. "I want you to know, I think what

you're doing is great." She inhaled and then exhaled. "What I'm trying to say is, I know how much your grandfather meant to you. You're only thirty years old, and you've worked your tail off over the past several years. You're too young to work yourself into the ground. Take this time. If I need help and can't reach you, I'll call on Zach."

My college roommate. I'd also worked with Zach since we'd both started at the firm, and I interned with him years before that. Unlike most of the sharks on Wall Street, who would sell you down the river faster than you could count to ten, I trusted Zach. And I'd helped him out of a few financial jams, once saving him millions. He owed me. *And* he was my best friend.

"Yes, use Zach for whatever you need. I've already given him a heads-up. Listen, I need to find a grocery store before they close up for the night, and I am forced to starve."

"Got it. Good luck." Jen disconnected the call.

* * *

As it turned out, Rolling Creek Grocery was open. The prices here were insane. Then again, I was used to NYC, one of the world's most expensive places to live. I couldn't remember the last time I had shopped for myself, food or otherwise. Jen and my housekeeper, Monica, handled all of that shit. I didn't burden myself with those details.

As I munched on a prepared chicken salad sandwich, which was actually pretty tasty, a small selection of Vermont brews caught my eye, and I loaded them into my cart. I also found some decent-looking white and red wine, a few bags of tortilla chips, and some salsa made in Vermont. I was the only patron at the moment, which someone seemed to notice.

"Are you new in town? Or vacationing?"

I turned toward an elderly woman with short gray hair and

kind blue eyes, a pair of reading glasses hanging from a small chain around her neck. She wore a mauve-colored apron with a faded grape pattern, a short-sleeved white shirt with stripes, and a skirt that was more of a cocoa color underneath. The shoes on her feet carried a thick tread, supporting legs with a slight bow to them and ankles that were borderline swollen.

"Uh, I'm staying at Callum Sullivan's place." I thought for a moment. "Off Route 2. It's down an old dirt road about ten miles from here."

Concentration labored across her brow, leaving a crease in its wake. "Whose place?"

I cleared my throat. "Uh, Callum. I can't remember the name of the road." And then a light bulb went off. "Old Oak Road."

Her eyes showing clarity, she nodded. "Oh, yes. Callum. Of course. We haven't seen him in a while. I hope he's well. He usually comes around in April if I remember correctly."

This was getting uncomfortable, mainly because I had to tell the woman why he hadn't returned. My grip tightened on the handle of my grocery cart. "He died late last year, actually." My gaze fell to the black-and-white tiled floor, which was faded and covered in black streaks (probably from grocery carts).

The woman's hand went to her mouth, alarm widening her eyes. "Oh, I'm sorry to hear that." She glanced toward the front. "Hey, Raymond, did you just hear that? Callum died."

Dressed in a loose-fitted button-down shirt with a dated pattern and a pair of baggy cotton pants in dark green—a black belt harnessed around his thick waist—a man of about the same age approached down one of four aisles in the store. "What was that you said, Martha?" He walked slowly, his shoulders hunched by age and probably a lifetime of hard work, a musty smell accompanying him.

Placing her hands into the pockets of her apron, Martha

raised her voice an octave. "Callum! You know, he lived over on Old Oak Road. He bought the Richardson place a few years back."

Raymond rubbed the gray scruff growing rampant along his jawline. "Oh, yeah." Under bushy gray eyebrows and a thick crop of tousled hair of the same color on his head, he narrowed his slate-colored eyes. "Hasn't been around for a time."

"Yes, this young man here just said he died late last year." Martha was practically yelling now.

That caused Raymond's eyes to expand. "Dead, you say? And who is *this* fella?" His gaze found me next. "You one of them city folk, plannin' to buy the place, fix 'er up, and sell it? We get a lot of that in this state. Not so much around here, though." He continued to size me up. "More of a Chittenden County sort of thing."

I shook my head. "I'm not sure what I plan to do." He was right about my intentions, but given the lack of amenity in his voice, I wasn't about to volunteer anything.

Martha took a step toward me, removing her hands from her pockets. "Where are my manners? I'm Martha, and this here is Raymond. We own this store. Been here forty-five years."

"Nice to meet you. I'm JC, Callum's grandson."

As though the sun had just come out, the vibe in the room warmed, Martha's and Raymond's faces relaxing into smiles. Martha took hold of my hand and shook it, her fingers bent from arthritis, the scent of something medicinal wafting off her skin. "Well, it's nice to meet ya. Callum spoke so highly of his grandkids. Showed us pictures of 'em a time or two." She let go of my hand and appraised me with her eyes. "You've sure grown some." She touched her lips. "If memory serves, you have two sisters?"

I nodded. "I do. Alyssa and Grace."

"They with you?" She slid her gaze to the front of the store as though Alyssa and Grace were out waiting in the car. "I believe they came for a short visit last summer. Didn't stay long."

"No, ma'am. They weren't able to come on this trip." I knew my sisters had been here last year. They tried to get me to join them. I was too busy. *Always too busy.*

Martha scanned the contents of my grocery cart. "How long you stayin'?"

"About a month or so."

"On your own?" Her gaze surveyed my cart some more.

I nodded. "Yes, ma'am."

"How much you willin' to spend? What's your budget?"

I made a face. "No budget. Money isn't an issue."

She flipped her hand in the air and grabbed the side of my cart, wiggling it out of my grasp. Then she practically bumped me out of the way. "Well, this won't do. Won't do at all. You need meat, fruit, and vegetables, soup, and sandwiches. And you don't even have any eggs!" She shooed me away with her hand. "I'll get you the necessities. You and Raymond can wait up front."

Used to people taking care of these types of *details*, I was relieved. I had no idea what essentials I'd need. I offered another "Yes, ma'am" and followed Raymond toward the front.

* * *

With my passenger seat and truck bed loaded down with bags of everything from toilet paper to Brunswick stew, still warm from Martha's kitchen—a dozen farm fresh eggs from her coop out back—I headed home. I had one more stop to make. As it turned out, the dilapidated house near mine didn't belong to a survivalist or a lost member of ZZ Top as I had imagined. It belonged to a woman named Iris.

As Raymond was ringing up my order, Martha approached. "Our employee, Becky, has a couple of days off. She's a gem. A real sweet woman. Retired mostly, but she works for us to keep a few bucks in her wallet and to visit with our customers. We've been friends for years. She's good with people, you know?" Martha paused as though to gather her thoughts. "Anyway, Becky is out at Pebble Beach at the state park with her grand-kids. No way to reach her. No cell service, either. The problem is we have an order that we deliver every two weeks, and she's the one who normally does it. We could wait until Becky comes back the day after tomorrow, but the place is actually near where you're staying. On your way home." Her cheeks flushed for a moment, and I wasn't sure why. "Would you be a dear and drop off our customer's order for her? It goes to a woman named Iris."

"Where exactly does she live? I don't know my way around here."

"She lives off Old Oak Road, right near where you're stayin'."

Hard to argue with that logic. She was *literally* on my way, not a figure of speech. I had assumed a man lived out there. Not sure why. It was just what came to mind. Maybe the German shepherd had made me think that.

"Sure, I can do that."

Raymond's bushy brow rose and fell as he rang up my groceries. *Bleep, bleep.* "Before he leaves, you better let this young man know what he's getting himself into, Martha."

That didn't sound good.

Martha began helping me bag up my groceries to clear the catch basin for more, her mind working on something.

At that moment, two young men came bursting through the

door, both with skinny bodies and soiled baseball caps on their heads, the scent of fresh hay wafting off their tattered T-shirts and jeans. Judging by the peach fuzz *trying* to grow along their jawlines and bodies that hadn't filled out much, my guess was they were in their mid-to-late teens.

"Hey, Nana, got any fresh sandwiches out back?" The teen with dirty-blond hair that grew far past his cap rubbed his stomach as if to make his point.

Yup, mid-to-late teens for sure.

"This is our grandson, Billy, and his friend, Warren." Martha gazed over at them both. "You boys go clean up. There are plenty of sandwiches in the kitchen." She spoke with authority in a no-messing-around sort of way.

Both boys removed their hats, their expressions more somber. "Yes, ma'am."

The kid with black hair and shifty eyes, named Warren, grabbed a banana from a basket near the register. "I'm starvin'." He gave me a once-over. "You some kind of movie star or stunt man or somethin'? You're stacked. What do ya bench?" His voice came out muffled, the banana puffing out his right cheek.

Now both of them were eyeing me.

Over three hundred pounds, so don't mess with me. "I can't remember. Not a movie star, just a city boy. Up here for a visit."

Martha then introduced me, offering my connection to Callum and his house. By now, Raymond was finishing up on the register, and Martha still hadn't told me what she wanted to say.

I cleared my throat. "Nice to meet you both." It wasn't nice. Something about these two struck me as typical country boys who were easily drawn into mischief.

Billy and Warren tipped their chins at me but didn't say much.

An awkward silence descended around us.

I focused back on Martha. "You were saying about Iris? And as I said, I don't mind dropping off her groceries. I know right where she lives."

Martha got all sheepish again. "Well, Iris is . . ." Her voice trailed off.

Iris is what? A troll? An alien? This was getting weird.

Her hesitation seemed to give Billy fodder to speak up. "Iris? *That* crazy loon? Complete nutcase if you ask me. I heard she thinks she's a witch, conjuring spells and shit."

"You got that right." Warren high-fived his friend. "A whack job for sure. What that fruitcake does in her shack of a house keeps me up at night."

Billy shoved Warren. "You pussy. Scared of Iris, are ya?" A grin spread wide across his young face.

Warren shoved him back, his cheeks flushed pink. "I ain't scared of no one, especially no freak."

Christ, the both of them looked about as dumb as a box of rocks. Using words like *witch* and *freak*, I felt as though I'd walked onto the set of a 1960s movie.

Martha rushed over to the young men, her hands flailing. "Now, hush! Both of you! I don't recall asking for your two cents. Go get something to eat, and I don't want to hear another word, or I'll let your father know how disrespectful you're being, Billy!"

Well, that shut them up. Spines now straight, both boys rushed away, "Sorry, Nana" under Billy's breath.

Crazier than a loon, huh? *Complete nutcase. Freak.* Were they being accurate or just immature? I envisioned the witch from the fairytale *Hansel and Gretel.*

Where was I? Derry, Maine? Stephen King wrote books about places like this.

Raymond finished ringing up the last of the groceries, which I then paid for. Thankfully, they took credit cards. The bags required two carts. Raymond steered one while I steered the other outside. With no customers left in the store, Martha went to check on the boys.

"We appreciate you dropping off Iris's order. She's not all that bad. Just don't stick around too long, is all. She don't take well to visitors." When we reached my truck, Raymond lent a tad more. "She's been known to get a bit *unfriendly*, you see. Used to yell at Becky from the living room window to drop off the groceries and go. A few years back, our grandson, Billy, delivered her order with Warren, and she pointed a gun out the window. Had my son's friend's son with them at the time. Nothin' came of it. All bark and no bite."

"She sounds *interesting*. Are you sure I'll be safe?" The gun portion of his story had me rethinking this venture.

"You leave these bags"—Raymond gestured toward the two he'd just hoisted into the back of the truck—"by her front steps and skedaddle out of there, and you'll be just fine. Becky grew to like her." He scratched his forehead. "Course, Becky likes most people."

"I met her dog. A German shepherd earlier. I *think* it was her dog. She came right up onto my dock."

Raymond nodded once as he stood back watching me finish loading the truck. "That would be Lily. Iris has another rough collie mix named Laddie and a little cockapoo named Maggie. According to Becky, all rescues. *I* haven't seen Iris in the better part of ten years." Sadness clouded his eyes. "That's her family. And you don't want to mess with Iris's family." He patted the back of my truck with a thud. "You all set, son?"

"I believe I am. Thank Martha for picking out all the things I'd need. I really appreciate it." She even included some home-made soups and a container of chicken salad that she sold in her small prepared-food section. Since the chicken salad was delicious, I suspected everything else would be as well. This was wholesome food, made from simple ingredients and love. The kind Gram used to make.

Raymond backed up a few steps, ready to turn and walk away. "The woman can't help but mother everyone she sees. She'll probably have you over for dinner before too long." He flipped his hand. "You take care now. And good luck." He disappeared into the store as a Jeep pulled into the parking lot, carrying a middle-aged man and woman.

Now, as my truck drew closer to Old Oak Road, I wondered if my offer to help them with Iris's delivery was really the best idea. According to Raymond, she was not violent. *All bark and no bite. Unfriendly.* Then again, he also claimed he hadn't seen her in ten years. And she *had* pulled a gun on his grandson for no apparent reason. Not good. If the woman shot at me, I'd have no way to defend myself. And as I made the turn onto this dreaded dirt road, and the bars on my phone abandoned me, I had to wonder. *What the hell have I gotten myself into?*

Chapter Three

JC

An old woman lived alone with her three dogs. *Did they say old, or did I imagine that part?* Either way, it all sounded so cliché. Once again, a fairy-tale-type character came to mind, warts and gray stringy hair . . . *a flying broom.* I was definitely stretching it. No way any of that could be true.

Those boys certainly knew about Iris. As immature as they were, they *had* encountered her wrath in the past. Hopefully, she'd mellowed since then. Even Raymond's worker, Becky, liked her. However strange or reclusive this woman was, she had to be accustomed to regular grocery orders. That said something. I'd drive up, drop off the goods, and get the fuck out of there.

The last time I took this road, it seemed to go on forever. Not anymore. Within no time, Iris's house sprang up in the distance.

My brain went into overdrive. What if something happened to me? Who would know? My phone showed zero bars. I chastised myself again for putting myself in this position.

Damn idiot. It's not your job to deliver the fucking groceries. Between the wine, beer, and ample amounts of pretty much everything Martha and Raymond had to offer, I'd dropped several hundred dollars there. Wasn't that enough?

That same sad-looking mailbox appeared, the driveway, a moment later. I took a deep breath and slowed the truck's engine. "If you're watching Gramps *and* Gram, I could sure use your protection right now. I didn't come all the way here to get killed on my first day."

With that, I turned into the drive, the wheels of the truck kicking up small stones and dirt. Perspiration gathered under my arms and on my forehead and neck. Shit, even my hands were sweating. But I kept going. I said I'd do this, and I was committed to getting the job done. If they ever asked me a favor of this nature again, I had my answer cocked and ready to fire: *Hell no!*

The truck's wheels ground to a stop, the cottage now in full view. Gramps hadn't touched his place in months, and it showed in the tall grass growing rampant around the yard and in the layers of dust collecting within the interior. The cottage before me didn't look much better. Someone had mowed portions of the lawn, but most grew untamed, intermixed with several species of wildflowers, reaching all the way to the road. It was pretty in a natural sort of way. Abundant with daisies and purple *somethings*. I wasn't much of a flower guy.

A flagstone path forked in two directions, one leading toward the front porch, where a wooden swing hung from the ceiling, and the other, circling around to the back of the house and out of view. The white paint and faded green shutters appeared older and more in need of a facelift than they had from the road. The barn equally so. But the windows were intact, and to my surprise, window boxes with actual flowers did their best to dress up the place, some of those same wildflowers from the field behind me offering a splash of color. A floral wreath hung from the front door, which appeared solid enough. No dents or awkward leanings. No vehicles cluttered up the small parking area, either. Did she keep a car inside the barn? Then again, if she needed groceries delivered, maybe she was too old or too feeble to drive.

I took a breath. "Here goes." I opened the truck door, cursing the squeaks brought on by old metal, something I hadn't paid much attention to before now. I latched it with careful hands and then hoisted Iris's grocery order from the bed of the pickup. I expected to hear barking. Three dogs. A lot of barking. But the only noise reaching my ears came from the birds and the crickets. A few mosquitoes hummed around my head. The front step of her covered porch was warped. Or maybe it was broken. That same swing watched over the place.

I set both bags on the deck, just above the steps and next to the railing, hoping that would provide just enough stability to keep them upright until the crazy lady had found them. No point in leaving a note. If she saw the note, she'd see the bags.

I turned to leave and found Lily standing there in front of my truck, watching me with the same expression she wore on my dock. Only this time, I wasn't afraid. Not of her. "Hey, Lily." I loved that I now knew her name.

She bounded over.

I scratched behind her ears. "So, this is your home, girl?" I squatted down to see her better.

Lily just stood there, allowing my hands to pet and pamper her. What was it about this dog? I already liked her. I almost wanted to take her home with me. Being alone wasn't something I had been accustomed to. Not lately. Lily would be a great companion. And if I suspected someone was abusing her, I would have done just that. But this dog was friendly, not guarded, and well cared for, judging by her disposition and her thick coat of fur. Abused dogs were mean. Lily was anything but.

"Maybe you can come see me again. Would you like that, girl?" I scrubbed around her ears some more and down her neck, which she seemed to like.

And then I realized I'd overstayed my welcome. What business did I have hanging around this place? I was far from *skedaddling* as Raymond had instructed.

I rose. "Okay, Lily. I've gotta go. You come over anytime you want to, okay? I gotcha some dog treats." *Do you expect her to answer you?*

I took a step toward my truck when the sound of a screen door opening and shutting came from the back of the house. My curiosity got the better of me, and I inched my way toward the front corner of the porch, assuring myself my truck was only a quick jaunt away. And I *was* prepared to run. Like the wind if I had to.

I just wanted to see what this . . . *person* looked like. All I could imagine was someone you'd buy tickets to see at a county fair. *Step right up, ladies and gentlemen, we've got a crazy loon for you.*

And then, she appeared, Lily running to her side.

"Hey, Miss Lily. You been wandering around again?" The woman was not old at all. She was probably younger than I was. She bent over and brushed her fingers through Lily's fur, and I found myself envious of the animal's care. "You wanna help me get these clothes down?" Various articles of clothing floated back and forth in the breeze.

Funny, she spoke to Lily as though she were another person. Just like I had. The late-day sun had paused just above the horizon, blanketing the scene before me in a sort of spotlight, only much softer than that, shades of pink, orange, and violet contributing to the spectrum.

I lost my breath or my ability to hold a single thought inside my head. Iris was . . . *beautiful?* No radiant. Honestly, there were no words. Was my mouth hanging open? I had no fucking idea. She stood sideways while pulling clothes off her line as the sunset filtered through her white cotton sundress, silhouetting a lean body and full breasts. A gentle breeze ran its fingers through her long locks of golden curls that cascaded all the way to her tiny waist. I wanted to touch it, then felt weird for wanting such a thing.

I dated beautiful women, some of them models. And if I were being honest, I wasn't so bad myself, or so I'd been told. But the vision of what stood before me spoke to somewhere deep within my soul, a place unknown and uncertain. I couldn't fathom what I was feeling in that moment. All I knew was that whatever it was, I was rendered helpless by its power.

Her profile highlighted a delicate nose that formed a small button at its tip. Her chin and neck were sculpted as if from sandstone, a golden tan glowing from her flawless skin. With long and delicate fingers, she unhooked a shirt and placed it in the wicker basket next to her feet. Her movements were graceful, almost rhythmic, and I couldn't for the life of me stop watching her. My feet remained rooted to the earth as my chest filled with something indescribable. My skin tingled. If I were still breathing, I was unaware.

The only thing I couldn't see were her eyes. It didn't matter, they could be jet black and she'd still be the most gorgeous creature I had ever seen.

Some sort of scuttle reached my ears from within the house, followed by a sharp series of high-pitched barking noises. That had to be the cockapoo. What did Raymond say its name was? *Manny?* I couldn't remember. I averted my eyes to the front door where the noise originated.

More yelping came from within the house. When my

gaze slid back to the clothesline, the woman had vanished, her basket sitting on the grass where she had left it half full. In what seemed like a split second later, Iris emerged, bursting through the front door, a small strawberry-blond-colored pup scampering at her feet, a larger dog with black fur on its back and red along its belly, keeping pace right behind her. Lily had returned, bringing up the rear.

"Who are you? And what do you want?"

This would have been a fine question to answer under normal circumstances, but not when the question had come from a woman holding a shotgun aimed at my head. A large hat pulled low shaded her face completely, those long, curly locks stuffed inside. And she wore a long trench-looking coat that covered her sleek body from shoulder to ankle. If I had seen *this* woman first, I would have understood what everyone was talking about.

"I said, 'What do you want?' And you have about five seconds to answer before I put a slug in your chest." She cocked the gun, the little pup hopping up and down, ear-piercing barks flying from its little mouth.

Jesus!

I finally found my voice, which came out all wimpy and rattled. "I-I'm s-so sorry. I was j-just, uh, dropping off your grocery order. You know, from Rolling Creek Grocery?"

Even though I still couldn't see her eyes, I was sure they were narrowed and focused on her target.

"They were shorthanded, so I offered to deliver it." That wasn't really true, but it was too late to correct myself. My chest was on fire, every pore in my body spewing sweat. If my heart pounded any harder, it would crack a rib. "I'm staying at Callum's place." I swallowed hard, hoping to moisten my parched throat. "He used to live just down the road." As I spoke, I made motions with my hands, even turning my body toward Gramps's place.

Like a statue, Iris stood there. She reminded me of a lioness assessing her prey. Was she going to shoot me now?

"Your dog, Lily, came to see me earlier." I chuckled. *Why?* I had no idea. *Jitters?* "Great dog."

The little pup kept her constant yipping. She was cute but loud. *Maggie?* That was her name. That meant the bigger black dog, some sort of mixed rough collie breed, had to be Laddie.

No words came from Iris. She just stood there watching me, her gun poised. The woman didn't so much as twitch, and that gun *had* to be heavy.

"Well, okay, then. I guess I'll be heading home. You have yourself a pleasant evening." Barely aware of my own words, I was in the truck on my way down the driveway before my brain had time to process what had just happened. My hands didn't stop shaking until I was safely in *my* driveway, where I sat for who knew how long. "What the fuck was that all about?"

As I unpacked all my bags and stocked the cupboards and fridge, my heart continued to pump at twice its normal rate. Even my fricking knees felt weak—too much lactic acid.

I pulled a box of dusters out of the bag. Martha must've known this place needed a serious cleaning. And given the adrenaline still coursing through my veins, I couldn't think of a better time to take care of it.

In a large closet by the front door, a vacuum, along with a mop and bucket, gave me just what I needed to get this place in shape. Gramps also had a full selection of cleaning supplies in the laundry room off the kitchen. No dusters, though, so Martha had set me up right. *Has she been here before?*

And so, I went to work, the image of Iris staring me down with a shotgun in her hands, pushing me forward. A braver soul would have confronted her about it. Or maybe that would have been a dumber soul. Would she have shot me? If she had, she would have found her ass in prison, where they *don't* take dogs.

The more I vacuumed, mopped, dusted, and straightened, the angrier I became. As I was throwing a set of sheets and towels of various sizes into the washer, my anger bubbled to the surface. "Who the fuck does she think she is?" I let out a flabbergasted breath. "This isn't the Wild West, and she's no Wyatt Earp. Pulling a gun on me like that." I stomped around the house like a gorilla. The housework helped, but I needed something else to take the edge off. I contemplated going for a run. Would she see me out there and then assume I was stalking her? *Great.* Now I felt trapped *and* angry. I was in one of the most remote places in the Northeast Kingdom, and I felt less safe than I had back in the city. Well, that just pissed me off even more.

I sucked down a few beers, and all that did was make me tired.

A shower, a fresh set of sheets on the bed, and I was ready to say sayonara to my first day in the wilderness. "What were you thinking, Gramps?" Tomorrow, I'd find a place to conduct business. And maybe a gym if one existed. What I really needed was a day on the greens. Golfing had a way of centering me. They had to have golf courses around here. *Right?*

With that thought in mind, I was off to bed and asleep before my head hit the pillow.

Iris stood before me, a summer sun hovering in the background, offering a perfect view of an incredible body barely covered by a sheer white dress. One of her spaghetti straps fell gently down her arm. She didn't adjust it. Instead, she let it hang there with the possibility of the rest of her dress following.

On graceful bare feet, Iris strolled toward me through the grass. Her full breasts swayed slightly as she drew near, her nipples poking through the tender fabric, aware of my presence.

Ringlets of hair, the color of corn silk, danced in the breeze as the light filtered through a small gap between legs that went on forever. All I wanted to do was touch and taste her sweet center. Bring her joy.

She brought her long, elegant fingers to her lips, her chin lowering in a bashful sort of way. And then she looked up at me. Those eyes, two sapphires, iridescent and vulnerable, had me riveted. I lost my breath. Whatever Iris wanted from me, I would happily give to her. She could have my soul if she so chose.

I not only wanted this woman. I needed her. My skin prickled for her touch, my heart aching to grab her and never let go. She was in front of me now, her lips parting, and her gaze flirting. She wanted me to kiss her. And I wanted nothing more than to oblige.

My fingers brushed along her collarbone of their own volition, her skin like satin beneath my touch. I slid my hand around the nape of her neck, trying not to lose myself entirely. She was a work of art, this woman, every inch of her pure perfection. And yet, her eyes up close revealed an inner struggle, insecurity, and heartache. Tears glistened. If only I could mend her sorrows.

With our eyes locked, I moved my lips closer, the distance between us causing me physical pain. I could almost taste her . . . feel her breath as light as a feather against my face. Our kiss would change everything. We would be one. And I was close . . . so close.

I bolted up in bed, a cold sweat soaking my sheets, my dick about ready to explode. The morning sun showered my bedroom in diffused light, a crow cawing outside my window.

"What in the hell?" I was panting. It was as if I had just run five miles in thirty minutes. With a hand to my forehead, I sat there calming my lungs and heart rate. Then I grabbed my cell, unhooked the charger, and noticed the time: 7:00 a.m. Still no bars.

I swung my feet over the side of the bed and hopped into a warm shower where I quickly took care of my throbbing dick. It didn't take much, considering Iris was still permeating my thoughts. Christ, I could almost taste her lips on my tongue. A couple of tugs and it was over. Only that didn't seem to satiate my sexual appetite. The dream was so damn real.

Was this place already making me nuts? One day here and I was fantasizing about a woman who had proven she had more than a few screws loose. "Yes, she's beautiful, but come on, dude. You've got plenty of women to think about. Models for fuck's sake." Hell, I could have called any one of them and had them here in a day or two. Phone sex was also at my disposal. I didn't need to think about women who were certifiable. I shook my head as I dried off and got dressed. Then threw my sodden sheets back into the washer. It was almost like having a fever dream, yet I wasn't sick.

I shook my head, disgusted.

As I made myself an egg and fried up some bacon to fill the empty cavern in my gut, I had to wonder what this woman's deal was. Those teenage boys in Rolling Creek Grocery, Billy and Warren, saw Iris as a complete nutcase. Never once had they mentioned what she looked like. Did they *know* what she looked like? Raymond had admitted he hadn't seen her in the better part of ten years. Any boy past adolescence would have *had* to have noticed. Crazy or not, the woman was a walking wet dream.

Then again, the babe I witnessed taking her clothes down off the line and the woman who burst through her front door holding a shotgun were two completely different characters. I recalled how gentle her voice was when she spoke to Lily, how her hands stroked her fur. But as she stared down at me from her front porch, all that tenderness had transformed into something ugly.

Don't overthink this. It was just a dream. And even though the image of her remained seared into my brain, she'd be gone from my thoughts soon enough. I'd had sex dreams before. All the time. This wasn't any different. Except for one very obvious point: it wasn't a sex dream. We'd never even touched. That was a new one for me.

Time to release this energy by doing yard work.

Chapter Four

Iris

The sound of Maggie scratching on the door roused my mind. I was still sitting at the kitchen table, my shotgun lying across its surface, and my head rested on my arms. I wiped sleep from my eyes, trying to keep them open. My back was stiff. My mind foggy. I arched, hoping to loosen the muscles clamping down on my lower back. And then Maggie started to whine.

"I'm so sorry, Maggie." I slid my chair back, stood, and rushed to the back door to let her, Lily, and Laddie out to do their business. Poor things, they must have been dying by now. Once darkness had fallen around us, I kept them inside, worried that strange man would return. Who was he? And why was he delivering my groceries? I was used to Becky.

Then I remembered he had said Martha and Raymond were shorthanded. "If that was true, why didn't they call me?" I had found my burner phone on the table last night and flipped it open. No calls. This wasn't our agreement. Becky brought the groceries. Period. I was used to her.

I thought my heart was going to stop when I was standing

at the clothesline with Lily, and I suddenly heard Maggie yipping. She only did that when she heard something. And then I saw him, his gaze focused on my front door. He was too old to be part of that group of teenagers who liked nothing more than to scare the life out of me and my dogs every Halloween. I hated them. Every last one of them. Yes, they were young, but evil at any age was a threat. And they were evil, especially that nasty-looking Warren, who was always the one stirring up trouble. I could see his dark, stringy hair now, extending far past his faded-out trucker hat, his camo shirt cut off at the shoulders to reveal pale arms with little muscle. He was a weasel of a guy, no more than eighteen or nineteen tops—a boy really—but one with a big truck and a small group of friends who followed him like sheep. Whenever I peered out at him through my living room window, his crooked smile and shifty dark eyes made me shiver for days.

It all started one afternoon three Halloweens ago, when Warren and Billy had delivered my groceries. I knew right away they were trouble, knocking on my door and yelling profanities.

"Leave the groceries and go," I'd said.

And then someone kicked the door, calling me rude and unworthy of their generosity. More kicking. I was afraid they'd break it down. The barrel of my gun through my living room window felt like my only recourse. That was when I saw him, a younger boy who couldn't have been older than twelve at the time. I didn't know who he was or why he was there, but I sensed that I had scared him, even though he had tried his best to yuck it up with Warren, who acted like the whole situation was hilarious. Warren stomped on my groceries, and then he threw a dozen eggs at my window before the three of them finally took off.

That night, Warren returned with his crew—minus the boy —to seek their revenge. And I had been on guard ever since.

Obviously not on guard enough, though. The stranger had caught me unaware. And he came in a truck, no less. Callum's truck. I was in the basement, the washer chugging away on a new load of clothes. Too much noise to hear properly. Laddie and Maggie were there with me.

I'd have to be more careful. And as angry as I was with myself, I realized the dogs hadn't heard him either. With the exception of Lily. She was already outside. Why hadn't she barked at him?

With their bladders empty, Lily, Maggie, and Laddie came bounding up to the screen door, which I opened to let them in. The sun was waking up to a new day, the birds finding their voices from various oak and maple trees flourishing with new leaves. Vermont springtime was often late, the temperatures struggling to climb out of the frost. But by June, the warmest season of the year bloomed all around me. The wildflowers I had planted over the years embellished my fields with speckles of white, orange, red, and purple. From a distance, they resembled butterflies, gathering for the season. I loved that. Thick clouds loomed with the promise of rain. I could smell the ozone.

"All better? Are you hungry?" I darted around my tiny kitchen, filling water bowls and ones for food. Laddie's water and food bowl sat by the back door, Lily's over by the fridge, and little Maggie's by the kitchen table. It had taken some strict training to get them all to respect each other's space when it came to meals, but I'd done it. The days of breaking up fights were long gone. And thank god for that.

While they lapped up the water and chomped on their dried food, I thought about that man again. Putting aside that he had scared five years off my lifespan, I could appreciate a handsome man when I saw one. And I hadn't seen one in quite some time. This one was tall and well built, his coral-colored polo outlining an impressive stack of muscles plumping up his arms and chest. Tan shorts revealed powerful-looking legs that supported his rugged body. Whoever he was, he definitely took fitness to another level, unlike the lowlifes who populated this neck of the woods. He kept his brown hair clipped short, a thin layer of scruff running along a defined jawline. Not dark enough to be considered brown, his eyes shone up at me, suggesting green. He spoke politely enough, his voice soft. And he hadn't approached. Then again, I had a shotgun aimed at his head. If he *had* come at me, he would have soon realized that my gun wasn't loaded. I wasn't a killer. I just wanted people to think I was, especially after what had happened last Halloween.

What I saw in those green eyes was fear and maybe a spark of confusion. He'd said he was staying at Callum's place. And he *was* driving his truck. Could that be why Lily went over there? My dogs weren't fans of strangers, yet Lily and even Laddie hadn't shown the slightest distaste toward this person. Not one bark came from their mouths.

Maggie? Well, she barked at everyone. Trying to compete with stepsiblings over twice her size, Maggie did her best to show her vigor, even if it didn't last long. She'd let Becky hold her on more than one occasion. And they all loved Callum, the only neighbor I'd had in years, even if he only came during the summer months. But Callum hadn't come this past spring to open up the place. Was it because of what had happened last fall? Was it my fault?

The stranger had referred to Callum as someone *who used to live just down the road.*

Used to, past tense.

There hadn't been any For Sale signs. No visiting traffic.

Had Callum passed away? I hoped not. Tears stung my eyes just thinking about it. And who was the new guy? An investor? A relative? Something in his facial structure reminded me of Callum, who was too old to be the man's father. *Grandfather?* Unbeknownst to me, had I just met his grandson? Callum had talked about JC a lot. I had never seen a picture, though.

Maybe that was why Lily took so kindly to him. Most men ran from a large German shepherd. They rarely stuck around long enough to make friends. *Great dog*, he'd said.

I scratched Lily's back while she ate. "You make a new friend, Lily?" I squatted down. "You think we can trust him?" I rose, the word *trust* curdling in my gut.

I'd trusted a man once. And I'd regretted it ever since. He'd cost me everything.

The breakfast nook window drew my attention, the one that overlooked my backyard. A patch of mowed grass surrounded by wildflowers and a good size rock I had found in the woods—that was my sanctuary—the Green Mountains off in the distance keeping an eye on us. "Good morning, beautiful." I would never leave this place. And no group of lowlifes was going to make me.

Memories of last Halloween resurfaced. The horror of it.

A winter chill had set in on that night, the sky clear, the moon offering a glimpse as the sun faded. I had sat out back on a blanket with my dogs, enjoying the sunset while I sipped on a mug of hot cocoa, my mind reminiscing. Growing up, my parents would often dress up right along with me (our costumes often historically or biblically related) to assist my trick-or-treating endeavors. We'd made candy apples. We'd carved pumpkins. I could almost smell the cinnamon from my mom's apple crisp baking in the oven. But they were gone now. Everyone was gone. Well, not everyone, I had assured myself as I snuggled with Maggie. Laddie and Lily lay close, the warmth from their bodies comforting me like a set of big, furry blankets. My family was right here.

And then, I heard something.

"Come out, come out, wherever you are." A sinister voice sent shivers down my spine. I dropped my mug on the grass and leaped to my feet.

Maggie yipped. Lily and Laddie sprang up on all fours, their ears pricked, a low growl gathering in their throats.

A stark reality slammed into me all at once, enough to take my breath away. We were unprotected outside. How could I be so careless?

The sun disappeared as the moon blazed on its path upward. It was the kind of night where you could see for miles.

"Let's get inside." I moved as swiftly and quietly as possible, ushering my pets into the house and locking the door where it was safe. Only, it wasn't safe that night.

"Come on out, come out. We're waiting, Iris." Those nasty calls came from Warren, their ringleader. I'd know that voice anywhere.

All three dogs rushed to the living room window facing my driveway and barked endlessly.

I crept around the house, shutting off lights, locking doors, and pulling down what blinds existed. I left the light out front on, hoping to intimidate. And then I peeked out from the same living room window, the only one uncovered. I recognized the curls of Billy's dirty-blond hair, in contrast to Warren's shoulder-length coal black hair that looked in desperate need of a trim. He was always squinting in a deceitful sort of way. Floyd and Bucky were brothers. I was sure of it. They had the same round faces and plump bellies, both donning short red hair, nearly shaved. Over the past two years, their conversations had carried, telling me exactly who everyone was.

Each one of them stood clad in old jeans and ribbed T-shirts. People called them wifebeaters. How fitting. I could see that in their futures, and I pitied the women who'd be stuck with a lifetime of abuse and neglect, raising kids who would grow up and behave just like their fathers. I didn't know Billy personally, but I knew his father, Tom. He used to be a deputy until he campaigned and won the seat for the local sheriff. Ironic, considering Tom's indiscretions, most of which the general public knew nothing about. Funny, rumors about me ran rampant, most of them untrue. I hadn't seen or spoken to Tom in a decade, but Becky worked for Martha and Raymond, Tom's parents and Billy's grandparents. She thought the world of that family and spoke of them often. I chose to keep my opinions to myself.

From what *I* remembered, Tom was a scary man. Righteous. Controlling. His parents were the opposite, both of them kind and giving. It appeared Billy was following in his father's footsteps. Or maybe he was rebelling against his authority. I remembered going through that phase myself. Only my rebellion had ruined my life and devastated my parents. My chest tightened at the thought of it.

Outside my living room window, a horrific scene unfolded. A gray pickup truck with wheels too big for its frame sat there. The beast that brought them to my home.

"Don't be shy. We came all the way here to see you. It's our tradition." That was Floyd, or maybe it was Bucky. They sounded so much alike.

"Get out of here! Or I'll shoot!" I sat on the floor and cranked open one of two casement windows, poking the barrel of my shotgun out. "I mean it. I'll shoot."

Warren fanned his hands out, his smile stretched wide. He slowly turned around, coming full circle. "Go ahead. Shoot." Such a rebel, that one. He faced my house, his chest puffed out like a skinny gorilla.

The eyes of everyone except for Warren registered worry.

What am I going to do now? I had thought. I didn't even have bullets. I'd found the gun in the basement when I moved in. I figured it might come in handy. What I should have done was purchase ammo and practice shooting. Hard to do when you never left your house.

"I seem to remember you saying the same thing last year and the year before that. Only, I've never heard that gun go off." Grabbing a bottle of something from the hood of his truck, Warren faced his friends. His hand movements caused the amber fluid to slosh around inside the bottle. He took an exaggerated chug and pulled the bottle away from his mouth. "Aah. That hits the spot. How bout you boys?" A burp flew from his lips as he wiped his mouth with the back of his hand. "Any of you ever hear a gun?"

"Nope," came from one, I thought Bucky, "never heard a sound."

"Probably not loaded," said Floyd.

Billy just stood there, trying to be cool, his shoulders slightly hunched, his grin tentative.

Warren turned back toward the house. "I thought witches didn't need guns anyway. Casting spells and all. You gonna fly out here on your broom for us? Give us a show. It's Halloween. And as I said, we came all this way. *Just for you.*"

Lily and Laddie continued to bark, the baritone resounding throughout my small house. Maggie was visibly shaking next to me.

Why they thought I was a witch was beyond me. A recluse, yes. Not a witch. I had tried to shoo them away from my home three years ago. That was my right. But I also knew how the rumor mill worked in this area. Who had started the witch rumor? I could think of several candidates.

If I had been a man out here on my own, I was sure those

jerks wouldn't have bothered me. One thing about bullies, they liked to pick on the weak and the scared. And in that moment, I struggled with both.

Soon, the voices all blended together. They slurred their speech, barely able to finish one sentence without laughing and dancing around like idiots. Unable to carry a tune, Warren tried singing "Witchy Woman" by the Eagles. He'd massacred it.

Lily, Maggie, and Laddie were in a frenzy over the commotion, running to this window and that, barking and growling. My dogs could sense the danger as much as I could. I pulled my gun back and took Maggie in my arms, trying to comfort her. "It's okay, Maggie. They'll be gone soon."

A large rock exploded through the window, glass shattering everywhere, a shard hitting my cheek.

Maggie flew out of my arms.

As my cheek burned, all three dogs barked at the large rock as though it were a creature, their ears pinned back.

Keeping my voice low, I tried to assuage their fears. "It's only a rock." I crawled over and grabbed it, shards of glass cutting into my knees. "See, it's only a rock." Something warm dripped down my cheek.

All I could think was I had to get this glass cleaned up before they were injured too.

With trepidation, Lily and Laddie approached and sniffed. Maggie kept a safe distance. Once they calmed down, I slid the glass into a pile, and using my jacket as a pouch, I carried the larger shards to the trash.

I swept up the rest as Warren continued to rant. "Come on, Iris. Don't you know what time it is? It's the *witching* hour. And we have crowned you our own personal witch."

The dogs were beside themselves once again. "It's okay. They'll leave soon." I tried to keep them close. It was like trying to herd ferrets. A cold breeze penetrated the house, the broken window sending ice into my veins.

The past two years, these jerks did nothing but yell, throw things, and then venture off, ready to drink more or pass out. But Warren wasn't having any of that. Not this time. "Let's torch the place. That'll draw her out." He giggled, his voice vibrating with excitement.

My heart dropped into my stomach. If they set my house on fire, my whole world would crumble. I had no other place to go. What would happen to us? I could call someone, but who? I was sure Callum had left for the season. I barely knew Becky.

I should have been able to call Billy's father, but I didn't trust the sheriff. For all I knew, Tom would have helped them finish the job. From what my high school friend, Haley, had told me many years ago, his temper was terrifying. I'd seen the bruises, even though she had tried to hide them. Tom was married—a pillar of the community. She was seventeen back then and, like me, easily led astray. Whatever happened between them was *her* fault. Just like whatever happened to me was mine. Public opinion said so. The only difference was Haley got out of here, but I never could.

"Nah, it's not worth it." The voice sounded like Billy's.

"Don't be such a pussy, Billy. I came here to see a witch, and I ain't leavin' till I see one."

"Jesus, Warren, you want to burn the old coot's place down? My dad finds out we're here, and he'll skin me alive."

"What about you, Floyd? Or you, Bucky? You two gonna wimp out on me too? Don't you wanna see a real-life witch up close?"

While they argued, I tried to form a plan in my mind. We could run out the back door and into the field and hide. Or into the barn. But I kept it locked. And the only way inside was through the front.

How would I keep Lily and Laddie from running at the commotion, ready to defend their home? I knew they'd behave that way just as I knew those morons would try to hurt them. I couldn't let that happen.

Where are those leashes? I returned to my feet and began searching the house, my back bent as low as it would go. With each step, my kneecaps throbbed. I wiped the blood from my cheek onto my lime-colored windbreaker, the sight of the red streak causing my stomach to turn. I pushed through the nausea.

"And then what, Warren? This place catches fire, and we're all gonna get thrown in jail for arson. I ain't goin' to prison just so you can see a freak show. In case you forgot, we ain't minors no more. You don't even know what the bitch looks like."

Warren mocked. "Well, genius, that's why we're here. And your dad ain't gonna send his only son to prison. So chill out, *Billy boy!*"

Billy didn't answer, and I was too afraid to peer out and see why.

Bucky or Floyd spoke instead. "No, he'll just kick the shit out of him. Seen *that* show a few times."

Billy's father was abusive to his son? No surprise.

"Shut up, Floyd. No one asked you." The ire in Warren's voice was palpable.

I found one leash curled up by the fireplace. *Where is the other one?* My gaze scanned the room until I spotted it on a small bench by the front door. All the way across the room. *Shit.*

Billy finally spoke up. "Those dogs haven't stopped barking since we got here. I hear one of them is a German shepherd. I don't need to get my ass chewed off." His voice softened just a tad. "Donna and Ashley said to come by, and they'd party with us. That sounds like a better deal than hanging around here."

Warren started hollering. "Come out, come out, you crazy bitch. We won't hurt you. We just wanna take a gander atcha." He paused, a clatter and then a clanking reaching my ears. "You come out or I'm gonna throw this Molotov cocktail right into that window I just broke. Now you don't want that, do you? I can't imagine those mutts would like fire too much. We just wanna see you."

"Come on, Warren. Cut the shit. Let's go!" Billy was finally taking a stand.

I grabbed the leash off the bench by the door. Then I hooked both of my big dogs. Maggie I would carry. "Come on, let's go." I whisper-yelled at my crew. "We're gonna make a run for it."

"Piss off, Billy. I came here to see a witch, and I ain't leavin' till I do!" Warren's harsh words were nothing but determined, not an ounce of humanity left.

I tiptoed toward the door, my cell phone secure in my back pocket. And then I realized, there *was* someone I could call: Dennis. Once I was clear of the house, I had planned to do just that. I knew he would help. The man had saved my life.

"What in the name of Sam Hill is goin' on here?" This voice was older.

Callum? It seemed he hadn't left as I had thought?

I paused and waited, my ears open and my body so tense I could barely stand the pain spearing through my shoulders.

"Now you boys weren't fixin' to catch this poor woman's house on fire, were ya?"

Complete silence.

"Did one of you break that window?"

"This is none of your business, old man." Warren again. Always the instigator.

"Well, when someone is threatening my neighbor, young

man, I *make it* my business. Harassing this poor woman, you all should be ashamed of yourselves."

I inched closer to the window and peered out as Callum held up a small phone. He had a baseball bat gripped in his other hand.

The dogs started barking again.

"And I suspect it will also be the sheriff's business who I just called on my way over here." His attention turned toward Billy. "If I'm not mistaken, that would be your father, wouldn't it, Billy? What got you all mixed up in this mess? Don't waste your life in prison, son. You're young. You got your whole life ahead of you."

The gang all stood there watching Callum. Their fidgeting and rapid blinks suggested they weren't sure what to do. And then Warren took a step toward my neighbor. *Oh no!* I worried he was going to hurt him.

Out of nowhere, the sound of a siren cut through the night air, blue-and-red lights flashing in the distance.

As though a firecracker had gone off under their feet, Warren and the gang headed for their truck. "You're too wasted, dipshit. I'll drive!" Billy pushed Warren out of the way and climbed into the driver's seat.

For once, Warren didn't argue. He rushed around the front of the truck and hoisted himself into the passenger seat, the door closing with a *slam.*

Bucky and Floyd hopped into the truck bed.

Floyd banged on the roof. "Hurry up! Let's get the fuck out of here!"

Tires spun up small rocks and dirt as the truck shot down my driveway as though a cannon had fired it. Blue lights shone in the distance for some time after that. I suspected the sheriff had cut them off before they had a chance to make it to the main road. Being Halloween and all, the blur of those blue-and-red lights cast an eerie glow into the night sky.

A knock on my door sent a jolt of electricity all the way down to my toes. I rushed over and flung it open.

"You okay, Iris?" There stood Callum, his brow creased from worry.

I flung my arms around the old man and cried. I was so scared. So helpless. But as much as I wanted to believe the world was rotten, it also included men like Callum. He was my friend.

The next day, he helped me repair the window. We used a large sheet of plywood at first.

"I can order you a window, and I'd be happy to install it." He beamed. "I've been told I'm pretty good with a hammer." His extensive tool selection supported his claim.

My neighbor *was* good with his hands and had quite a skill set, especially about matters I knew nothing about—handyman stuff. Within a week, I had a new window. I let him handle it all, still reeling from the whole experience. It had been a long time since anyone had been so kind. I was used to handling things on my own. This was a refreshing change.

"I spoke to the sheriff. He assured me those boys won't be comin' around again." Using a nail gun, he secured the window while I helped hold it in place. "You can press charges if you'd like." *Pfft.* Another nail sank into the wood.

I had put the dogs in my bedroom to avoid the noise, something Maggie in particular didn't care for. And it kept them out of the way, safe from swallowing things not meant for doggy bellies.

"Do you think I should?"

Callum seemed to ponder my question as he continued to work. When he finished, he stood back, his hands braced on his hips, a tool belt hanging lopsided around his waist. "Well, according to the sheriff, they were just blowing off steam. He said he spoke to them and assured me they wouldn't be any more of a problem. And they did pay for the window."

That much I knew.

"I'll stick around for a few more weeks yet and make sure things are okay." He crossed his arms and offered me a comforting smile. "I think the worst is over. I reported the incident. If they cause any more trouble, you call the sheriff right away." He wagged a fatherly finger at me. "And call me as well. I'll make sure someone gets out here to arrest them."

An orchestra of scratching and whining came from my bedroom door.

"You better let those dogs out or you may have several messes to clean up."

And that was the end of our conversation.

True to his word, Callum had stayed until just before Thanksgiving. And in those few short weeks, I'd made him two dinners, both at my house. We took chilly walks with the dogs. They loved that. And we talked . . . a lot. I opened up to Callum in a way I hadn't done in many years. I probably told him too much. I wanted to share who I was before I slipped away entirely. Or who I used to be. In all honesty, I wasn't sure who I was anymore. Callum listened and offered what advice he could.

"You're awfully young, Iris, to live out here all alone. And if you don't mind me sayin', quite a looker." His eyes twinkled. "You're just starting your life. Don't waste any more of it. Time has a way of rushing by, and soon, you'll realize it's almost over. What I wouldn't give for one more moment with my Evie."

I was envious of his deceased wife, Evie. He talked about her all the time. And as sorry as I was for his loss, Callum and his beloved had known what true love had felt like—having that one person in the world who not only had your back but cherished you. That was more than I could ever hope for. I lived for my pups. One day, they'd be gone, too, and I'd be truly alone. It was hard for me to imagine a future beyond that point. And so I put the thought out of my head.

I would live here. And I would die here.

As I thought about it all now, I wondered about the man who had come here yesterday. If he was Callum's grandson, he had to be a good man too.

The trouble was that I had no idea who he was. And until I could find out, he had better stay away from me and my pets.

Chapter Five

JC

I spent my Sunday mowing the grass and trimming the edges. I also washed my SUV and checked over Evie to make sure she was ready for an afternoon of fishing. Not today, I had too many other things to take care of, but soon.

Despite my misgivings about Iris and her trigger-happy tendencies, I went for a run. My muscles needed loosening, and running had a way of calming my nerves. I made sure to stretch before I left and planned to finish my workout with a set of push-ups, sit-ups, and whatever else I could muster with the resources around me. I'd have to either find a gym or purchase a set of free weights and maybe a pull-up bar to help keep me in shape. These were details I should have thought of *before* I had left. I'd gotten lazy at fending for myself when it came to anything outside of work, like mowing lawns and cleaning houses from top to bottom. (I made a mental note to offer my cleaning lady a much-deserved raise.) Maybe this trip would be better for me than I had thought. I needed to get back to self-sufficiency, like I used to be when I was younger.

Out on my run, I made sure to keep a steady pace, not

slowing or peering over when I drew near Iris's place. (I even jogged on the opposite side of the road.) That was until Lily came bounding out from the driveway to run with me. *Were you waiting for me, girl?*

"Hey, Lily." I was glad to see her, but at the same time, pensive about what this could mean. From my GPS, I knew this dirt road ran three-and-a-half miles from my place to the main road. I wouldn't take Lily that far. I'd cut off half a mile before the dirt met blacktop and then head home. (Having an analytical mind, I'd mentally logged all of this.) That would be a six-mile round trip of cardio. I just hoped Lily would go home when it was time. I didn't need her mother out looking for her, shotgun in hand.

As much as I wanted to deny it, I was attracted to that woman. Well, attracted to her looks, anyway. Her personality was about as appealing as a bat to the head. Yet, the memory of her standing at the clothesline taking down her laundry was hard to shake. And that dream. Somehow, Iris had stirred something deep within me. I struggled to understand my feelings. I was a city guy. I lived in the fast lane, and I *loved* in the fast lane as well. I didn't have time for infatuations that made absolutely no sense to me. But as I jogged along, the image of the woman living in the cottage refused to relent. Truth be told, she was in my thoughts almost constantly. At some point, I'd have to find out who she was. Maybe that would break the spell.

To my delight, Lily did return home as I jogged past for a second time. I watched her trot up the driveway, already missing her. What was it about that dog? She felt like a companion to me. If only her owner wasn't quite so . . . nuts? Using that word made me feel in-line with Billy and Warren, the two yahoos from Rolling Creek Grocery who seemed to enjoy labeling people like Iris. They reminded me of a not-so-fun time in my own life.

There weren't a lot of things I didn't like about going to see Gram and Gramps during my summer vacations when I was younger, with the exception of one thing—a dude named Ernie Parker. About ten years older than I was and with arms the size of tree trunks—not the brightest bulb in the box—Ernie was my bona fide bully.

Gramps had bought me a bike for when I wanted to venture out on my own. There was a general store a couple of miles away, and I'd ride over and buy candy or a soda when free time allowed. And being that he lived in rural Massachusetts, Gramps must've figured I would be safe enough.

I *was* safe enough—until I ran into Ernie. Like literally ran into what appeared to be a pickup truck that used to be a wagon. Add in a set of oversized wheels, and the contraption looked like something you'd construct with a bucket of leftover Legos.

I was watching some horses in a distant field and collided smack-dab into the back bumper of his vehicle. And even though I apologized for not watching where I was going, Ernie still gave me a bloody nose and a fat lip for my efforts. After that, I swore the asshole kept a watch out for me. If Gramps was with me, like say at the feed supply store, Ernie kept his distance. Gramps wasn't so old that he couldn't give that prick a run for his money. Not that I ever told Gramps about where the bloody noses, fat lips, and even a cracked rib had come from (blamed on various biking accidents). I might have been a bit scrawny back then, but I was no snitch. I suspected Gramps either thought I was a complete klutz or lying.

In a lot of ways, Ernie was the reason I was built like a brick shithouse now. I didn't like the power he held over me. That was when I started pumping iron, as they say. And I grew like a weed. My bulk and height helped me get on the high school football team, which in turn worked well with the ladies. And even though my interest in girls contributed greatly to my absence from my grandparents' lives, Ernie had played a hand.

When Warren and Billy had burst through the door of Rolling Creek Grocery, their voices loud, their eyes bloodshot from hay fever or too many bong hits, Ernie came to mind. The only difference was that I had at least ten years on Warren and Billy and a whole lot more muscle. Christ, I could knock their heads together without much effort. Not that I would. I just liked knowing that I *could*. Immature for a thirty-year-old, but some wounds never quite healed.

By nightfall, the rain had returned, washing away some of the loose grass clumping up the lawn and dropping the temperature from the high 60s to the high 50s. Jesus, this state was cold. But it wasn't all bad. I found some wood in the shed/garage that I used to start a fire (thanks to my fire safety merit badge) and settled onto the soft leather couch. I still had ample amounts of Brunswick stew, which I warmed up and coupled with a turkey, ham, and cheddar sandwich. And man, did that taste good. I also grabbed a microbrew from the fridge.

"Okay, now what?"

Without Internet, I sampled a couple of my grandfather's books to pass the time, and a glass of red wine to chase the beer I had just finished. At least I had some music downloaded on my phone, easing the isolation bug.

As I stood in front of one of two bookcases sifting through the volumes, I recalled the book Gramps had used to win over Gram's heart, *The Old Man and the Sea*, but I couldn't find a copy. The quote he recited from the book never left me. "*A man is not made for defeat. A man can be destroyed but not defeated.*" For Gramps, it was a turning point between him and the love of his life. For me, it meant never giving up, no matter how often you failed. Little did he know, I had printed that quote, laminated it, and stored it in my wallet. Some people kept family photos. I had this. I also had a copy of the book but not with me. Whenever I felt the foot of life stomping on my neck, I'd think about those profound words and buck the hell up.

I grabbed *The Adventures of Huckleberry Finn* instead. I got about ten pages in before my eyes grew heavy. I awoke at 3:00 a.m. and dragged my sorry ass to bed.

On Monday, I managed to find a few things that were working in my favor. Gramps did have cable *and* Internet. He'd had both shut off for the winter season. The attendant at the cable company told me I'd definitely have Wi-Fi inside the house. "You won't have much beyond that. Not out there." With indigo-colored hair framing a face full of freckles, Willow (according to her nametag) smiled at me, her cheeks flushed. She wore a V-necked T-shirt in pale yellow, a yin-yang symbol at its center, and a long maxi skirt with a blue floral print, a pair of two-strap sandals on her feet. Where I worked, everyone wore a suit, the women in pantsuits or dresses. In some ways, this was a refreshing change.

"I can handle that." I didn't have to find rentable office space. Nothing was close here, and I wasn't too pumped about driving all over the friggin place to conduct business. Or work in my SUV. My hours were often long and outside the parameters of a forty-hour work week. I could work when the market opened or late into the night and weekends without worry. Although, I would make every effort to curb my workaholic lifestyle while I was here. Gramps wouldn't appreciate anything less.

"Hey, any gyms or golf courses around here?"

Even though Willow was fairly lean, she didn't strike me as the golfing type—or someone who would frequent a gym. Maybe it was the black lipstick and the studs in her lip and nose.

Willow twirled her indigo hair with her fingers, remnants of her teal-colored nail polish nearly picked away. But she was nice enough, so no complaints. "Yeah, I can see you're a guy who works out. How long are you here?" Her gaze lingered on my biceps, partially covered by my light-blue polo.

"About a month."

"Oh." Her tone rose in a hopeful manner, her eyes welcoming. "I think there's a gym and golf course around here. Let me ask my boss, Sammy. She's out back." She pushed an order form across the counter toward me, then grabbed a pen. "If you could fill this out, I'll be right back." She smiled again, and I was pretty sure she was batting her eyes at me.

Willow was a nice kid, but not my type. And *way* too young. If I needed to let off any sexual steam, I'd call Morgan, my ex. Unlike some of my other so-called relationships, my breakup with Morgan was mutual. A stockbroker herself, Morgan ran on high octane. Just like I did. And she didn't burden herself with who called whom or where our relationship was headed. We both knew going into this wouldn't be a game changer. But man could that woman fuck, every which way but Wednesday. Long, dark-brown hair and big brown eyes, an ass that could crack wood, and tits that cost in the thousands, she was the perfect woman for whenever I needed a lift. My dick sure enjoyed her. I often wished my feelings ran deeper where Morgan was concerned, but the heart wanted what the heart wanted—or didn't want, in my case. There were no Evies in my life, and there never had been. A problem for another decade. Right now, I was too young to care.

My gaze wandered to the storefront where rain pattered the floor-to-ceiling windows. It had been a cloudy drive into town, so this wasn't a shocker. According to the app on my phone, it was supposed to clear off. I hoped Mother Nature would allow me some golfing later today.

Willow returned, her sandals shuffling across the industrial carpet. "Sammy wrote down the names of two golf courses in the area and one gym, but she said the gym has shitty equipment that is always breaking down, though."

I imagined the owner running something out of his garage.

She quirked a brow. "Sorry. That's the best I can do." She leaned over the counter, revealing a slight hint of cleavage. "So, you're a golfer, huh? I've always wanted to try golf."

Does she mean miniature golf? "Sure am, and thanks for checking for me. All done." I slid the form back and handed her my credit card.

She stood upright and slid the card through the machine. "Sammy said since you already have service hooked up, it will only take twenty-four hours or less to turn it back on." She gave me back my credit card and leaned over the counter again. "If you need to use the Internet, my apartment isn't far from here."

Nope. Not going there. "Thanks, Willow. I'm good for now. Hey, is there a Walmart nearby or a Dick's Sporting Goods?" I figured the latter was pretty unlikely.

Willow nodded. "Sure is. There's a Walmart in Berlin, and a Dick's in Williston."

While I had Wi-Fi, I grabbed my cell phone and started looking up addresses.

She smiled. "I'd be happy to write down directions for you."

Friendly girl. "Thanks." I held my phone up. "I've got it."

* * *

I drove directly to Dick's Sporting Goods in the town of Williston, which turned out to be close to an hour away. I purchased a cart full of free weights, a mat, and whatever I could envision needing to stay in shape, including a pull-up bar. Running would take care of the cardio. Fitness wasn't something I was willing to squander, not for an entire month. I had no intention of returning to the city with a beer gut. In a month, I could always donate what I had to that shitty gym Willow had told me about.

According to my phone, there was a golf store not too far from Dick's, so I made my way there next. I had already checked out the selection at Dick's, knowing I might return. The owner fitted me with a decent set of clubs, and I thanked him by purchasing a full set with a bag, along with balls, shoes, and attire, plus a duffel to carry it all in. Needless to say, I dropped a few coins at his place. His smile and enthusiastic wave when I left told me he appreciated the business. These newfound treasures would also be donated when the time came.

Another hour on the road, and I found the closest golf course to my house, which wasn't that far, as it turned out. (It still felt weird calling it *my house* and not Gramps's place, but I had to adjust.) The rain had stopped, patches of blue sky poking through the fluff, the sun encouraging the temperatures to climb into the low 70s. Definitely doable for golf. My shoulders were ready to work, so I was down. I also craved social interaction. Other than the many phone calls I had made to Jen, whenever I had bars, I was feeling pretty lonely. According to my assistant, things were running smoothly, my clients doing just fine. And by tomorrow, I'd have Internet and could take care of things on my own.

A large building appeared with green-and-white-striped awnings over each window and a portico out front. A burnt-orange roof offset the black shutters and white siding. I followed the signs to the Green Mountain Country Club parking lot, which remained half full. It *was* a Monday after all.

I parked and hauled my golf bag and attire from the back of

the SUV. Voices intermixed with country music carried from one side of the building devoted to a restaurant, a large deck with a roof overlooking the course. Waitstaff walked around with trays, some taking orders while two golf carts rode along a paved path weaving through the greens. I took a comforting sigh of relief. This was a good idea.

The awning above one of the glass doors out front indicated where the pro shop was, so I made tracks. I pulled the glass door open, a bell ringing over my head, and stepped inside.

"Welcome to Green Mountain Country Club," said a young guy with short blond hair, decked out in a tangerine polo with yellow golf pants. He stood behind a glass encasement. *Summer job?* Unlike Warren and Billy, this kid was clean-cut and friendly. Well dressed.

"Thanks." I crossed the modest-sized room in no time, the scent of fresh leather with a hint of rubber ripening the air. Clusters of clothing racks, shelving for shoes, and racks of golfing equipment crowded the confined space.

"I'd like to schedule a tee time if you have anything available. Also, do you offer monthly memberships?" I approached the counter and unburdened myself of my golf bag, which made a *plunk* against the tiled floor.

Donning a bright-colored paisley polo and matching skirt, a woman with a blond bob—one of those white plastic visors crowning her head—searched a clothing rack nearby while two men with thinning hair examined the men's shoes section, as small as it was.

"Sure. Let me check my book. My name is Emmett."

"Hi, Emmett, I'm JC."

Emmett turned toward the back wall, taking a black binder off a counter that reached waist high, supported by several cabinets underneath. "I don't know if we offer monthly memberships, but I'll check with my manager." Turning toward me, he placed the binder down and flipped it open. "I've got a three o'clock open. I've booked my 3:15 and 3:30. Do you have a foursome or are you golfing on your own?"

"I don't have a group, but I'll see if I can join one. Are those foursomes scheduled for 3:15 and 3:30?"

Emmett examined the schedule in front of him. "Yup. Do you want me to have the marshal ask if they have an opening? Sometimes people don't show up."

"Nah. I'll ask around, and if I can't find anyone, I can maintain a pretty good pace. I won't get in anyone's way. Put me down for the three o'clock."

I'd golfed at some of the finest courses in the world and rubbed elbows with a few champions. I wasn't worried about slowing anyone down. Although, I hoped I could find a group for the interaction. Someone to share a beer with afterward.

"Go ahead and sign in here." Emmett pointed at another book that contained log sheets and times, a pen ready to take my name down.

I did as he asked.

"It's fifty for the day. If we're able to do a monthly membership, I'll subtract what you paid today from the total."

"Sounds fair."

As it turned out, the country club didn't offer monthly memberships. I was fine with it. I'd pay whatever and whenever—perks of having a bloated bank account. By the time I was finished paying the fees and had changed into my new golf attire (I'd rented a locker there), I had fifteen minutes to kill.

I stepped out into the Vermont sunshine, appreciating how fresh the air felt and smelled up here (when out of smelling distance of a working farm). You didn't get *that* in the city, where the smog had the potential to coat your face with grime on a daily basis. A group of small black birds chased one another from the roof of the clubhouse to a few trees nearby, grackles, if my eyes weren't deceiving me. At the edge of the woods, a bunny rabbit hopped into the thicket. I half expected a deer to show up next.

As I turned the corner, a puff of cigar smoke wafted past my nose, the sound of several men chatting within earshot, two groups of men to be specific. They had to be the 3:15 and 3:30 tee times. Silver hair and sweater vests contributed to the style of one group, the other slightly younger. Nearby, a small parking lot of empty golf carts sat at the ready.

I approached the younger group, mainly because they were closest to me. Plus, there only appeared to be three of them. Was it wishful thinking that I could be their fourth?

"Any of you gentlemen looking for a fourth?" Clad in a turquoise polo and dark-gray shorts, a tall dude with a decent build and black hair that curled out from under his dark-gray golf hat, turned to face me. "Sure. We were just saying we were short today. Our buddy, Kurt, couldn't make it. You play much? I'm Brody, by the way, Brody Larson." He reached his right hand out, the one wearing a performance glove, for me to shake, which I did.

"Jacob. My friends call me JC. Nice to meet you. Yeah, I've been known to hit a few balls around." My gaze found a golf cart already loaded up, its proximity closer than the rest. "That your cart?"

"Sure is." Dressed in a white polo with a few colorful stripes running across the breast area and a pair of khakis, another man with broad shoulders stepped forward. Slivers of gray weaved throughout his brown hair, cut short, his steely eyes discerning. He pulled the cigar out of his mouth and reached his hand out, also covered by a glove, for me to shake, the tobacco sending hints of wood and spice into the air around us. "Tom Bradley. I'm the sheriff in town." Tom had a square head, his jawline giving the impression he could bite through metal. He had the kind of look one would imagine a sergeant in the military would share. Perfect for a sheriff, I would assume. And his body was also big. Not in a muscular sort of way, but more big-boned with a slight belly to him that fell just over his belt.

I shook his hand and smiled. "Good to meet you, Sheriff."

He motioned toward a third man with dark skin and a bald head, who was about my height, give or take an inch. A textured dark-maroon polo and navy golf pants outfitted this guy. What I noticed most about him was his friendly smile and welcoming brown eyes. "This here is Dennis."

Once again, I made pleasantries.

"You on vacation here?" Brody asked. "I don't recall seeing you before." He fiddled with his glove for a better fit.

I was about to answer when Emmett, sporting a white golfer's cap, poked his head out of a side entrance to the club-house. "I couldn't find anyone, JC. But I can play if you need a double."

Dennis turned toward him. "We're all set, Emmett." He put his hand on my shoulder for a brief moment. "We're also short one, so JC will be our fourth. Thank you just the same, young man."

"Okay, well, you can begin anytime. We didn't fill the 3:00 slot." Emmett withdrew back into the clubhouse.

Dennis approached the cart. The rest of us followed, and soon we were underway. I offered to tee off last, but Brody insisted I go first, being I was "a guest and all." I hit the ball with a *whack*, leaving my mates standing by with their mouths hanging open. My ball bounced along the fairway, avoiding hazards and setting up my next shot nicely.

Brody took off his hat, his mouth slightly open, then returned it to his head. "Hit a few balls, huh? Well, I guess *so*. Either that, or you have one hell of a beginner's luck." He squinted toward the green where my ball awaited its next shot. "Where did you say you were from?"

"New York City. Stockbroker. I golf a lot with clients. Or I used to when I had the time."

Tom and Brody both exchanged a look, their eyebrows raised.

Unfortunately, my new friends weren't quite so lucky. Brody and Dennis managed a straight enough shot, but ran short of the fairway, and Tom's ball landed in a swath of tall grass next to the woods.

"Well, this is gonna be fun." Dennis beamed. "It's not every day we have a golf pro with us."

I tried to wave that comment off. "Oh, I'm not a pro." I'd just golfed with pros, which I chose not to mention.

"Yeah, right," Brody said as he jumped behind the wheel.

Dennis took a little more time getting in. He seemed to have trouble with one of his knees, which was probably why he always took the passenger seat: more legroom. Even though he was the biggest man of the lot, the sheriff sat in the back seat with me.

"I'll have the clubhouse run us down some beers." Brody peered over his shoulder at me. "You do drink beer, dontcha, city boy?"

"Absolutely." I sat back, enjoying the soft breeze against my face. A beer would be just about perfect right now. I took in the scenery and the abundance of trees surrounding the course, the mountain range off in the distance. Everything was green and lush. "Nice course. I was hoping they did monthly memberships, since I'm only in town for the next four weeks. But I'll give you all my cell number if you want another fourth again."

"Four weeks, huh?" That was Dennis. "I'm sure Brody can help you out with a short-term membership." He gazed over at our driver. "Isn't that right, Brody?"

That piqued my interest. "Oh, yeah? You got some clout here?" I stared at the back of his head, his black curls bouncing in the breeze beneath his hat.

I wished I had brought *my* hat, but it was in the SUV. I wasn't too worried about sunburn or glare, the clouds helping me out today. Plus, this was Vermont, not Kiawah Island.

Brody stopped at our first hole. "I sure hope so since I own the place."

We all climbed out. "Well, lucky me. Glad I was able to tag along with your group." I was surprised; however, he didn't golf better. Then again, we'd only taken one shot so far.

Brody grinned. "Before I make any promises, we'll see how you handle this course." He pulled out his 3 wood and raised it up, twisting it this way and that. "I gotta feeling we may be playing with a sandbagger."

"A sandbagger? Nah. I have my days, believe me." But when I scored two under par on the first hole, I wasn't sure any of them bought my argument anymore.

* * *

I finished the day with a seventy-five, Brody, an eighty-six. Dennis and Tom earned a ninety-two and a ninety-eight respectively. As the afternoon wore on, I learned that Dennis, who favored his right knee more than his left, was also a veterinarian—one of the best, according to Tom. I found myself gravitating toward Dennis, maybe because Brody was rather stressed about his game. Tom did his best to assuage his friend's rumblings.

They asked me to join them for another beer on the deck afterward, and I almost declined considering Brody's sour mood. "Shit!" "Fuck!" flew out of his mouth at almost every hole. The movie *Happy Gilmore* came to mind, although Brody hadn't resorted to slamming his club down on the greens or throwing it into the woods.

Then I realized I wasn't one to shy away from difficult people, not his type of difficult. Pissing contests were a part of my life, and I was up for the challenge.

"I thought I was a good golfer . . . but you showed me I have a lot of work to do." Brody had just ordered a round of beers along with almost everything off the pub bar menu. The young waitress who took his order had to be in high school. Donning long and straight blond hair, her figure thin, she had a propensity to giggle at just about everything Brody said. "Good to see you, Harper. I saw you play in that field hockey game last week. You were on fire. I just love watching you play."

Dial back the creep factor, dude. You're her boss.

Something in his eyes told me he'd like to watch Harper do a few other things. It was the only time he'd smiled all afternoon.

In no time, the staff had loaded our table down with nachos, wings, baskets of fries and onion rings, along with fish and chips. I wasn't much into fried food, but I sampled as I sipped my beer, the Green Mountain Country Club emblem etched across my pilsner glass. The IPA I was drinking came dense with hops, chased by a hint of citrus. It was good. Hearty.

"I guess you golf a lot being a broker, huh?" Sitting next to me, Brody removed his hat, revealing a faint tan line running across his forehead, his black curly hair matted down from sweat.

I set my pint down on the round table. "Not as much as I'd like. I've been pretty busy the past couple of years."

"Doing what? Making millions? What are you, twenty-eight? Thirty?" Brody continued to grill me like this. Something in his voice carried a slight edge to it. Was he jealous? Pale-blue eyes and a handsome face, Brody wasn't stacked like I was, but he was fit enough. No beer belly that I could see. That would be Tom. And the dude also owned a country club.

I shrugged his comment off. "I'm probably not making any more than you are, Brody." I took another sip of my IPA.

Tom just sat there watching me. He'd barely said two words all afternoon. Not to me, anyway. He'd stuck to his buddy Brody.

"Don't knock the young man for making himself a good living." Dennis smiled over at me as he grabbed an onion ring and popped it into his mouth. He swallowed his food. "Better than most of the younger generation who want everyone else to do their work for them." He palmed his pint, his eyes focused on the glass. "Or bail them out when they have nothing better to do than to cause trouble."

Both Dennis and Brody got a funny look on their faces, their eyes avoiding Tom.

Huh, what is this all about?

"No offense, Tom," Dennis said as he focused on his beer.

Tom flipped his hand slightly, which he'd had rested on the table. "None taken. I'm well aware of my son's mistakes, Dennis." His voice was less than kind.

So, his kid's a troublemaker? I read last week about a kid who had shot up a school in Texas. The son of a deputy. *Hmm.*

Just then, an attractive woman with shoulder-length blond hair and a tight body—big tits—approached. Her grayish-blue eyes slanted toward bitch and so did her stiff brow, but I wasn't certain.

"Hey, fellas." She stood next to Brody, placing her hand on his shoulder, a huge rock shining from her ring finger. "Warren and Billy are here to help Rudy with the grounds." She stared down at Brody.

Warren and Billy worked here? Or did they take odd jobs? I could have sworn they were out haying when I last saw them.

"Tell Billy, his mother is not happy with him about the condition he left her car in yesterday. She's called me five times about it. So he better clean it up *pronto*, or there will be hell to pay." Tom set his jaw, his brow bearing down.

Sounded like Billy was related to the sheriff? And then I remembered something Martha had said when I was at Rolling Creek Grocery. *Go get something to eat, and I don't want to hear another word, or I'll let your father know how disrespectful you're being!* Tom had to be Billy's father. I'd estimated all of these dudes were in their mid-to-late forties. Brody could be younger, but not by much.

"Will do, Tom." Her gaze found me next. "Who might you be, handsome?" Her blue eyes brightened, and I swore she even thrust her chest out a tad, her tits the product of a good plastic surgeon, I was sure.

Keeping his face tight, Brody sat up in his seat. "This is JC. He's staying in town for the next month." He glanced over at me and made a gesture with his hand. "JC, this is my wife, Nicole." His voice was about as deadpan as it got.

Clad in one of those tennis skirts and a sleeveless polo, both in pink, Nicole smiled at me. "Nice to meet you, JC."

I returned her smile. "Nice to meet you too."

"Where are you from?"

I sat up and gave her my full attention, something I sensed she craved. Privilege sat on her shoulders well, her tone sharp and authoritative. I had always been good at reading people, which helped given my profession. Nicole struck me as a force to be reckoned with. I got the same vibe from Tom. Other than my golf game, Brody didn't seem to care about much else. I could have been wrong about all of this, but I hadn't made the money I had by not understanding what made people tick. "I live in New York City. Been there for about eight years now."

She tipped her head to one side, her mouth making a funny

quirk. "Wow. New York City. To what do we owe this pleasure that brought you all the way here?" Her eyes sparkled with curiosity, her finger running along her lower lip, the one covered in cranberry-colored lipstick.

"My grandfather died last winter, and he left me his vacation home not too far from here."

Now, everyone was staring.

Dennis was the first one to speak. "I'm sorry to hear that, JC. Were you two close?"

"Yeah, we were." A lump gathered in my throat, which I washed down with another sip of my IPA. I took a breath. "He was a great man."

Dennis placed his forearms on the table and leaned into them. "I'm sure he was. Do you mind me asking how he died?" He blinked, sympathy weighing heavily in his dark-brown eyes.

"Heart attack. From what I heard, he went quickly. He died in Massachusetts where he lived. My gram died a while back, so he was alone. He bought a place up off Old Oak Road. It's about twenty minutes from here."

Everyone around the table suddenly looked away as though I had said something wrong—everyone except for Nicole, whose wide smile had morphed into a definite scowl.

"Old. Oak. Road?" She stared me down, her eyes as cold as an iceberg. "Near that crazy-ass bitch, Iris?" With flushed cheeks, Brody's wife was practically spitting venom. "I can't believe that psycho still lives there. She is nothing but trouble. If it were up to me, I'd have her ass hauled out of town. Or arrested. Pulling a gun on Dylan like that. A twelve-year-old. Can you imagine?" She scoffed, her hand flailing. "And she's nothing but a freeloader from what I hear."

Dylan had to be her son. So Iris had pulled a gun on him too? A twelve-year-old? Why? The woman was definitely unstable. I suddenly felt lucky I had gotten away from her alive.

Chapter Six

JC

Who'd have thought that the subject of where I was staying would have caused a vein to poke through Nicole's forehead the way it had, her face as tight as a drum. Brody and Tom just sat there, expressions flat as though they were trying to avoid poking the bear— the one who loomed over us with her thick perfume. Dennis didn't speak, either; he just stared down at his plate full of food.

I couldn't blame Nicole. If someone had pulled a gun on one of my relatives, I'd be pretty pissed too. I wasn't crazy about the idea of it happening to me either. "I'm sorry to hear that about your son. But I do live at the end of Old Oak Road. I'm from New York City, where crazy is a way of life." That was my feeble attempt at humor, something that was lacking at the moment. "I can handle strange neighbors." *Could I?* I had this vision of Iris creeping around my house, watching me, her gun fully loaded. "When did this happen?"

"Three years ago," Brody said with a blank expression. "And Dylan shouldn't have been there in the first place." He glared up at Nicole.

Was it the same day that Iris had pulled a gun on Billy and Warren? Were they together? That must have been his son's friend's son that Raymond was talking about.

I was pretty sure a *hmph* came from Nicole's lips. I hoped she would snap out of the storm raging behind her bluish-gray eyes. I agreed with her, but at the same time was ready to move on from this conversation.

"Have you met *her*?" She crossed her arms over her bountiful chest.

Her voice came out all *mean girl*. And judging by Iris's appearance, I was sure it must've played a factor. Still, Iris had pulled a gun.

I could have told her what had happened to me, but I didn't want to stoke those fires. Raymond had said Becky liked Iris. That meant she hadn't been treating *everyone* that way. Was it just men in general? Regardless, I needed to defuse the situation.

"No, ma'am. I haven't met her. And since I'm only here for a month, I doubt I ever will. I'll be sure to be careful, though." Something occurred to me. If Tom was Billy's dad, that meant he was also Martha and Raymond's son. *Would they tell him I had dropped off groceries at Iris's place?* I cleared my throat. "I mean, I dropped off a grocery order for Martha the other day, but I never saw Iris." *Nice one.* They wouldn't know about the incident unless they talked to Iris, which I suspected they would never do. *Why am I protecting her?* I had seen firsthand how violent Iris could be. I couldn't help but wonder what had made her that way. She was clearly alone. Other than her dogs.

"Well, you're lucky you survived." Her jaw working, Nicole stared off.

After he took another sip of his beer, Brody peered over the balcony at a man driving up in a small ATV. "There's Rudy now." He stood and bent over the railing. "Hey, Rudy, Warren and Billy are at the maintenance shed waiting for you."

Coordinated in a dark-green baseball cap with matching polo, both carrying the golf course emblem and a pair of tan work pants, Rudy signaled back with a salute from his ATV. "On my way there now."

Tom rushed over to the balcony next. "Tell Billy he better clean up his mother's car or his ass is grass. Woman won't stop calling me about it."

Nicole joined the fray.

Rudy is a popular guy.

"And tell Warren, I need to see him before he leaves."

Brody faced his wife. "Why? What do you want with Warren?" His brows drew together.

"Nothing. I want to give him his paycheck and go over a few other smaller jobs at the house that need taking care of. The rain gutters need cleaning, and there is that shutter that blew off during last month's storm. I want him to fix it." She plunked both hands on her narrow hips. "Why? What difference does it make?"

Standing between his wife and his friend, Brody swiveled his body accordingly. "No offense to you, Tom, but I'm not all that keen on Warren hanging around my house with Aubrey around. And I don't want Dylan hanging around him either."

Aubrey had to be his daughter. I wondered how old she was.

Brody saw no problem flirting with young waitresses, yet was protective of his daughter? *Hypocrite* came to mind.

Tom straightened his belt. "No offense taken. I've been working on the Warren *problem* myself. Billy is as stubborn as his freeloading mother." An arrogant smirk curled his lips. "Kid may think he knows what he's doing, but he's no match for me.

And I don't care what Sandra threatens. He's a legal adult now. And he *will* be treated as such."

Sandra? Ex-wife?

"Yeah, I've had my own talks with Dylan. Missing curfews and assignments at school. Kids are gonna put us in an early grave. Try having twins who will be driving age next year." Brody blew out his lips. "I can feel the gray hairs filling in already."

Standing behind her husband, Nicole rolled her eyes.

Brody shook his head subtly and turned toward me as he gestured with his hands. "If you're done with your beer, JC, we can get that membership application taken care of."

And that was the end of the family drama. Another reminder that I was destined for eternal bachelorhood.

I was loading my SUV when Dennis came over. "Hey, JC. Getting' ready to head out?" Beads of sweat beaded across his forehead as he secured his golf bag on his shoulder.

"Oh, hey, Dennis. Sure am. Brody hooked me up. Looking forward to another day on the greens soon." I hauled my golf bag into the back.

"Sounds good, son. I'll be ready for more lessons from our new pro." He flashed that friendly smile of his. "You have yourself a nice day. It's not supposed to rain for three whole days." His bag was starting to slip, so he slung it back over his shoulder as he began to walk away. "After I check back at the clinic, I've got loads of yardwork waitin' for me before the rain returns." His smile stretched wider as he patted his belly. "All this activity keeps me in shape for the Mrs., you know."

I pushed the button to close the hatch and chuckled. "I can see that. Hey, before you go, can I ask you something?"

"Sure thing. What's on your mind, son? You got a pet that needs looking after? My daughter is managing the day-to-day at the clinic these days, and I have two partners who are more than competent. We'd be happy to help you out."

I shook my head. "No, nothing like that. I did meet Iris's dog, though. Lily. She came to my place and has gone running with me along Old Oak Road. She's a great dog."

Dennis's face lit up. "Oh, Lily's a gem. She's a rescue, you know. A family just up and left her about eight years ago. Poor pup was lost when I found her. A bit malnourished and scared as a deer in the headlights. Shakin' like a leaf. I've always said there is a special place in hell for people who abuse animals, children, and the elderly."

Hmm. That had my wheels turning. "Lily is Iris's dog, though, right?

Dennis's expression flattened toward serious. "Sure is."

"Did you give Lily to her?" I looked around for prying eyes, especially Nicole's. Other than a group of men walking into the clubhouse, we were alone. "I wasn't totally honest about meeting Iris. I did meet her. Well, she shooed me off her property. I've never had a conversation with the woman. And she seemed very standoffish. But Lily seems like a great dog."

I was hoping Dennis could shed some light on what made my neighbor tick.

He nodded. "Yes, all of Iris's dogs are good pups. Well-mannered. She's done a wonderful job raising them. And don't believe everything you hear."

"Do you mean about Iris? Can you elaborate?"

Dennis took a small cloth that I just noticed was in his hands and wiped his forehead. Then he reached into his back pocket, pulled out his wallet, and handed me his business card. "I don't mean to be rude, JC, but I'm in a bit of a hurry. Too much to do." He walked away, favoring that same leg. "Enjoy this beautiful day Mother Nature has provided for us." He fanned one hand out on his trek toward his truck, which he identified with a beep of his key fob.

"Thanks. You too."

Don't believe everything you hear. Why wouldn't Dennis explain himself? Was he really in a hurry to get home to do chores, or was he uncomfortable talking about Iris, a woman he knew and trusted enough to take his rescues?

As I drove home, the situation continued to trouble me. Iris had enemies and for good reason. Yet, Martha and Raymond hadn't minded her, other than being slightly scared of what she might do. I was with them on that front. I glanced over at Dennis's business card, sitting on my console. Like Gramps, Dennis had an easy way about him. A warmth that told me he was a good man. Brody was nice, too, albeit a tad cocky, and Tom was just plain intimidating—a brooder. I sure wouldn't want to be Billy if he didn't clean up his mother's car.

When I arrived home, I had Internet. I was pumped. "Son of a bitch! I'm back in business!" I grabbed my laptop and placed it on the kitchen table, charged my phone, and even tried the TV in the living room. I had paid for premium cable, knowing there would be lots of lonely nights out here.

"That deserves a drink." I dialed Morgan's number, hoping to have a little fun while I was at it.

I spotted Becky delivering groceries to Iris's place one afternoon, marking my two-week stay. No gunshots to speak of. It was the same day my sister, Alyssa, called to bitch and moan about her soon-to-be ex. "Do you believe he wants me to sell the house?"

Alyssa and Greg had purchased a home against my dire

warnings. "You've only been married eight months, Alyssa. Why the hell did you buy a house with him?" I felt bad about my told-you-so attitude, but this was her second divorce, and the woman was still in her twenties. She liked to jump into relationships with her eyes closed. *I could tell Greg wasn't going to be a lifer from the start. Whenever I saw them together, he barely listened to a word she'd said. (In his defense, Alyssa was a talker.) A guy can tell when another guy isn't *that* into his spouse, and Greg had struck me that way. So had Brody. As far as Greg was concerned, he was more interested in himself. Being a trainer, he took fitness beyond even my expectations. For a time, Alyssa had dabbled in physical exercise, too, trying out a gym membership, where she had met Greg. The membership hadn't lasted long, nor had their marriage.

She huffed. "I get it, JC. Geez. I didn't call to have you read me the riot act."

I softened my tone and let her rant, which she did for the next ten minutes. That was my role as her big brother.

"How is it up there? The lake is great, isn't it? Gramps took us out fishing a few times last summer."

Ouch! That stung. I knew she didn't mean it that way, but it just about killed me to know that she was able to experience something with Gramps that I had selfishly missed. "Yeah, the place is great. Listen, Alyssa, I gotta get back to work."

"Okay, let me know if you want me to come up. I have some time off for the Fourth."

"I'm good, but thanks. I kinda want to take this time alone. You understand, right?"

"Of course."

"Call me anytime." And I ended the call.

The following night, Zach called to give me shit about missing the nightlife. "When are you coming home, dude? I can't handle all these women by myself."

I laughed and assured him it wouldn't be much longer. *Two more weeks.*

The days seemed to sail by, my life embracing a routine I could live with. I golfed when I felt like it, worked most mornings and nights, and fished nearly every day it hadn't rained. It definitely wasn't the same without Gramps here, but I made the best of it. I even grocery shopped, filling my fridge and cupboards with appetizing food and drink.

Earlier in the week on Thursday, Kurt had shown up, a heavyset guy with nearly white hair and a flushed skin tone—the kind often brought on by high blood pressure—broken capillaries on his nose and cheeks. He turned our foursome into a fivesome. But being the owner, Brody allowed it.

Kurt liked to joke around, his belly bouncing right along with his laughter. "What the hell is this? I'm gone for one week, and you've already replaced me with this new stud?" His jocular tone implied he was kidding. "Going for the young buck, I see. Where'd you find this guy, Hollywood?"

At first, I wasn't sure I should stay. I was horning in here. "Hey, listen. I can play on my own."

"Oh, come on, now, Hollywood." Kurt fanned his hands out, then whacked me on the back. "I'm just havin' a little fun. Plus, you look fit enough to jog behind our golf cart." The dude was having a good time cracking himself up.

Brody came up beside me, wrapping his arm around my shoulders. "This is our new friend, JC. Here for a couple more weeks. And he's from New York City, not Hollywood. Big-time stockbroker."

I never said *big time.*

"Well, you don't say. Maybe you can give me some tips, JC, so I can save a few pennies before my ex-wife drains me dry." He put his hands around his throat and made an obnoxious choking sound, enough to turn heads.

I had to admit, the man *was* funny.

Dennis had been inside the clubhouse but came out. "I got an extra cart for JC and me. You all can take the one with Brody."

And so the game was underway, Kurt talking nonstop the entire course. "Who taught you to hit a ball like that? . . . I thought your last one was going to hit the stratosphere. . . . You ever play with any pros? . . . What does a young guy like you make in a year?"

The first time we played, I wasn't sure if these men were having a bad day of golf or were just *bad golfers*. The more we played, the more I realized it was the latter. I even fudged a few shots to avoid showing them up shamefully. *Again.* With the game behind us, we had our traditional beer on the balcony shooting the shit. Country music emanated from all four corners of the open-air room.

"You look like a guy who scores pretty well with the ladies. I bet those city women are wild." Kurt was at it again. He munched on some fries, taking swigs of his beer to wash them down.

I sat back in my chair. "Oh, I do alright."

"I bet you do. Not married though." Kurt wagged a finger. "Smart man. You're young. Get all the tail you can first." He took another swig of his beer and burped. This was his third. "Once you walk down that aisle, your balls won't belong to you anymore . . . neither will your bank account."

I nodded as I swiped a drizzle of condensation from my glass with my finger. "I couldn't agree more. I have no intention of putting on *those* shackles."

"Stop filling his head with your bad advice. Not all marriages are bad, *Kurt*. Vanessa is the best thing that ever happened to me." From across the table, Dennis sat up straighter in his seat and shot Kurt the stink eye.

"Yeah, we know, *Dennis*. But you've never been divorced. Tom gets it. Ex-wives are the devil."

Tom offered a hint of a nod.

"How bout you, Brody. You lovin' marriage after fifteen years?"

Brody didn't answer right away. Instead, he chewed on his nachos. "What I'd like to know is if you could stop jibber-jabbing for five goddamn minutes. Honestly, dude, you're worse than ever. You gotta crush on JC here?" He nudged his friend with his elbow.

Kurt's cheeks fired up, his complexion the color of a tomato. Against his white hair, his face nearly glowed.

Jesus, *does* he have a crush on me?

"Fuck off, Brody. Just tryin' to be friendly." Kurt took out his cell phone and averted his attention. It took his cheeks several minutes to return to their normal red.

Both Dennis and Brody covered their mouths with their hands. Tom just sat there brooding like he always did. But where Kurt couldn't seem to stop himself from chatting nonstop, Tom never had much to say, other than, "It's a hot one today." Or "Been right wet lately. Farmers are having trouble with their crops."

I had friends in the city who were cops—one who was a detective. Good men. I wasn't so sure about Tom. Something about him didn't sit right with me, but I couldn't put my finger on it.

And then there was Brody. When he wasn't flirting with waitresses or women at the club, the dude liked to brag. "I'm planning on opening another club in the southern part of the state. . . . Did I tell you? I also own some property in town. I'm considering building a restaurant on one. Maybe you can give me some tips on the financials. I already own a shitload of land in Shelburne, prime real estate. . . . You ever seen the Burlington area?"

"Not yet. Is that where Lake Champlain is located?"

"Sure is. A few colleges up there too." He wiggled his eyebrows at me. "Maybe we can hit some bars together and check out those *hot* college chicks." He grinned before he continued to snack on those same nachos, taking a few short sips of his beer in between.

Dennis shot Brody a look. "Don't let Nicole hear you say that." He shook his head and then exhaled. "She'll castrate you."

Brody raised both palms as if in surrender. "I wasn't sayin' I'd do anything. But you can't blame a guy for looking. And besides, JC here is single. Ever heard of a wingman?"

Dennis shook his head again. "Son, there is no need to play with fire. You've got a good life, don't mess it up."

Their conversation was light enough, but somehow, I sensed Dennis was trying to warn Brody. Had he cheated on Nicole before? Given the way Brody seemed to notice anytime a remotely attractive woman passed by us at the club, I suspected as much. I knew a lot of men like him in the city. And my parents were never faithful. It was yet another reason I chose to stay single. *Marriage is bullshit.*

On the following Tuesday, Brody took me out for dinner. It was just the two of us this time. The restaurant looked like it used to be a train station, converted into an eatery that boasted organic food, most of it sensitive to specific allergies or preferences. We sat at a booth with red cushions near the bar, the clatter of several conversations swirling around us. Two TVs at each end of the room showed basketball and golf.

Our waitress was young with caramel highlights in her shoulder-length brown hair, her body curvy in all the right ways. Dressed in a white button-down blouse and black pants, she zeroed in on Brody right away.

"Well, hello, stranger. Where ya been? I haven't seen you much lately." Her eyelashes batted.

Brody beamed at her. "Hey there, Tracy, I've been showing my new friend, JC, around town. How ya been, gorgeous?"

A pink hue flushed her cheeks. "I've been good. Missing my best customer, though." As she spoke, she wiggled her shoulders a tad.

The two of them continued to flirt with each other until Tracy took out a small pad of paper. "What can I get you two gentlemen tonight?"

Having hit my limit with bar food, I said, "I'll take the Thai chicken salad. And an order of brussels sprouts."

She wrote down my order. "And to drink?"

"A glass of bourbon. Whatever you've got. No ice."

Brody placed his order next, which turned out to be a steak with a baked potato. He also ordered bourbon.

"Be right back with your drinks."

As Tracy sauntered off, Brody blew out his lips. "She's a firecracker, that one. Knows how to party."

"Is that right? You been hitting that hard, have you, Brody?" I was curious about the condition of his marriage. Was he a cheater, or did he just like to window shop? Not that it mattered to me one way or another.

He hesitated for a moment, then seemed to catch himself. "Nah. Just lookin'. You know how it is? Oh, wait, you don't know. *You're* not married."

Tracy brought our drinks over. "Here you go, fellas. Food will be out soon."

Maybe it was the way Brody couldn't seem to peel his eyes away from our waitress's tits or her ass as she walked away, I wasn't convinced.

"I'm sure we don't have the babes here that you find in the city. And judging by the look of you, I'd say you get more than your share of tail."

Tail? He sounded like Kurt. I got his meaning, but it wasn't a word I had heard a lot.

I took a sip of my bourbon, enjoying the spicy rush of heat against my throat. "I'm not complaining." He was right. New York City had some of the most beautiful women in the world. Hard to find in this remote of an area. I'd only seen one woman whose looks rose to that level. Too bad she was bat shit.

"So how are things over on Old Oak Road? Seen your nutty neighbor yet?" He wiped a hand across his mouth. "Talk about a firecracker. And not in a good way." He raised his eyebrows.

This was a complicated subject, and I had to admit, I was curious about Iris, but given how these people felt about her, I chose to keep the conversation simple. *Don't get involved. You're not here much longer.* "Nope. Not yet. Seen her dog, Lily, though. She likes to run with me." It had become a regular thing with Lily and me. I looked forward to seeing her every day. The other big dog, Laddie, and little Maggie never showed up. Probably a good thing. It would be hard to corral all three of them. Plus, Iris would most certainly notice if *all* her pets went missing. I got the sense Lily wandered around a lot.

"How'd you know her name was Lily?" Brody took a sip of his bourbon, his eyes narrowing slightly.

"Raymond had told me her name when I delivered those groceries I had told you about." Against my better judgment, a question forced its way out of my mouth. "What is the deal with her anyway?"

"What do you mean?" Brody turned his glass back and forth between his hands.

"When I went to Rolling Creek Grocery, I met Warren and Billy. They informed me that 'Iris is crazier than a loon' and that she was probably a witch. They don't actually think she's a witch, do they? I mean, that's really out there." I laughed and shook my head.

Brody didn't seem to think my comment was funny.

I realized why and felt like an asshole for bringing it up. "Did your son tell you why she had pulled a gun on him?"

"Probably because he was there with Warren and Billy that day. Nicole used to let Dylan hang out with them from time to time. Until I put a stop to it." He bared his teeth a little. "Warren and Billy are lowlifes with too much free time on their hands. They are always gettin' themselves into trouble. And I don't want Dylan getting caught up in their bullshit. Tom has been beside himself dealing with Billy. Imagine bein' the sheriff and havin' to bail your kid out of jail? I don't know why Nicole keeps hiring them to do odd jobs around the club *or* our house. Personally, I don't like having them around." His voice raised. "But what do I know? The woman never listens to me, anyway." He took a sip of his bourbon and practically slammed the glass down on the table.

"That sucks." I thought for a moment. "Did Iris actually shoot at them?" How close had I come to death or serious injury?

Brody seemed to dismiss my question. "I don't know. I'm assuming Billy and Warren had a hand in whatever happened." Defiance sparked in his eyes as he pointed at me as though I had transformed into Nicole. His nostrils flared. "I told her, under no uncertain terms—*not* to let Dylan hang around them after that." It took a moment for the blood to drain from his cheeks.

"Yeah, I get it. Martha and Raymond also warned me about Iris, you know. Told me to drop off the groceries and go." I came *this* close to fessing up about my own altercation with her, but something stopped me. Maybe it was because I had lied about it before. Not a good way to begin a friendship.

A faraway look captured Brody's eyes, his hand rubbing along his jaw in a thoughtful manner. "I really don't know Iris. I just know that she was involved with a married man about ten years ago. She was like that. Always looking for a thrill. . . . At least, that was what I had heard about her." He palmed his drink. "She got around, if you know what I mean. I guess her parents were bible thumpers. Apparently, the married dude was a dentist from Stowe. She nearly broke up his marriage." He snapped his fingers. "Nathan was his name. Rich dude. He left town with his wife and kids after that. And she's lived out there by herself ever since."

Iris was losing ground in my mind. Other than her beauty, she was violent with a questionable character. I wasn't exactly a Boy Scout, but I had never pulled a gun on anyone (although if I had, it would have been on Ernie Parker) or tried to break up a marriage. My desire to learn more about her was dwindling.

Tracy arrived with our food and was gone in a flash. This time, Brody focused on his plate and not her ass.

I mixed the peanut dressing into my salad. "You think I should pay her a visit? She *is* my only neighbor. Or do you think that would be dangerous?" I took a bite of my salad, savoring the explosion of peanut, ginger, and too many other flavors to identify. The brussels sprouts paired nicely.

Brody sliced into the ribeye he had ordered.

"Everything to your liking?" Tracy had returned. She aimed her question right at Brody, who barely looked up at her. "We're good. Thanks, Tracy." His tone lacked the enthusiasm it once had a moment ago.

I got the sense Warren and Billy were stressing this guy out, especially where his son was concerned.

I nodded in agreement as I savored my food. "Yup. Very good, thanks."

The sparkle in Tracy's eyes dimmed as she wandered off to take another order.

"Did I hear correctly, you have twins?"

"Yup. Dylan and Aubrey are fifteen. When he's minding, Dylan is my pal." He spoke with pride as he cut his next bite of steak. "Aubrey is just like her mother. When those two go at it." He made a cringy face. "You don't want to be anywhere near them. World War III at our house." He mixed butter into his baked potato. "I'm assuming you don't have kids. How old are you, anyway?"

"Thirty. No kids, and I don't plan on having any."

Brody washed a bite of potato down with a sip from his water that Tracy had brought us, along with our menus and utensils when we had arrived. "Ah, you're young. I'm pushing forty-six. You've got plenty of time for that shit." His perma-smile had returned. "Haven't met the right woman yet, huh? Been too busy meetin' *all* the right women, if you know what I mean." He reached across the table and slapped my arm play-fully. "Man, to be you. I can't imagine what life must be like for a handsome dude like yourself."

And so the conversation rattled on. We discussed the area and more of Brody's potential projects. As we were walking out to our cars, he stopped for a moment. "Hey, thanks for coming out. And about your questions regarding your neighbor. Best to leave that one alone. I don't know what Iris is capable of these days. And I wouldn't want you to get caught up in any trouble during the short time you're here. You know the saying 'best to let sleeping dogs lie?' "

"Yup." Interesting choice of words, considering Iris had three dogs. But he was probably right. I had two weeks remain-ing. I'd already started browsing real estate agents.

He took his key fob out of his pocket and unlocked the doors to his cherry red Corvette, a car that suited a man like him. "Hey, we're having a shindig at the club on the Fourth. You oughta come. Nicole hired a band, and this place"—he pointed toward the restaurant we had just exited—"is catering." He reached out for a handshake. "Should be a lot of fun. If you get too wasted, we have rooms above the club we use for weddings. You can crash there." He headed for his car. "That's where *I'll* be sleeping." I couldn't help but notice that he hadn't said *we*. I also wondered if one of those young waitresses from the club would be joining him.

"I'll think about it. Thanks for dinner. See you soon." I unlocked my SUV.

My new friend sank into the seat of his sports car, fired up the engine, and then pulled up beside me. He rolled his window down. "One of these days, I'm gonna beat your ass on *my* course. I'll wager a fine bottle of scotch over it." He revved his little toy for effect.

I waved him off. "Sounds good, man." Even with my eyes closed, I could golf circles around these dudes. *No point in stating the obvious.*

The next morning, I ran four laps back and forth, surpassing my previous goals. I was up to twelve miles now, Lily with me the entire way. Iris kept to herself, which was fine by me.

I worked most nights after the sun went down, keeping myself privy to any market fluctuations. I fished. I read. I watched Colbert for laughs and porn whenever my dick required attention. Mostly, I enjoyed this time away. It reminded me that a world was still out there full of moments that didn't require a laptop or a dollar sign. Other than when I was running, I slowed my pace, the sights and sounds of nature taking over my consciousness. And I kinda liked how it felt. Not a bad way to live.

I questioned whether or not I wanted to sell the house anymore. What was wrong with a vacation getaway? Deep down, I suspected that once I immersed myself in city life again, this place would lose its appeal.

Morgan offered to visit. "You sound lonely," she'd said during our last conversation, which usually turned into phone sex. "Want me to come up there and keep you company? I've got the weekend off for the Fourth." It was Thursday already— the Fourth landing tomorrow—so the weekend was practically here.

Man, did that sound good. Morgan also loved to golf. I could take her to Brody's Fourth of July party and show her around the club and the area. The guys at the club would fall over backward over Morgan, especially Brody. We could skinny-dip in the pond out back and fuck ourselves silly.

My response wasn't easy for me to say. But this wasn't about me. "I appreciate that, Morgan, but I made myself a promise, I'd stick this out for my grandfather. I hope you understand."

She exhaled. "I get it. Just don't forget what you have waiting for you when you get back." A smile filled her voice. "Maybe we can start seeing each other again. You know, outside of the bedroom." Something in her tone was different from what I had grown accustomed to. Vulnerable. Was Morgan wanting a relationship with me? So unlike her.

Not knowing how to follow that proposal, I layered on the sarcasm. "Outside of the bedroom? You've got to be kidding me? But you're so damn good at it. The best!" I paused. "You should see the size of my dick right now. I don't ever want to leave the bedroom when you're around."

She giggled. "You're so bad. Okay, well, enjoy your time in the wilderness. See you soon, stud."

Wait, no phone sex? It was too late, the line had gone dead, and I wasn't such a prick that I could protest.

On the Fourth, I attended Brody's party solo. Unfortunately, every female I encountered was either married, much older, or way too young. Neither Tom nor Dennis showed up. The holiday might have required law enforcement to be in full force. But Kurt was there with his boisterous personality. By ten o'clock, the man had drunk himself into a stupor. He could barely speak. *Or walk*, for that matter.

Needless to say, I didn't stay long. I left just after the fireworks, which went off about the same time Nicole and Brody were getting into a major argument in the parking lot. From what I could hear, it sounded as though Brody's eye had wandered at the party. I still wasn't sure how far he took things with these other women.

A flirt? Hell, yeah. I'd seen him do that at the club many times. A cheater? The jury was still out on that one. He was a good friend, and so was Dennis. I liked the bond forming between us all.

A few nights after the Fourth, I was sitting out back answering a bunch of texts and emails on my phone while enjoying a glass of wine when I heard *something*. When you're accustomed to the sounds of frogs croaking and the birds and crickets creating their own chatter, an unusual sound stands out. And this one had. *Is that a truck horn?* The noise remained off in the distance, but I could still hear it. No way was it coming from the main road. That was three-and-a-half miles away. I put my wine glass in the house, threw on my sneakers, and jogged up the road to find out where it was coming from.

It was definitely a vehicle of some sort—a truck by the sound of it. And then I heard laughter. Only it wasn't benign. It was rowdy. I quickened my pace, mainly because only one other house existed on this road.

Did Iris have friends over? That didn't seem to fit her hermit lifestyle.

I drew closer.

"Come out, come out, wherever you are, you crazy bitch. We wanna see you. And this time, we ain't leavin' until we do."

This time?

As I came around the corner, a truck was driving all over the field in front of Iris's place, large tires digging up the wild-flowers and sending them into the air along with dirt and debris. Round and round the truck went, its high beams cutting through the night, *woo-hoos* adding to the drama. "Come out, come out, wherever you are."

Who was that? In the truck's bed, two guys I hadn't seen before hung on as the truck fishtailed. They continued to laugh and hoot from the thrill. I couldn't see who was in the front, although my gut told me it was Warren and maybe Billy. The horn blasted obnoxiously loud.

These motherfuckers are harassing one woman? Real nice. My blood boiled as I thought about Ernie and the power he held over me. With sweat dripping down my back, I ramped my jog into a sprint just as Iris's black dog, Laddie, came running around the back of her house.

Outfitted in a pair of shorts and a simple tank, Iris came bounding out the front door, pushing her other two dogs inside. I could hear them barking from an open window.

I waved my arms over my head. "What are you doing? Stay in the house!" I was too far away for her to hear or see me. Especially when the truck was making such a racket, dirt flying up behind its large wheels. High beams bolted to a bar on the roof provided a perfect view of the destruction.

I pushed my legs to run faster as I closed in on the

disturbing scene, a full moon above casting eerie shadows from the tall oaks and maples bearing witness to this shit. It was a horror show.

"Get out of here!" Iris shot after Laddie, who was running dangerously close to the truck's wheels, the ones that had just turned her beautiful field into a dirt track. She clapped her hands. "Come here, Laddie! Right now! Laddie, you're going to get hit!"

The truck came to a halt in front of her house just as the sound of a disturbing yelp reached my ears. *Fuck!*

"Laddie!" The pain in Iris's voice sent a shiver down my sweaty back. "You hit my dog! Oh my god. Laddie!"

I had reached the foot of her driveway. I'd be there in less than a minute.

"Well, well, well. What do we have here?" Doors opened and closed, Warren's voice taunting. "Isn't this a surprise. I didn't know our witch was such a babe." He leered at Iris.

Billy climbed out of the passenger seat, as two other doofuses stood in the bed watching.

When he reached the front of the truck, Billy waved Warren over. "Let's go. You just hit her fucking dog. We need to get out of here!"

Iris dropped to her knees near Laddie's body, weeping, her hair pulled up into a high ponytail. "Come on, Laddie, wake up." She stared up at Warren, her cheeks drenched with tears, strands of blond curls floating around her face.

Knowing her distress, I felt guilty about how goddamn good she looked.

Lily and Maggie filled the air with barks of distress in the background.

"How could you do this to an innocent dog?"

Warren loomed over her, practically salivating, his long hair—the color of an oil spill—matted against his forehead.

Iris's outfit was skimpy, her feet bare, and I was pretty sure she didn't have a bra on. It was ten o'clock. She was probably getting ready for bed, allowing Laddie one last trip to the bathroom. None of that was going to help her now.

But *I* was.

"Well, whose fault is that? I asked you to come out, sweet cheeks." Warren rubbed his jaw and tilted his head. "And man, you certainly do have some sweet cheeks."

"Get the fuck away from her!" I closed in on them, words struggling to form against the lack of oxygen in my lungs. My body still worked, and so I used it. I ran right up to Warren and shoved him to the ground. He reeked of alcohol. "What is the matter with you?" I glared at Billy and the two bumpkins standing in the truck's bed watching the show as if they were at the drive-in on a Friday night. "What is wrong with all of you? You just hit her fucking dog. You just destroyed her yard. You have no right to be here."

Iris stayed bent over Laddie, her voice soft and soothing. "You're okay, boy. We'll get you fixed up. You'll be okay." She stroked his fur, her voice shaky and uncertain.

This wasn't at all what I had imagined was going on. Iris was the victim here, not the perpetrator. And they'd been here before. These assholes *deserved* a gun pointed at them.

Chapter Seven

JC

Warren climbed to his feet. "Mind your own goddamn—"

Thwack. I let my fist fly, colliding with the lowlife's face like a wrecking ball. I leaned over him, grabbed the collar of his T-shirt, and smacked him again as he lay on the ground.

Warren screamed and covered his face from further damage. He whimpered like a baby. "Yeah, you're a big man when it comes to attacking innocent women, but you're not so tough *now*, are you?" For years, I had wanted to say something similar to Ernie. I never got the chance. According to Gramps, he had died of an overdose years later. A big story in a small town.

I straightened up and pointed at the rest of the riffraff. "Unless you want what Warren just got, I suggest the four of you get the hell out of here before I kick the living shit out of you." I clenched my fists and stood firm, my gaze finding each and every one of those assholes. I'd never fought four on one before—although I *had* taken boxing lessons—but something told me I could take them all without much trouble. Billy and Warren were scrawny, and the two standing in the truck's bed had the kind of pudge that came with too little exercise and too much junk food.

They all stared back at me, dumbstruck.

"Now!"

With a jolt, they seemed to snap out of their haze. Billy ran over to Warren. "Come on, let's get out of here." He pulled him up, blood spewing from Warren's nose. He was lucky he had a nose.

Billy ushered Warren into the passenger seat and then ran around the front of the truck before he climbed in behind the steering wheel. The other two idiots sat on the wheel wells with their hands braced on the edge of the bed.

Before he pulled away, Billy looked down at Iris, still huddled over Laddie. "I'm sorry. We didn't mean to—"

"Get. The. Fuck. Out. Of. Here!" I had never been so angry in my life. Four men bullying one helpless woman? What were they planning? Rape? I forced the thought from my mind as the truck rushed down the driveway and out of sight.

Why didn't Iris use her shotgun? My reasonable side answered. If she had, this situation could have gotten even more out of hand. Tom was Billy's father. If she'd shot them, her freedom would be over.

I stared down at a most devastating scene, the other canines barking with abandon from the house.

Iris sobbed over Laddie, who wasn't moving. "It's okay, boy. You'll be okay." She kissed his head. She stroked his dark fur. Her gaze scanned his limp body in desperation. The heartache in her cries had me tearing up with her.

Even though I was pretty sure Laddie was dead, I had to do something to help. I inched closer, not wanting to crowd or scare her. Why did they do this? *Why her?* That question clawed at my mind. Was Tom aware of what his kid was doing? The man had spoken about five words to me all the times I'd golfed with him.

Brody was right about this bunch of kids. Bad news. In all the conversations I'd had about Iris, not one person had described a scenario like this one. According to them, she was pulling guns on people for no apparent reason. I just saw for myself that wasn't the case.

"I have a car, Iris. And I know a vet. I believe you know him too. I can run home and be back here in just a few minutes. I'll drive you there. The vet's name is—"

"D-Dennis?" Tears of anguish dripped off her chin.

"Yes. Dennis. I'll call him from my house and get my car. I'll be right back." I stepped away. "Don't worry. Everything is going to be okay."

I sprinted off, hoping I was right. The idea of leaving Iris alone and vulnerable made me question everything I was doing. I had to believe those lowlifes were long gone. Hopefully, they were shitting themselves with fear over getting caught.

Billy had been the only one of them who had shown an ounce of remorse. *I'm sorry*, he'd said, as if that would excuse what they had just done. Warren was a lost cause. *Psycho*. The two in the back were sheep who would follow their demented leader anywhere.

I didn't know who the other parents were, but I did know Billy's. If I were to venture a guess, I'd say Tom was crazy strict and probably abusive. What did he say would happen if Billy didn't clean up his ex-wife's car? *There would be hell to pay.* "Yeah, I bet there would be. Nice job, Tom, you raised a real fucking winner."

When I had bars, I dialed Dennis. Thank god he answered.

"Hey, JC. Whatcha up to on this fine evening?"

"Iris's dog, Laddie, has been hit by a truck. Warren, Billy, and two other assholes were tearing up her yard and hit him. Iris is beside herself. I just left her there to get my SUV." I ran onto my porch as I spoke, my sneakers slapping against the wooden planks. "I don't think Laddie is alive, but can we bring him over to you?"

Dennis's voice changed to a more serious tone. "Of course. The clinic's address is on that business card I gave you. I'll meet you there." He paused. "Take care of Iris. That young lady has been through a lot."

I wanted to ask him what he meant, but more urgent matters required my attention. "I will."

* * *

After carefully placing an unconscious Laddie onto Iris's lap, I opened the back door of my SUV for Lily and Maggie to hop inside. I didn't want to leave them there after what they had just witnessed. Maggie looked especially stressed, and Iris was too distraught to comfort them. I wasn't sure how long we were going to be gone either. With the engine purring, I lowered the back windows enough to offer both dogs fresh air, and we were off.

The drive to Dennis's clinic seemed to take forever. Iris continued to speak softly to Laddie, providing love and comfort. She'd cried so much, her beautiful sapphire eyes were all red and puffy. Somehow, I knew they were blue; I just couldn't explain how I knew.

Dennis's clinic was about five miles from Brody's club. I had frequented the area enough to know where I was. I pulled into the modest-sized parking lot to find Dennis standing by his sedan. A building stood before us with an A-shaped roof and brick exterior. The words *Washington County Animal Hospital* completed a sign hanging over the door. He rushed over to us as I shifted the car into park.

Lights inside the building came on just before a woman appeared and opened the front door made of glass, etched with the same signage. Dressed in a peach-colored kaftan dress decorated in an African print with some sort of silk headscarf wrapped around her hair, the woman watched Dennis with a hand to her mouth. She was attractive. Was she Vanessa, Dennis's wife? She kept the door open for easy entry, her brown eyes focused on our movements.

"D-Dennis, they hit him. He's not moving. P-please help him. I can't lose him too. Please, Dennis."

Dennis eased the passenger door open. "It's okay, Iris. We're gonna take good care of Laddie. Right, boy?" With skilled hands, he lifted Laddie from Iris's lap.

"He's breathing, and I can feel his heart beating." Did Iris believe what she was saying? Or was she hoping it was so?

"That's a good sign, Iris. I can feel his heartbeat as well. It's strong. He's probably in shock."

That was a relief.

I didn't think it was possible for Iris to cry any harder, but she did. Clinging to hope could do that to a person.

With his arms loaded down, Dennis walked slowly into the clinic, the woman at the door following him inside.

Lily and Maggie were all over my back seat, not sure what to do with themselves. Maggie was whining. Poor thing. My heart broke for them. All I could think was, no wonder Iris didn't talk to strangers. How many times had those assholes paid her a visit? How had she escaped harm before? She had to have been terrified. Everything about her guarded behavior made sense.

I wasn't sure what to do. *Comfort.* I rushed out of the driver's seat and came around to her side of the SUV, the door still open. "He's alive, Iris, and Dennis will do everything he can to help him." I touched her arm. "Let's get you and the dogs inside where it's safe." I eased her out of the car.

Lily and Maggie leaped over the console and were out a millisecond later.

* * *

Sitting in molded plastic lime-green chairs, the walls half white, half pale yellow, and with posters of various animals staring down at us, we awaited news.

Within a short time, the woman came out with two bowls of water for Lily and Maggie. "If you need to take them out to use the bathroom, I have leashes, so they won't run off." She sat next to Iris, who kept her head bowed. "The back area is also fenced in."

The crying had stopped, but Iris's silence was almost deafening. Laddie wasn't the only one in shock from what I could see.

"I'm so sorry, dear. Dennis will take good care of Laddie. I know we've never met, but Dennis has told me a lot about you over the years. He cares very much about you and the dogs. He knows what to do." She placed her hand on Iris's thigh. "Can I get you anything? Coffee? Tea?"

Iris nearly whimpered her answer. "No, thanks."

"Okay." The woman gazed over at me, sitting on Iris's right. "Hi, JC, I'm Vanessa, Dennis's wife. He's told me a lot about you." She smiled at me, but it was strained, given the circumstances.

"Nice to meet you, Vanessa. He's talked about you as well. Dennis is a great guy."

"He sure is. Listen, there is a small break room just down the hall. I put on a pot of coffee, and there is a fridge full of bottled waters. Help yourself. There are all sorts of leashes hung on the wall in there. Take whatever you need. We won't open until seven-thirty tomorrow, so you've got plenty of time before then. I should get back to help Dennis. Come get me if you need anything."

I glanced down at my cell phone, eleven o'clock flashing back at me. "Thank you."

Vanessa rushed off, leaving me and Iris alone.

This was beyond awkward for me. I knew Dennis from my time at the club. He was Brody's friend. We made small talk. In the time I'd been here, this was the second time I had seen or had any contact with Iris. She was a stranger. But that didn't stop me from wanting to help her. After Vanessa had returned to the back, I pet Lily. Maggie was visibly shaking on the floor.

"Should you hold Maggie? She looks pretty upset."

Iris nodded and picked her up. "It's okay, girl. Don't worry. Laddie will be okay. Dennis will help her. You remember Dennis, dontcha?" Her voice came out hollow and weak.

Maggie was all too happy to snuggle into her mother's lap. She looked like a small strawberry blond puffball.

"She seems better now." I pet Maggie, who looked up with the most adorable puppy dog eyes I had ever seen. "You're better now, right, girl? Just needed Mommy?"

Lily came over and placed her chin on my lap. I gave her some love too. And I felt love for that dog. I'd spent nearly every morning with her since I'd arrived.

For the first time since we'd met, Iris looked over at me.

It was everything I could do not to find a mirror and check how disheveled I had to appear. *WTF?* I was a guy. We didn't think about shit like that.

"Where did you come from? How did you know what was happening?"

I continued to stroke Lily's crown as I thought about my answer. "I could hear them from my place. So, I came to help."

Iris's sapphire eyes held so much pain. It rippled off her body like waves of sound.

"Thank you," she said. "I don't know what we would have . . ." She pressed her lips together, her face drawn tight as though trying to block out what could have happened tonight.

Feeling we'd crossed a communication barrier, I placed my arm around her shoulders, making sure to remove it if she showed any sign of discomfort. "I'm glad I was here. I'm sorry, Iris." She felt so delicate, like a flower, underneath my touch. I quickly pulled my arm away, not wanting to linger.

She blew out a breath and shook her head. Then, she met my eyes again.

Jesus, were those eyes blue. *Breathtaking.*

"No, *I'm* sorry. I wasn't very nice to you before. I didn't know who you were. And I don't even own bullets for that gun."

That explained a lot. Iris never shot at anyone. She tried to scare them away. And from what I had just witnessed, she had good reason. What had they done the last time? Warren implied there had been multiple visits.

She seemed to ponder something. "Who *are* you, by the way? Are you related to Callum?"

"Yes. My name is Jacob. People call me JC. I'm Callum's grandson. I take it you knew Callum?"

"Knew? Did Callum die?" Her eyes glistened with new tears, and I hated that I was the one causing them.

I nodded as my chest grew heavy. "He did. He passed away last winter." This time, I supported her tears with some of my own. And I *never* cried. Not in front of people. But this night was too much for anyone. I'd have to be made of stone to get through the experience without feeling its impact.

I wiped her tears away with my fingers. "It's okay, Iris. He lived a good life. And now he's with my gram. She was the—"

"Love of his life." She nodded, a humorless giggle escaping from her pouty lips, the ones I couldn't for the life of me stop gawking at.

Her long, curly hair was left half gathered up, the stress of the night evident by the ponytail that was slowly falling out. Smudges of dirt collected on her high cheekbones, and she was barely dressed, a soiled white tank and skimpy gray shorts (probably her pj's). Honestly, she was the most beautiful woman I had ever seen. New York City be damned.

She turned in her seat and reached her hand out. "Can we start over? Hi, Jacob, my name is Iris Flynn. So nice to meet you." She attempted to smile, but the stress weighed too much.

I shook her hand. "Nice to meet you, Iris Flynn. My name is Jacob Sullivan, but my friends call me JC."

I watched as she stroked her pup. Iris was gentle in her movements, soft-spoken, and she was pulling me into her orbit at warp speed. On her feet, she wore a pair of faded yellow flip-flops she must've grabbed when I was gone, retrieving my vehicle. She'd also put on a bra. Once again, I was ashamed of myself for noticing such things.

While she comforted Maggie, my gaze glided up a set of legs designed to render any man helpless, say nothing about her tiny waist and tits, ample enough to fondle and treasure—a perfect body in my mind, all of it God-given from what I could see. And then there were those eyes, the ones that reached into my soul and tormented me. That dream came to mind. What I wouldn't give to be in her bed, pleasing her over and over again, chasing away all of her sorrows.

"I know about Evelyn. Callum talked about his Evie all the time."

Thank you for getting my mind onto other things.

The last thing I needed right now was a goddamn hard-on, although my dick was already pushing against the zipper of my shorts.

"He spoke about you too. Said how proud he was." She altered her voice. " 'Taking New York City by storm.' " She smirked, and I wanted to wrap my arms around her and hold her close. "So, you own his place now? Are you staying the summer like Callum used to do?" She continued to pet Maggie as she spoke. Lily stayed at my feet.

"Um. I'm not sure. I was supposed to only stay until the middle of July." That was a week from now.

Iris looked away. "Oh." Her voice slumped right along with her shoulders.

Was she disappointed? How could she be? She barely knew me. And I barely knew her. The thought of disappointing this woman had me scrambling.

"But I'm thinking of staying longer." Where the hell had that come from? I had no idea. I was a money guy. I thrived on adrenaline and challenge. I'd traveled a good portion of the world due to my success. I fucked. I didn't fall in love. And I was happy with that life until now . . . until *her*.

Chapter Eight

Iris

As 1:00 a.m. approached, Dennis came out dressed in a long white lab coat over a pair of aqua-colored scrubs.

Lily sprang up on all fours.

I handed Maggie over to Jacob without realizing what I had done. To my surprise, Maggie curled up in Jacob's big, strong arms as though she had known him forever.

I hopped to my feet, my head light, and my knees not as strong as they should be. "How is he?" I steeled myself for what Dennis was about to say.

"It's late. Let's have a seat."

I did as he asked, even more alarmed than I was before. People only told you to *have a seat* when they were about to deliver bad news.

This gave Lily an excuse to lie back down right next to Jacob, her new friend. Poor girl was tired.

"First and foremost, he's gonna be okay."

All the stiff muscles in my body turned to jelly, my lungs expelling a lengthy breath. My heart filled with hope again.

"He has a fractured leg and a bruised pelvis. I was worried he might have some internal bleeding, but I didn't see anything on the CT scan. The good news is the truck hit him on the backside. No head injuries. He's pretty banged up, but with proper rest and time, he'll be running around soon enough. I'll prescribe some pain medication for him. Do you still have his crate?"

I thought about that. "Yes, it's in the guest room. They all sleep on pallets on the floor in my room, except for Maggie, who sleeps in bed with me."

"That may be fine, but if Laddie tries to get up too much, you will need to crate him to keep him still. Bring the crate into your bedroom just in case. His injuries should heal within the next two to four weeks. And leash him when he goes out to do his business. Make sure the leash is short for the time being. The more you can keep him still, the faster the bone will heal." He stifled a yawn, his eyelids drooping. And then he ran a hand over his beautiful bald head.

I felt so bad for putting him through this. And in the middle of the night, no less. Dennis worked hard during daylight hours. He had to be exhausted.

"He's got a couple of cuts that I bandaged. But if he starts to lick or chew on them, we'll have to put a cone on him."

I leaned over and hugged Dennis, the man who brought me my wonderful dogs and gave me a reason to live again. "Thank you, Dennis. I can't tell you how grateful I am. I'll find a way to pay you."

"Send me the bill, Dennis, I'll take care of it." I turned toward Jacob, my gaze zoning in on his tender fingers stroking Maggie's fur. For just a moment, I was envious. It had been so long since anyone had touched me. I wasn't sure what it felt like anymore.

"I can't let you do that, Jacob."

Dennis cleared his throat, drawing my attention. He raised a palm slightly. "No need. You took these dogs out of the goodness of your heart, Iris. No charge."

"Thank you, Dennis. Can I see him?" I glanced over at Jacob, who seemed to anticipate my next question.

"Go ahead. I'll watch the dogs." He peered down at Maggie. "You'll be okay with me, right, girl?" Jacob spoke so gently to Maggie, and part of me couldn't help but feel awed.

It didn't take long for me to realize that Callum was a good man. I felt the same way about Jacob. The only difference was that Jacob was young and handsome. Dreamy even. Anyone with a pulse could see that. I had thought his eyes were green at first, but upon closer inspection, I learned they were more hazel or olive. I'd already noticed that he kept his light-brown hair relatively short. What I hadn't paid attention to before was the dimple that centered his strong jawline, all of it covered in a layer of sexy scruff. Large biceps and pronounced pectorals stretched his mint-colored polo in all the right directions, his skin tanned by summer. My excuse for swooning to this degree was never having the opportunity to see people, gorgeous or otherwise. I read books. I watched what TV I could get in focus. This was different. Jacob was flesh and blood. And he was here.

Maybe it was a hero complex, but whenever he looked into my eyes, my heart couldn't help but carry itself away. He was leaving soon. And he didn't need to get swept up in my complicated life. I could appreciate Jacob as a friend, and that alone was a big step for me.

I followed Dennis toward the back, aching to kiss and love on my Laddie. When I saw him lying on the table, all motionless, I dashed over and showered him with my affection. I'd cried so much my throat ached. "You're gonna be okay, Laddie.

Dennis got you all fixed up. And I'll take good care of you at home." He barely moved, his mind zonked out.

Standing beside me, Dennis cleared his throat again. "I'd like to keep him here for the next twenty-four hours if that's okay with you."

I lifted my head off my dog. "Why? You said he's okay, right?"

Dennis nodded as Vanessa stepped into the room. "He's fine. But I'd like to monitor him anyway. Make sure there isn't something I've missed."

Vanessa came up behind me, her hands landing gently on my shoulders. The gesture reminded me of my mother. It had been so long since I had seen her.

"Go home, Iris, and get some rest. You have to be exhausted. We'll take good care of Laddie." Her voice was soft and supportive.

"I appreciate all you've done for him, Dennis . . . and Vanessa. I just don't want him to wake up alone." The thought made me want to cry, only there were no tears left. The strain of the night still weighed on my chest like a cinderblock.

Vanessa turned me around to face her.

I'd never met Dennis's wife before or his daughter, who was all grown up now. I just knew they existed. I gazed into her soft-brown eyes and saw nothing but kindness, which wasn't surprising considering how great Dennis was.

"I promise you. I'll be here when he wakes up. And we'll send you regular texts about his progress. He's going to be pretty out of it for a while."

Dennis positioned himself next to his wife. He blinked, his face softening. "I gave Laddie to you. And I've been providing all your dogs' care for a very long time." He offered me a fatherly smile, reminding me of another parent devoid in my life. "He's in good hands. I don't have a busy day ahead, and I've been letting my partners handle some of my patients for the summer. Bethany's managing the staff and the schedules over her summer break."

As I understood it, Bethany was studying to become a vet herself, eventually running the place when her father retired down the road. Dennis had mentioned these things when he'd come to give my dogs shots or checkups over the years, which wasn't that often. He'd made sure they had tick and heart meds as well. And where I lived, that was important.

Other than one person who had stolen my heart and nearly shattered it, I knew three people as of late: Dennis, Callum, and Becky, who delivered the groceries. Everyone else I knew *of*. Those unsavory characters, I chose not to think about

Now I could add Jacob to that list, someone I would look forward to seeing every summer. That was, if he planned to return. The thought of him leaving and never coming back brought emotions to the surface that scared the hell out of me. Ten years ago, I'd have been crushing big time, trying to find him on socials or asking about him in town. *Does he like me? Will he call or text?* I didn't have the strength for such foolishness anymore.

I agreed to let Dennis keep Laddie. I knew he had my dog's best interest at heart, and that was something I didn't take for granted. Dennis had saved my life in more ways than one. I trusted Vanessa by default. And I was comfortable with that.

With Laddie settled, the four of us ventured back to my house, Jacob yawning several times along the way. We arrived at 1:30 a.m., my yard looking like it had become part of a construction project. All those beautiful wildflowers were gone, ruts carving up the land.

I let the dogs out, who quickly emptied their bladders.

Jacob stayed in the driver's seat, so I approached. "Let me put the dogs inside, and I'll be right back."

"Sure. Take your time."

When I returned outside, Jacob was standing on the driveway in front of my porch, just like he was doing the first time I had encountered him. Feelings of guilt clenched my stomach as we both stood there, awkward and not speaking.

I was about to thank him again when he spoke up with me. Our voices collided in the air between us.

Then we both smiled bashfully at each other. "I was going to thank you for all you've done."

Jacob didn't respond right away. I could see his jaw working on something. "Would it be okay . . ." He stopped himself. "Never mind. It's late." He waved his statement off into the air.

I took a step forward. "No, go ahead. What were you going to say?" I hung on his next words.

He peered up at me. "Could I come in for a moment? I promise I won't stay long."

I was thrilled. And what a strange feeling *that* was. "Sure." I gestured with my hand. "Come on in. I could make you some coffee, or I've got water."

Once inside, I put my pups to bed, who didn't argue. Normally, they'd want me to accompany them, but they were too tired to protest. Lily fell fast asleep on her dog bed, and Maggie did the same on my human bed. A quick glance in my bathroom mirror horrified me. I redid my ponytail and tried my best to wipe the dirt from my cheeks.

I didn't want to be gone too long and encourage Jacob to leave. So I rushed back out.

When I returned to the kitchen, Jacob had taken the liberty of pulling out two glasses, which he filled with water. He handed one glass over to me. "I figured you were thirsty."

"Thank you." I took a sip, my throat appreciating the much-needed hydration. Then, I took another one.

I followed Jacob into my living room, equipped with a

plush sofa, an easy chair, and a few tables and lamps. Adorning my eggshell walls, I had purchased a few pieces of artwork from yard sales that I had found ten years ago when I first moved in. We stood at my picture window, gazing out at the remnants of what used to be my lawn.

I could still hear Warren and his friends laughing as they teased and taunted me and my dogs.

"Is this window new?"

Distracted by my thoughts, I gazed over at Jacob. "Huh?"

Jacob pointed downward. "The trim is framed in natural wood, unlike your other windows that are all painted white. I was just curious if this is new."

I nodded. "It is new. Callum helped me install it last fall."

Jacob took a sip of his water. "Yeah, Gramps was good at home improvement projects. I suspect he paneled the lake house in pine before he died. Have you seen his place?"

I shook my head. "Not really. I've walked down that way and seen the outside. Once, Callum was fishing, and I watched with my dogs." Paranoia had me fidgeting. "We weren't peeping or anything. We were just out for a walk. The house had been vacant for a very long while. I didn't even know who Callum was at the time."

"No worries, and no need to explain. It's all good." Jacob looked down at the window again. "This window may be the last project Gramps worked on." His eyes grew distant as he stood beside me.

I wanted to take his hand and offer my condolences, but I was too shy.

"Why did those lowlifes come here, Iris? Have they been here before?" The inflection in his tone suggested he knew they had.

A lump formed in my throat as anxiety heated up my chest, which was already quite warm. But what was the use in lying at this point? Jacob had seen what these people were capable of. "They started coming here three years ago on Halloween. First, to deliver groceries. That time, they waited outside my house, yelling profanities and kicking my door. Warren stomped on my groceries and then threw eggs at my windows. Later that night, they came back. This time, accusing me of being a witch." I set my glass down on an end table behind me. "I don't know where they got that idea. It's crazy, right?" I suspected where the idea originated, but I had no proof. "They've come every Halloween since. Last year was the worst."

"Did you tell Raymond and Martha what happened? And what happened last year?"

Why hold back? Tell him.

"No, I didn't tell anyone."

"Why not? You're their customer. They should have known what their grandson was doing."

I looked away, my head shaking from the absurdity. "No one is going to believe me, Jacob. Billy would deny it or make up some story about me being the aggressor. You don't understand how people work around here."

Jacob nodded. He seemed to understand what I was saying. I wondered if he'd already heard stories about me. Ten years later, were they still circulating? *Of course they are. You are now a witch!*

"What happened last year?" Jacob asked again.

I took a stabilizing breath. "They threw a large rock through this window. And they threatened to burn the place down if I didn't come out." I had never explained this to anyone before. Not even to Callum, who had seen it for himself. "Your grandfather came to my rescue. He had called the police." While part of me was nervous and uneasy about admitting what this nightmare had been like, another part of me wanted to unburden myself. "That was why Callum helped me fix the window. I don't know what I would have done without him. It would have been a very cold winter. That's for sure." I attempted a smile that didn't last long. And when Jacob didn't respond, I gazed over at him with trepidation. Was this something he didn't want to deal with? I knew *I* wouldn't. Only that wasn't the expression etched all over his face.

Eyes wide and jaw clenched, he finally found his words. "What did the police do about it?"

I shook my head again. "Not much. Paid for the window. The sheriff is Billy's father. He was the one who—"

"I know who Billy is, and I also know Tom."

How? Jacob hadn't been here long enough. I didn't like hearing those words. Were they friends? Now I knew he had heard things. How could he have not? And I had pulled a gun on Jacob. I shuddered at what he must've thought of me. And yet, he came to my rescue anyway.

He continued to stare me down, his eyes narrowing. *Is he angry with me?* Was he about to shatter my image of him? Wouldn't be the first time this had happened to me.

"Iris, this isn't normal. You know that, right?" His cheeks tinted toward pink. So did his neck.

"Of course, I know that, Jacob! But what am I supposed to do about it? Do you think Tom is going to arrest his precious son? I used to know Tom, and he wasn't much better back then."

"Back when? Why do you live out here by yourself? Where is your family? And why are those assholes out to hurt you?" He flailed a hand in the air, his volume increasing. "How can you live this way?"

My teeth ground together. What was this? Blame everything on Iris? It sure felt that way. That was exactly what everyone else had done ten years ago. I was seventeen—a kid. Once again, I worried I had misjudged Jacob. And he was inside my house now, leaving me totally vulnerable. *But he is Callum's grandson.*

"I don't have to explain myself to you!" I pointed. "And my life is none of your business!" I stormed over to the door. "Thank you for helping us. But I think it's time you leave."

How disappointing. I never should have let myself get sucked in by a man like Jacob. He was kind, but he had no right to judge me. My parents had judged me. Everyone I had cared about had done the same. There was a reason I was alone. People weren't worth the effort.

Jacob dropped his head. He placed his empty water glass next to mine on the side table and approached, his tone more compassionate. "I'm sorry. You're right. I just met you." He reached his hand out as a gesture of what appeared to be good-will. "Let me tell you what I know so far. . . . You are unbeliev-ably loving to your pets. You are cautious with people, and from what I witnessed tonight, I can understand why. You are strong, probably a lot stronger than you give yourself credit for. And you appear to be alone. What bothers me most? You are also so very sad."

My lower lip trembled, tears threatening my tired eyes. I was ready to crumble right there in front of him.

He came closer, his fingers brushing a few strands of hair away from my face. "And you are the most beautiful woman I have ever seen." His olive eyes grew intense, the color more vibrant. "I don't know your story, Iris, but if you feel comfort-able enough someday, I hope you will share it with me."

I wanted so badly to fall into his arms and weep. I hugged my waist instead, my cheeks soaked by tears brought on by his unexpected sympathy.

"I am not going to do anything to hurt you. And I am not hitting on you either, even if I really, really want to." The ghost of a smirk played on his handsome lips. "But I am not leaving you here alone. I can sleep on the couch, or you can bring the dogs and come stay with me. I have a guest room. Until I understand the threat you are dealing with, I am sticking to you like glue."

Again, not what I had expected.

I wasn't sure if I had ever heard words more welcoming to my heart. Being alone, I had shut a part of myself down. I was twenty-seven, yet I felt as though I had lived three lifetimes. Did I dare to trust that Jacob wouldn't do to me what the others had done? How could I step back into the light, only to have it blocked out again?

I wanted to tell him this, but years of despair and solitude forbade it. Wounds ran so deep, I wasn't sure I would survive reopening them again. How could he know all of those things about me? *But he doesn't know everything, does he?* Secrets hidden in my past would surely change his mind about the person he *thought* I was. Secrets I could never reveal. We were friends, and it would have to stay that way. Soon, he'd be leaving.

He could have the couch. But I would never let Jacob have my heart. For his protection as well as my own.

Chapter Nine

I was making love to Iris. We were on my dock, no one around as water lapped against the pylons, my tongue savoring her sexiness. Naked and perfect, she was below me, her long legs spread wide. I sampled her sweet nectar, my dick about ready to explode. We worshipped each other with touch and taste. She stroked me; she suckled me, her pouty lips and tongue driving me wild. Our bodies tangled together, every touch pushing me to the limits of my control. She was everything I had ever wanted and more. So gorgeous. So sexy. So mine.

No longer on the dock, we were now in my johnboat, the swells swaying our bodies back and forth with their powerful rhythm. The pond was much larger now and deeper. It wasn't the pond after all. We were in the ocean. Something slammed into us. Warren stared down from a higher peak, his grin sardonic, and his eyes predatory. "Those are my sweet cheeks. Enough playing, Hollywood. Hand her over."

I rose as Tom's fist collided with my jaw. I fell back into the cold water, my hands flailing to keep my body afloat. The water was heavy, pulling me under.

Iris fought against her attackers, but she was too weak. The boat grew larger and out of reach, Tom peering down at me from the same bow, its height unfathomable. They had her. She was gone. And she would never return. Water slapped my face, trying to muzzle my nose and mouth. My limbs grew heavy and slow.

And then my eyes sprang open, Lily pressing her wet nose into my cheek. It took me a moment to comprehend what was happening. I took several heavy breaths, relieved I was safe. *Jesus Christ!*

Lily whimpered as she prodded me again with her nose.

"Oh, hey, girl," I said through a foggy mind and panting lungs. With a raging dick, I hopped up off the couch and let her out to empty her bladder, self-conscious of the extremely large bulge protruding through my shorts.

I had told Iris I wasn't hitting on her. This would *not* support my argument. *Where is Maggie?*

I crept closer to realize Iris's bedroom door sat open, no sound coming from her room. *Hmm.* The remnants of my dream implied she was in danger, but I knew that probably wasn't the case. I mentally shook off the haze as I returned to the back door. "Come on, girl."

Lily trotted inside and right over to her water bowl to get a drink.

While she did so, I grabbed my leather duffle bag from the floor bordering the living room and took advantage of Iris's half bath located off the kitchen. It wasn't ideal, but I had to give my dick time to calm down. Not having sex in weeks was my excuse. *Porn and phone sex doesn't count.* It was all bullshit anyway. It was that dream. And I'd had several. Not of someone accosting Iris, but of her in general, most of the time naked, and bringing me to the peaks of my sexual fantasies. In my subconscious, we'd been intimate a number of times already.

I washed my face and armpits as best I could, brushed my teeth, and changed into a fresh white T-shirt with a pair of gray gym shorts. Casual was becoming my new vibe. I'd brought a couple of suits with me, mainly because I was so used to wearing them. This was not a place for formalities.

When I came out, Iris was waiting for me in the kitchen, Maggie at her feet. For a moment, I struggled to maintain eye contact.

Glad you can't read my thoughts, Iris. Or peer into my dreams. She'd kick my sorry ass out for being a pervert.

"Good morning," she said with a smile. "Did you sleep okay on the couch?" Her hair was slightly wet, the scent of something sweet, apricot maybe, flattering the air between us. She stood before me in a floral satin robe that barely reached her knees, a pair of black ankle socks cushioning her feet. I could tell she had a T-shirt and shorts on underneath. No naked body just waiting to be ravaged. Pervert or not, when it came to her, *nothing* got past me.

"Yeah, I slept okay."

She giggled. "I couldn't get Lily to leave you alone to go outside and pee. I think you have a new girlfriend. I heard you let her out. Thank you." Unexpectedly, she approached and pushed up on her toes to plant a sweet kiss on my cheek.

Did I want to grab her around the nape of her neck and follow that kiss with one of my own that was sure to impact us both? That went without saying. *Not why I'm here.*

"Would you like some eggs for breakfast? I think I may have some bacon, but I'd need to thaw it." She approached the freezer above her fridge, opened the door, and peered inside, her long legs and perfect ass taunting me. *Jesus, get a grip, dude.*

And then I thought about Warren, and my selfish desires took a tumble.

"Eggs sound great. And I have plenty of bacon back at my place. Want me to run home and get some?"

She waved me off. "Nah, maybe another time. Did you want to take a shower? You can use my bathroom."

"Uh, sure. I washed up, but I could really use a shower." *And a moment to get my pathetic shit together so I can be in the same room with you.* "Be back in ten."

* * *

When I came out of her bathroom feeling clean and refreshed, my nose welcomed the smoky scent of bacon. I entered the kitchen for a second time, where Iris had set a table for two, a small vase displaying an arrangement of wildflowers at its center. Just beyond the table, a small window overlooked her backyard, creating a cozy scene for me to appreciate. Picturesque. On the stove, a pan of scrambled eggs sat warm as Iris bent over to open the oven, pulling out a tray of bacon that she flipped with a pair of tongs.

"Thanks for making breakfast. I thought you said the bacon was frozen." I headed for a short section of countertop next to the fridge, where a coffee pot called out to me. "Mind if I grab a cup?" The nutty aroma was as welcoming as an old friend.

"Help yourself. And I found a way to thaw the bacon quickly. It's still gonna be a few minutes yet."

As she flipped the bacon, she tipped her chin toward another area of the kitchen where a toaster rested next to a loaf of bread and a glass butter dish. "Hey, would you mind making the toast? Everything you need is right there."

"Sure. No problem. But you have to agree to let me make dinner for you sometime to return the favor."

She placed the bacon back in the oven. "Deal."

Morgan had made breakfast for me. So had a few other dozen women. Somehow, this morning felt different—as though I belonged here with Iris. But that was crazy, right? *Just your hormones, big boy. Chill out.*

Before long, we were sitting at her table, filling our faces while the dogs, who had already eaten, rested on the beige ceramic-tiled floor, watching us.

Iris had opened the window, allowing a light breeze to lift the sheer fabric of the white curtain with each breath. With no air conditioning, I noticed all her windows remained open, inviting cross breezes to refresh the air.

Facing east, rays of morning sunshine ran along the vertical paneling in faded green that dressed her kitchen nicely. She'd chosen open shelving on the upper walls, which appeared to hold her plates and drinkware, plus a small collection of spices and large containers of food. Optimum for limited space. Her countertops were made of Formica in light gray, several drawers and cabinets underneath, allowing additional storage for the compact room. She didn't appear to have a dishwasher, but she did have an oven and also a microwave, which peered down from above her stove.

It was quaint.

"So you said the couch was okay?" Iris forked a bite of her eggs. "I hope it wasn't too uncomfortable."

If I were being honest, my lower back wasn't a fan. "No, it was fine." I'd have to figure out a way to make this work. I wasn't used to sleeping on couches, especially long term— meaning more than one night.

"I do have a guest room, but not an extra bed. I mainly use it for storage."

I gazed out the window at a circular area of lawn that Iris had mowed, a small boulder with a somewhat flat surface facing a bench. Wildflowers grew heavy along the perimeter, framing it all in, a mountain range set off in the distance. "That's a nice little spot you got out there. Was that boulder here when you moved in?"

"No, I rolled it here from the woods." Iris tore her toast in half, taking a bite.

What woods? Other than a few clusters of trees, tall grass spanned quite a distance. Did she mean from across the road? My eyes grew wide. "Wow! That must've taken some effort." Iris was stronger than she looked.

She lifted one shoulder and continued eating.

"That boulder reminds me of a time when I was at my grandparents' house one summer. I was little, I can't recall my exact age, and I had wandered out into their cow pasture. Gramps wasn't far off, but he'd turned his head for a moment, and I was curious about the cows. Until I got closer and saw how much larger they were than I was." The memory caused me to grin at myself. "Anyway, there was a boulder in the center of the pasture, much like yours, only bigger. The cows seemed just as fascinated with me as I was with them. Once I realized that, I jumped up on the boulder, thinking I would be safe."

Iris popped the rest of her toast into her mouth. "What happened?"

"By the time Gramps got to where I was, the cows had surrounded me. But being on the rock helped me feel taller. I didn't mind that quite so much. According to my Gramps, I acted like I was king of the world. He said I wouldn't stop talking about it for days. All I needed was a wooden sword in my hands."

We shared a moment of laughter.

"That's adorable." Iris sipped her coffee.

I stared back out the window. "Your boulder is smaller than

the one I was on. It's nice, though. Gives that little seating area some character."

She placed her mug down on the table and stared out the window with me. "It took me all day to get it here. But I had to have it." Her chin lowered, the smile she'd been flashing melting away. "That spot is my sanctuary. It's my favorite place in the whole world." She grew quiet, her eyes unfocused as though her mind had traveled to another place.

Had something about this conversation sparked an unpleasant memory, or was it the opposite? I wasn't sure what to make of it. But then again, I wasn't sure what to make of a lot of things here. I took a sip of my coffee, enjoying the caffeine rush and the thick, nutty taste. "I see you have a barn. What do you store in there? If anything."

Iris shook herself into focus. "I have a car in there. A compact. My dad left it for me. I just don't know how to . . ." She pursed her lips as heat rushed to her cheeks.

I had lifted my mug to my mouth for another sip and paused. "Don't know how to what, drive?" Was it possible that a woman her age and in the twenty-first century didn't know such things? Once again, I reminded myself where I was.

She peered down at her food. "Nope. I studied for the test, but I never learned how to actually drive." Using her fork, she pushed a few small clumps of egg around her plate.

I had finished my breakfast and sat back in my chair. "Do you mind me asking you why not? How old are you?"

"Twenty-seven." Letting go of her fork, she wrapped her palms around her coffee mug as though she needed the support. And she wouldn't even look at me, her shoulders starting to droop.

"That's nothing to be ashamed of. I know lots of people in the city who don't drive." I placed my hands on the edge of the table. "Want me to teach you?"

She peered up into my eyes, leaving me breathless. *How do you keep doing that?* I'd seen women wear contact lenses that made their eyes the color Iris was born with. It wasn't just the color that stirred my insides. It was something else I couldn't pinpoint.

"Really? You would be willing to do that?"

"Of course." I pushed my chair back and rose, taking my plate along with hers to the farmhouse sink. "I've got a decent enough SUV. Or we can use your car if you want." I set the plates by the sink and then searched for some dishwashing liquid in the cabinet below.

Iris grabbed our utensils, the glasses, and the mugs, and joined me at the sink. "My car isn't registered or inspected. I'm not even sure it would start. I used to start it often, but it's been years."

I gazed out another small window above the sink at all her open land. "We can give it a try, and if it doesn't start, I have my SUV. And we can practice on Old Oak Road. As long as you drive along the edge in some areas, you can avoid the ruts." I'd become rather masterful about this topic in the time I'd traveled back and forth. "You'll have the whole place to yourself. And if you want, I can even help get your car inspected and whatnot. Or get it to a garage if it needs repair. I do know that once cars sit for too long, they can develop issues."

From next to me, Iris placed her hand over mine by the sink, a tiny wrinkle forming between her brows. "Why? Why would you do that for me? You don't even know me."

I hadn't offered her *that* much, so her question caught me off guard. It wasn't as if I had promised to teach her how to fly a plane, which I also knew how to do. It made me sad for her, how isolated she'd become, her life uneventful. Except for scary lowlifes.

I stood back; my hands braced on my hips. "Maybe I'm

doing it because I like you. Hasn't anyone done something nice for you before?" I meant my comment to be funny, but it wasn't received that way, judging by the distress crinkling the edges of Iris's eyes.

She bowed her head, something I was starting to notice she did a lot. "With the exception of Dennis"—she fanned one hand out—"and Callum, of course, no one has done anything like that for a very long time."

I returned to the sink, making sure to avoid staring directly at her. If we kept busy, maybe she would open up to me. "I'll wash. You dry?"

She grabbed a hand towel off a hook by the sink. "Deal."

She already had a small plastic tub inside the large sink for washing, so I squeezed a fair amount of soap into the tub and turned the faucet on to fill it. The other portion of the sink I'd use for rinsing. "What about your parents?" I grabbed a sponge from a small caddie and scrubbed a plate as I spoke. "You said your dad left you the car. Did your parents move away or something?" I hoped they weren't dead. If they were, so was this conversation.

"Yeah, something like that." She took one plate from my hands, rinsed it, and then dried it with her towel before placing it on the counter. "They moved away ten years ago."

Okay, good. Not dead.

I washed the second plate. "But you said you're twenty-seven, right?"

"Yeah."

"Your parents moved away when you were seventeen? Why didn't they take you with them?" I handed her the second plate to rinse and dry.

She inhaled, and in a stressful sort of way. "Because I refused to go with them."

"Why not?" I dropped the small stack of utensils into the

tub, making them clank together. This didn't make sense. What parents would leave a seventeen-year-old behind?

"Because I couldn't." A lone tear ran down her cheek, an indication of how painful this conversation had become for her.

"Were you involved with someone at the time? In love?" I was pushing it, no doubt, but something told me Iris needed pushing. She'd kept herself holed up in this house without the ability to drive for ten years. She was a young woman who was living the life of a hermit. It broke my heart.

"I was involved with someone back then. But that wasn't the only reason."

I placed the washed utensils at the bottom of the sink next to the tub for her.

"Does the reason have anything to do with what happened last night?" Had she been with someone abusive, and they weren't willing to let her go? I could see that happening in a place like this. Even in the city Iris would be fawned over.

"No. I told you. They started coming here three years ago, and for some reason, they think I'm a witch." She tossed her hand towel down onto the counter. "I don't see how they could think that unless someone put that idea into their stupid heads. I think they are just trying to . . ." She placed her hand to her mouth.

"What?" It was all I could do to refrain from shaking her to get more answers.

"Run me out of town."

"Why? You're a single woman living alone. You're not hurting anyone."

She backed away from me, her arms hugging her waist. "Not everyone sees me that way. Some people think I'm a horrible person."

I leaned against the sink and crossed my arms. "That's

crazy, Iris. Clearly, you aren't a horrible person. *You* don't believe that, do you?" *What happened to you?*

She gazed up at me, the sadness in her eyes returning. "Maybe I *do* believe that. I am not who you think I am." Her body seemed to shrink into itself.

I shook my head at the absurdity of her words. "Iris. You are not a bad person."

"How would you know? Yes, I am."

"Look, I don't know what happened ten years ago. But nothing short of murder would excuse the treatment you're receiving." I uncrossed my arms and took a step closer. "I'm a pretty good judge of character, and I can tell with 100 percent certainty that you are a good person. You have had some bad things happen to you. Hell, bad things happen to everyone. But that doesn't mean you deserve what's happening here. That's on them. Warren and his gang are bullies. Don't own their crazy behavior. That's not who you are." I ran a hand down my face, trying to collect my thoughts. "And if you were involved with someone who made you believe you were less than spectacular, that's also on *them*." I touched her upper arms. "I don't know your parents, but anyone who would leave their seventeen-year-old child behind has to take some responsibility as well." I took a moment, before I shared some of my own shit. "My parents were abusive to each other, and they were angry pretty much all the time, but they never left us." I had to admit, there were times when I almost wished they had. Growing up in an angry house had changed my sisters and me. Made it harder for us to trust people.

More tears ran down her cheeks. "But I broke their hearts. And I might not have murdered anyone, but that doesn't mean I wasn't responsible for someone's death."

What does that mean, Iris? The woman was a jigsaw puzzle, the invisible pieces of her past scattered all over the floor.

Her whole body shook, telling me this session was now over. I wrapped my arms around her frame and let her get it out. How in the hell had she survived like this for ten years?

And then, it occurred to me: the dogs. They became her family. Even Raymond knew as much. They were her every-thing. The realization made what Warren had done to Laddie all the more brutal.

She sobbed in my embrace, and I was in no hurry to rush it along. Clearly, she needed to get this out. Her arms reached around my waist to reciprocate my hug, and that was when I knew I was getting somewhere. This wasn't a woman who allowed people to get close. It made me appreciate the gesture all the more. And we would have stayed that way if we hadn't heard the sound of a truck approaching. Or maybe it was multiple trucks by the thunderous racket it was creating down Old Oak Road.

No one came out here. It was a dead-end road. That had to mean it was those fuckheads, and from the sounds of it, this time, they'd brought friends.

Chapter Ten

JC

Iris and I pulled our bodies apart immediately, terror carved all over her face.

"Are you sure you don't have any bullets for that gun?" I asked.

She shook her head. "I-I found the gun in the basement when I moved in. There could be bullets down there, I just never looked."

I touched her arm, trying not to freak her *or myself* out. "Where is the door to the basement?"

She dashed out of the kitchen and grabbed said gun from her foyer closet. Then she led me toward a short hallway that bordered the living room. On the far end, a door sat open that must've been the spare bedroom she had mentioned. But we didn't go that far. Instead, she opened another door, also near the foyer, a musty smell riding up the wooden stairs. Together, we bounded down to the basement, Iris closing the door so the dogs couldn't join us.

"The dogs may be safer down here." When I reached the bottom, I scanned the room.

"That's true, but I don't know exactly what's down here, and I don't want them getting into something dangerous. And we won't be down here long, right?"

"Right. Good thinking."

The space was pretty basic. A cement floor and walls, a washer and dryer sat in one corner next to a clothes hamper and some clothesline to hang garments indoors. A furnace, equipped with a large tank (probably of oil), required the far side of the room. *Who pays for her fuel? Who pays for any of this?* Nathan the dentist? Her parents? From what I gathered, Iris didn't have a job. No income.

My eyes scanned the area, landing on a pile of boxes stacked haphazardly near a cellar door that I assumed brought you back to the surface. We called them bulkhead doors at my grandparents' house.

"Is that where you found the gun?"

She nodded.

I rushed over and ransacked what was there, coming up with a small box of shells at the bottom of the last box. Being underground had muted the noise from the road, giving us a false sense of security.

"Do you know how to use it?" Iris was pale, her eyes wide with worry.

"I don't know what shape this gun is in. It looks like no one has cleaned it in years. But, yes, I've shot guns before when I went to my grandfather's place during the summers. I also had a client who liked to hunt pheasant on his estate." I opened the box and loaded the gun with two slugs, then handed the box over to Iris in case we needed more ammo. "I don't plan on shooting anyone today, but maybe a few shots over their heads will change their minds about what they are planning." I thought about Warren's injuries, imagining him stewing over it.

I had thwarted his efforts to get at Iris, and I had probably embarrassed him as well.

Upstairs, the dogs began barking, the sound of their claws racing across the floor above us.

"We better get up there." I filled my lungs with oxygen and paused. "Are you okay? You can stay down here if you wish. I've got this." And then, I remembered my cell phone on the kitchen table. "Shit!"

Iris startled. "What?" Her hands were shaking.

"Sorry. My cell phone is in the kitchen. When we get upstairs, grab it and call 911." I knew she had service because I'd checked.

"Okay. I have a phone too. A burner."

Somehow, that surprised me, but I didn't have time to ponder it. Holding the shotgun, I hurried to the stairs, ascending two at a time.

A cacophony of barks, both low and high, filled the main floor. "It's okay, Lily and Maggie." I don't know why I bothered reasoning with them; they weren't listening.

Doing as I asked, Iris ran into the kitchen to make the call, the box of bullets shaking around in her grip.

I approached the front door, my hand clenched tight around the gun. My heart was racing, my breathing shallow, but I ignored that right along with the stiff muscles aching along my back and neck. It sounded like an army of vehicles traveling our way. I just hoped the police would get here in time before things got out of hand. Even with a loaded shotgun, I realized I was vastly outnumbered as I slid my feet into my loafers.

I stepped out onto the front porch, not sure of what I was seeing. A pickup truck followed by another truck pulling a trailer came barreling down the driveway. Leading the front of the brigade was a black-and-white SUV with a sheriff's emblem stamped on each door, emergency lighting across the roof. It appeared the police were already here. *Tom?*

"Iris, hold off on that phone call!"

When the vehicles all came to a halt, dust flying up around them, Tom climbed out of his SUV. I'd never seen him in his sheriff's uniform, mainly because he was golfing every Thursday afternoon—sometimes on Monday—depending on his schedule. His shirt and pants were dark green, the word *Sheriff* embroidered just below a shiny gold badge across his left breast, some sort of walkie-talkie slung over the same shoulder.

I focused on the holstered gun over his right hip. Maggie and Lily continued to make themselves known, their barks of protest flying out of the open windows flanking the large picture window in the living room, the one they had thrown a rock through last Halloween. Gramps had come to her aid, and now I was taking up the charge. Somehow, that gave me strength, knowing he would be in this with me.

"Mornin', JC. I didn't expect to see *you* here." Tom approached the porch, the other drivers and passengers staying within their vehicles. "Dennis informed me that there was quite a commotion over here last night."

He stared up at me, his hands anchored on each hip, one of them inches from his weapon.

"Uh, more like a hostile takeover, Tom." I navigated the stairs until I was right in front of him. Dennis and Brody were closer to my height but with less body mass. Tom was built like a tank, with shoulders broad and resilient. "Your boy was here."

The front door opened, Iris emerging in a pair of denim shorts and a V-neck, short-sleeved fuchsia top. Those same pale-yellow flip-flops cushioned her feet. As she fastened her curly hair up in a high ponytail, she came to the edge of the porch, stopping by one of the posts. Remaining inside the house, the dogs continued to fill the air with their distress.

"Mornin', Iris." Tom gazed up at her.

She didn't return his pleasantries, as limited as they were.

"I'm awful sorry about what went down. I sure am glad your pup is gonna be okay. And I reprimanded Billy for his hand in what happened." Tom pivoted his body toward the front field. "This their handiwork?"

Once again, Iris didn't answer.

"It sure is." I crossed my arms and widened my stance. "Those boys were drunk, Tom. And one of them, Warren, was the instigator of it all. He's trouble. If I were you, I wouldn't let Billy anywhere near him. That kid should be locked up." I wanted to say that he was about to harm Iris, but with her standing there watching us, I chose not to. That was a conversation for another time.

Tom stood back on his heels and rubbed his jaw. "I know all about Warren, JC. Father was a drunk. Mother died of an overdose. Not that it excuses anything. Kid's had a tough life is all. Needs a man around to knock him silly every now and then." His gaze found Iris again. "Been a long time, Iris. You look . . . well."

The woman stood there expressionless. It reminded me of how she'd appeared the first time we had met.

What was the history between these two? Aside from Billy, how did Tom know her? Iris didn't trust the sheriff. Why? This area wasn't overly populated. People knew each other. Then again, it was also rural, miles between them. A perfect place for secrets to hide. Iris was at least fifteen to twenty years younger than Tom was.

And then, there were the stories about Iris. Brody had them, and so did his wife. Even Raymond had warned me about her. What story had Nicole's son, Dylan, concocted about his visit to her house? People like Nicole wouldn't think to question. He was her son. Iris was a stranger. Was that it? Or was there something more going on here? *I may not have murdered anyone, but that doesn't mean I wasn't responsible for someone's death.* That chilling confession would take some time for me to process. All I could imagine was Iris at seventeen, young and rebellious. Did she cause someone to die through negligence or irresponsible actions? Did it have anything to do with her affair with Nathan? Brody had said Nathan and his family had moved away. A dentist would have a full list of patients. It wouldn't be easy for him to just up and leave.

Tom scratched at his ear. "Well, we came here to fix the yard. I've got a landscaper ready to rototill and level out all the ruts, and then we'll spread grass seed before the rain comes in later on today. That okay with you, Iris?" He peered up at her.

Instead of speaking, she offered one nod and then returned inside the house, the dogs halting their barking, which my ears secretly thanked them for.

"Did you know that they've been harassing her every Halloween for the past three years?" I stared Tom down, who met my gaze, his eyes the color of cold steel. I motioned toward the house. "They threw a rock through her picture window last fall and were about to catch the place on fire if it hadn't been for my grandfather showing up and stopping them." As I spoke, the cords in my neck grew taut. How could anyone do this to a young woman who never bothered anyone and lived by herself? They had it in for her, and I was determined to find out why.

"I am well aware of the shenanigans from last fall, JC." Tom had that authoritarian voice, meant to dismantle criminals and intimidate.

It wasn't working on me.

"Maybe not the details, but the horsing around."

I laughed without an ounce of humor in my voice. "Horsing around? Is that what you want to call it?"

"This isn't the time, JC. I have work to do."

Tom waved his arms at the trucks, and that was when all the doors opened, three men in the back circling around the rear of the trailer to take the equipment down. To my surprise, the three men who exited the middle truck were Billy and his husky two cohorts. I didn't see Warren.

Boasting a sizable black eye, Billy approached, his head bowed, his dirty-blond hair tousled, Kurt Cobain-style.

Nice one, Tom. Beat the kid to what, make him angrier? My respect for the sheriff had plummeted. No more golf games for me. I had better things to do than hang out with assholes. Iris didn't trust him, and neither did I anymore. How did Dennis and Brody deal with him? Then again, having the sheriff on your side could come in handy.

Tom watched his son like a hawk as he came up beside him. "You boys got something to say?"

Billy thrust his hands into the front pockets of his jeans, the other two redheads with shaved scalps standing back a few steps, staring at their feet. Jeans and T-shirts, stained and holey from overuse, were their fashion trend. "I'm real sorry about what happened." Avoiding eye contact, Billy kicked at the gravel beneath work boots that remained untied.

Tom loomed nearby before he bellowed, "And?"

Christ, Billy was practically leaning away from his father as though worried he might receive another beating. "I'm real glad the dog is gonna be okay. I'll pay for the vet care."

Tom's gray eyes locked on the two in the back. "Bucky and Floyd? You got something to add?"

That gave me their names. Which one was which, I had no idea.

"We're sorry too." No one met my eyes or Tom's. They

were too scared. The one they should have been apologizing to was inside the house, but something told me she was watching *and* listening. I wasn't about to ask her to come out here again.

Tom whacked Billy across the back of his head, much like a feisty grandmother would do. It wasn't hard, although his message was clear. *Do as I say or else.* "Go on, now. Do whatever Frank tells you to do. Don't come home until you've finished the job!"

The three of them sauntered off with their symbolic tails between their legs. And then everyone got to work.

* * *

Tom stayed around for about half an hour before he took off, leaving the work crew to do their jobs. He introduced me to Frank, who was in charge of landscaping. We tried to make small talk with each other, but it didn't go well. Especially when I had asked him how he had known Iris, and his answer was "Small town."

I went back inside to see how Iris was doing, which wasn't good. I found her in the kitchen picking up a broken glass from the ceramic-tiled floor. Lily's and Maggie's front paws stayed glued to the sill of the picture window, watching the activity out front.

"Ouch." Iris thrust her finger into her mouth and sucked on it.

I crouched down to help her pick up the glass. "You okay? Need a Band-Aid?" I picked up the fragments and headed to the trash can.

"I don't want Lily and Maggie to get cut."

I poured some water onto a paper towel and returned to where she squatted on the floor. "They're making so much noise outside,

I'm sure the dogs didn't even hear you drop the glass. Here, this is a trick my mother taught me." I blotted the area of small shavings, which stuck to the dampened paper towel perfectly.

"I'll grab the vacuum." Iris went to the hall closet and was back in a flash.

Mess cleaned up and finger bandaged, Iris went to put some glasses back on the shelf. That's when I noticed her hands shaking so badly that she nearly dropped another one, which I caught before it could reach the floor.

"Do you have leashes for the dogs?"

"Yeah, but I don't think a walk is a good idea right now."

"No, I was thinking we can take them to my place. We'll drive. It's a lot quieter there. We can bring their food bowls and leashes." I lifted my voice and smiled. "I'd love to show you the place, anyway. You said you hadn't seen it, right?"

She nodded, but it was subtle. Not only was her complexion about as pasty as a bowl of cooked oatmeal, but her shoulders were tight, her eyes slanted with worry. Every loud noise seemed to make her jolt. It wasn't healthy to be this stressed.

"Okay, then." I moved around the house to help pack up what we'd need.

Iris stood in the center of the kitchen as though frozen in place.

I stopped working. "What's wrong?"

"I don't trust them to be here alone. What if they break in or . . ."

Catch the place on fire? Break more windows? Tear the place apart, piece by piece? I had already entertained those same thoughts. Even if we stayed, I was only one man. Warren could also show up, or Billy and his minions could have a change of heart. With Tom gone, who knew what they might do? I doubted that would happen, but nothing was certain. I'd given up on underestimating these people.

"Well, from what I witnessed, Billy is pretty scared of his father. And so were the other two. I also talked with the landscaper. His name is Frank, and he has two workers with him. They all seemed like decent people.

The dogs started barking again every time the vehicles drew near the house. It was quite a racket. I could barely hear myself think, a phrase Gramps would often say when my sisters and I were chasing each other around his house or had the TV on too loud. Now, I understood what he meant.

Iris's hands refused to stop shaking. That bothered me more.

"I think it will be fine. We'll lock up. I'll bring the gun with us. I can even drop you guys off and come back here and keep a watch on the place. We've got cell service at your house and mine. We can call for help if we need to." I paused. "Does any of that sound like something you'd be comfortable with?"

Lily started whimpering. She dashed over to the back door. "Oh no, she's gotta go out again." Iris grabbed a leash and hooked her up. "Okay. We can do that. And thank you, Jacob. I'm sorry about everything." Once she had both dogs leashed, she took them out while I continued to watch out front.

Why was I doing this? I wasn't sure. I had to keep reminding myself that I didn't know Iris. For the moment, I was here. And I was engaged in whatever this calamity turned out to be. Gramps had helped her, and I was following in his footsteps. For the moment, that had to be enough.

My feelings were another issue, but I told myself I'd know what to do about them when the time was right. The reason Morgan and I had lasted was because we never put any attachments on what we had. We saw each other when it was convenient. With the other women from my past, we'd had a moment of combustible attraction that would always dwindle before long.

Maybe the reason I was still so tuned in with Iris was *because* we hadn't slept together. She remained elusive, mysterious. I was also out of my element here. Everything was different.

* * *

I tried my best to lighten the mood as I drove over to my place. "Gramps did a nice job decorating the house. And the view out back is incredible. I can't wait to show it to you." It took all of two minutes to get there.

We leashed the dogs and let them walk around to sniff and discover. I knew Lily would especially appreciate this.

"Before you grab your things, come around back." I led the group along the path that brought us to the dock. And there we stood, both dogs in front of us. "This is where I first met Lily."

"Really?" Iris's eyes widened with wonder. She turned her head back and forth to take in the pond and the lush vegetation growing rampant up and down the small mountain in front of us. The sounds of nature welcomed a partly sunny sky. However, a thick layer of clouds waited off in the distance, warning a storm would approach. "This is just beautiful, Jacob. We used to walk around here a lot before Callum bought the place. I can understand why Lily would come here." She ran her long, elegant fingers through Lily's fur as she knelt closer to her. "Is this your special place, Lily?" She kissed her dog.

Allowing her this moment, I snatched Maggie up in my arms before she could interfere, which I was certain she was about to do.

Iris rose. "Thank you for bringing us, Jacob."

I set Maggie down. "You know, you're the only person who

calls me that. All my friends *and family* call me JC." I kept my tone playful.

Iris took a long breath, one that seemed to center her. "Well, that's because, to them, you *are* JC."

I had to process that one. "Oh, yeah? So what am I to you?" Without meaning to, I'd loaded my question with verbal explosives, but it was out, so nothing I could do to rein it back in now. I went with humor. "Knight in shining armor, superhero . . ." I paused for comedic purposes.

She giggled, and it felt like the air suddenly cleared, the sun brightening just a little. "No, silly." With her index finger, she touched the cleft in my chin. "You're Jacob."

I hated to admit how much I liked hearing her say my name, especially with a smile on her face. I wanted to ask her to repeat it over and over again—while I was satisfying her every sexual want and need—but I realized I was getting weird. This girl had endured enough weird.

Chapter Eleven

JC

No, silly, you're Jacob.

I thought about those words for the rest of the day. What was she feeling, thinking, or wanting? It was driving me insane. And yet, I didn't have the power to shut it down, not without seeing where we were headed.

We brought in her things, along with the dogs' food bowls. It didn't take long. "Do you think the dogs would be okay for a short time if I took you out on the boat? It's supposed to rain later, but we have a window before it hits. And I can show you around the pond."

She answered immediately. "Sure!"

I rowed this woman around the water as though we were back in the 1800s. The only thing missing was her parasol. We ventured over to the other side, where the trees grew tall, choking out the grass. It allowed me to see deep within the woods as it extended upward. A Robin Hood woods was what came to mind. When I was a boy, I would have loved nothing more than to explore the terrain and pretend I was the heroic outlaw, a long stick in my hand as a sword.

"It would be fun to go swimming here when the water warms up." Iris pointed out several areas where sand appeared near the shore. "The dogs would love *that* area. . . . I bet it would be great to bring a picnic lunch. . . . I believe that mountain is called Red Spruce Mountain for all the red spruce that grows along it. . . . I wonder if the surface of the pond freezes over during winter. I've never checked. But it would be fun to skate out here if it does."

Honestly, I don't think the woman sat still for a minute while we were out there. She kept turning and gazing and pointing. "Look at that? Is that an eagle?"

As it turned out, it *was* an eagle. And I had never seen one in the wild before.

"Is that a woodchuck?" And so the eye-spy game continued. The only thing Iris didn't do was cover her mouth in amazement, but I suspected she wanted to. It was exhilarating to watch her take in the scenery.

"Oh my god, Jacob. I think I see a black bear." She pointed. "Look up that incline. See it? In that tree?"

We were nearing the edge, the vegetation drawing near. I stopped rowing and peered in as best I could, my eyes squinting out the last of the sun to see better. I even leaned over, my hand on the edge of the boat to steady myself. I was a little freaked out that bears lived out here, but it *was* on the other side of the pond. And we were in the wilderness. I'd have to keep an eye out when I went running. As I pondered that thought, a sudden "Rah!" exploded in my ears as Iris grabbed my arm for impact.

My heartbeat raced with a sudden burst of adrenaline that had me just about falling off my bench. I had to take a breath. "What the hell was that?"

And then Iris started laughing. "You should have seen your face." She pantomimed my startled expression, her face exaggeratingly wide with surprise.

"Oh, yeah. You think you're pretty funny, do you?" I reached down and splashed cold water onto her chest and arms.

"Eek." She gasped. "That's freezing, you brat!"

She splashed me back, and I then understood her shock. "Don't start what you can't finish." My second splash came with more water this time. I hit her face and hair. *Oops!*

With an open mouth and hands flailing, she took a breath and then soaked me back.

Now it was my turn to gasp. "Jesus Christ, this water is cold."

More laughing, both of us cracking up. When I regained my bearings, I quirked a brow. "Did you *really* see a bear?" My expression became serious, but it didn't stay that way for long.

She jiggled her shoulders a tad. "Don't worry, Jacob. I'll fight it off for you." She tilted her head to one side, and it was all I could do not to kiss her. Take her right into my arms and let her know just how gorgeous she was.

"I've seen bears out here before." She touched my knee. "But no, I didn't see one just now. Unless you go near a mother bear and her cubs, they won't bother you anyway. I think you're safe for now." She propped her elbows on her knees, positioning her body closer to mine.

We shared a moment, gazing into each other's eyes, not a word coming from either one of our mouths. The sun dazzled her baby blues, creating two pools of luminescence. I was awestruck.

Gramps had told me how *smitten* he was when he had first seen Gram. Love at first sight. Was that what this was? Was I falling in love with Iris? Or was it just an infatuation that would fade over time? Everything in my world had become so atypical when it came to her.

Finally, I straightened up. "We've been gone for a while

now. We should probably head back and check on the dogs, don't you think?"

Iris sat up, the edges of her pouty lips crimping downward. "Yeah. Good idea." Her voice was nothing short of deadpan.

Don't be disappointed, Iris. You have no idea how much I want you. I just can't string a woman like you along. I would never forgive myself.

When we returned to my dock, Iris helped me secure the boat to the cleats. And then she didn't seem to know what to do with herself. She let the dogs out, and she walked around the house with them. She had also stopped looking at me. Was she embarrassed? She had no reason to be.

A thought came to mind.

"How about I go check on things at your place. You can come with me if you want. And then, let me make you dinner. You could even stay here if you'd like. I've got a full guest room and a spare bathroom."

In front of my house, she picked a small cluster of Queen Anne's lace growing by the front porch as she seemed to consider my offer. "Are you sure that's not too much of an imposition? Especially with the dogs?" Her vibrant blue eyes studied me.

"Not at all. And to be honest, I'd be much more comfortable in my own bed versus the couch." I raised a palm. "But only if you're okay with that. I can sleep on your couch if you need me to."

She shrugged. "Okay. I mean, sure."

And off we went. We left the dogs in the house again, arriving at her place two minutes later. Frank was just finishing up with the seeding when lightning flashed in the distance, the sky still fairly bright on our side. It lent the sky a surreal, almost heavenly appearance. Billy and his buds had already left. I wondered how much they had actually helped.

Wearing a tan sun-protective hat with a wide brim, a long-sleeved shirt in the same color, and pants made with thick canvas material, Frank trudged over in his work boots while his two workers loaded up the trailer. "Seed's down. I left a small bag by the barn in case you notice some bare spots, but given all the rain we're gettin' this season, the grass should fill in well." He took his hat off and wiped his brow with his hand, the scent of perspiration and hay encapsulating his laborious day. "As you can see, I put straw down to keep the birds from eatin' all the seed."

They'd covered most of the front field in straw, with the exception of the outer edges where Warren's truck hadn't ventured.

Frank handed Iris his business card. "If you need anything else done, here's my cell number."

"Thank you." Iris kept her tone friendly, telling me she probably hadn't met Frank before. "It looks great. And the cost?"

Waving her off, Frank turned to walk away. "All taken care of. I'm hoping to get my equipment under cover before the next rainstorm hits. Have a nice night."

Without the dogs to slow us down, we packed things up in short order. Of course, all I had to grab was my leather duffle, but I helped Iris get what she needed for the dogs, leaving her personal things for her to take care of on her own.

When we were leaving, she locked the front door and stood there with a strange expression on her face. I had reached the bottom step of her porch and turned. "Everything okay?"

She didn't answer right away.

"Iris?"

She rattled her head a bit. "It's nothing. It's just that I haven't stayed away from this house in ten years. Isn't that crazy?"

I loved that she was starting to see that. It showed growth.

"Time to change things up, right? And wait till you taste what I'm cooking you for dinner." I continued on my way, trying not to make a big deal about this. The less said, the better, I reasoned.

Back at my place, I did an inventory of the food in my kitchen. I'd been to the grocery store—a real grocery store—so I was stocked. A few years ago, I had taken a cooking class with a woman I was seeing. (Unlike me, Ling liked to cook.) The romance didn't last long, but the recipes I'd learned how to make did. One in particular came to mind. Since I'd scored some local sausage, I decided on baked rigatoni with country sausage. Gramps had a gas grill out back, and I planned to try my hand at grilled corn on the cob. For dessert, I pulled a half dozen cupcakes, covered in buttercream icing and Fourth of July sprinkles, from the freezer and got busy.

Iris stood in the center of the room. "Okay. Put me to work."

I guided her over to the kitchen table and sat her down. "Nope. You just sit there and keep me company."

"What? No! I want to help."

I stared her down, noticing her cotton fuchsia top had collected some algae from the water fight. "You may want to wash your shirt. Sorry, I didn't realize the pond water would stain."

She peered down at her chest. "Oh, I hadn't noticed." Then she smelled her hair and grimaced. "Would you mind if I took a quick shower in your guest bathroom? I can wash my shirt out in the sink."

"Sure, go ahead. There are towels and washcloths in the cabinet." I pointed toward the laundry room. "And there's detergent in the laundry room right over there. You may want to pretreat it and then put it through the wash. I'll probably do the same with my clothes." I caught a scent of the same algae and wrinkled my nose at it.

After I grilled, I'd be taking my own shower.

* * *

Iris came strolling into the kitchen as the scents of garlic, tomato sauce, and maple sausage had taken over the room.

"Wow, it smells delicious in here. Also, I spoke with Dennis, and Laddie is about the same. He said I can bring him home tomorrow. I told him I was here with you, and he said to thank you for all your help." Dressed in a sleeveless white shirt and fitted black shorts, revealing legs that went on forever, Iris made her way over to Lily and Maggie, who were lying on an area rug by the back door watching me work, her bare feet padding against the kitchen tile. Her curly blond hair was already starting to dry at the tips, her scent entertaining my nose with notes of apricot from either her shampoo or body wash as she sauntered past. "You girls hoping Jacob will give you some treats?"

The mere mention of the word *treat* had their heads lifted and their ears perked.

"I wasn't sure what they could have, so I didn't feed them anything other than the dried food in their bowls."

"Good. I don't feed them from the table. It just makes things more difficult. After dinner, I'll take them out to potty and give them a few extra treats tonight." She returned to the kitchen and inhaled through her nose. "Whatcha making?" She came up beside me, placing her hand lightly against my lower back.

My mind struggled to concentrate on much else.

"Uh, let's see." I opened the oven door, allowing more succulent scents to escape into the air. "I've got baked rigatoni with maple sausage." I tipped my head toward the corn wrapped in their husks on a large platter near the sink. "I'm planning on grilling the corn. And I have the fixings for a salad if you're hungry for one."

"That sounds great. My mouth is watering. Hey, while you're grilling the corn, I'll fix the salad." A radiant smile spread across her face. "Is everything I need in the fridge?" She plunked her hands on her hips and then wagged a finger at me. "No arguments!"

* * *

When I came in the back door smelling of grill and holding a tray of steaming corn, Iris had made a fresh salad and set the table. "Looking good in here. I have placemats?" A set of ceramic plates, decorated with roosters, sat atop cloth placemats in red checkerboard. Totally country. And totally Gram.

She grinned. "Yes, you do. I found them in that top cupboard." She pointed to a cupboard above the fridge.

She'd also found everything from utensils to glasses and even the paper napkins I had bought, which I had stored in the lazy Susan where the cupboards met in the corner of the room.

I placed the corn in the center of the table. "Corn's done."

"Looks great."

I approached a high cupboard where I pulled out two small juice glasses. Gramps didn't drink wine, so these would have to do. "How about I open us a bottle of wine? What kind do you like? I've got both red and white."

Once again, a funny expression slid across her face. "I'm not sure. I used to drink beer when I was younger, but that was a long time ago. I don't think I've ever had wine." Each time she'd made these types of proclamations, she seemed to shrink into herself a little.

"I'll open a Riesling I have stored in the fridge. It's somewhat sweet . . . for beginners." I winked at her, which seemed to settle her nerves or whatever was bothering her. "And if you don't like it, I have some iced tea or water."

Soon, dinner was underway. Sitting across from Iris was always a tad awkward for me. Our eyes met and then blinked away. Conversation started out a little sparse. "The casserole tastes yummy" from her. "You did a great job making the salad" from me.

"Cheers!" I raised my designated wine glass to clank against hers.

When she took a sip, I watched for any sour expressions but didn't notice any. She seemed to savor the Riesling for a moment. "It's good. It has a citrus flavor if I'm not mistaken. Maybe grapefruit? And do I detect apple?"

I nodded my approval. "Nicely done. Yes, both are in this wine." I had chosen an expensive bottle with subtle notes of various fruits. Iris had a discerning palette.

As we ate, I tried my best not to focus on her mouth as she chewed on her food, especially when she rolled her eyes from the flavor.

I'd like to make those eyes roll for another reason. It had been too long without sex for me. I was hard up for sure.

"This is scrumptious, Jacob. You're a good cook." She tucked another bite of casserole into her mouth.

I took a sip of wine before I picked up my corn cob and began chewing away on it, butter dripping off the kernels. The pleasantries had halted for the moment. I saw it as a chance to dig a little deeper into her life.

"Do you mind if I ask you something?" I wiped the melted butter from my mouth. (I'd gone through three napkins already.)

Iris straightened up in her chair. "I guess so."

"How do you know Tom? You do know him, right?"

She had been chewing on her salad, which she visibly swallowed, placing her fork beside her plate. "Yes, I do know him. He's the sheriff. But I knew him before he ran for office. When he was a deputy."

I didn't respond. Mainly because I wanted to hear more. I just nodded and tried to show my interest.

"Back when I was younger, I went through a rebellious phase. I had worked really hard in school. Made honor roll. I was runner-up for valedictorian." Her shoulders rose with pride, which was a refreshing change. "I'd applied to several colleges. And I actually got into Cornell. But my parents couldn't afford it, and I wasn't able to receive enough financial aid." She rolled the edge of her paper napkin between her thumb and forefinger, her gaze averted.

"What did your parents do for work?"

"My mom used to work as a bookkeeper for an accountant in town, and my dad was an equipment operator for the road crew." She took a breath and raised her brow. "*Very* religious. That wasn't it, though. You see, my mother had been sick. She's better now. At least, I think she's better. But her medical bills were a lot." Her voice trailed off. "College wasn't an option for me." She sighed. "So, I lashed out. Did things I never should have done. I got involved with the wrong people. Tom was one of them. He was cheating on his wife, Sandra, with one of my friends named Haley. He and Sandra later divorced. And from what Haley had told me, Tom was abusive." She chewed on her lower lip. "I knew he was abusive. I could see the bruises on Haley's arms."

What a scumbag Tom turned out to be. Having sex with a minor. And this man was the sheriff? He gave good cops a bad name. I was growing less fond of the people here, not all, but some. At the same time, I was relieved Iris hadn't slept with him. Not that it would have been a deal-breaker. Maybe a deal-*denter?*

Something else occurred to me. "Was he ever abusive with you?"

Iris stared down at her half-empty plate. "No, not with me. I made plenty of my own mistakes, though—like also dating a married man." Her cheeks flared as she looked away. "And then, everything fell apart."

I knew it was Nathan, but I still wished Iris felt comfortable telling me about it herself. She was opening up to me, and that was huge from a person who had been so guarded. I suspected for years.

"If it's any consolation, all teenagers go through a rebellious phase. And we all make our share of mistakes. I lost a buddy who drove his car into a tree going one hundred miles per hour. Died instantly. Took out the power for an entire planned community. And another friend who died of alcohol poisoning. Hell, I smashed up my dad's truck one night driving into a ditch." In my defense, I wasn't experienced and allowed myself to be distracted by friends riding with me.

My words didn't seem to penetrate whatever battle was going on inside Iris's head. "And I'm sorry, but having sex with a minor is against the law, much less abusing them. Someone should have brought Tom up on charges."

This beautiful woman, holding so much pain in her heart, finally looked up at me. "That's true."

"Did the person you were seeing hurt you as well . . . you know, physically?" I hated to ask, mainly because I wasn't sure I wanted the answer.

Her subtle nod had my jaw clenched so tight, I feared I'd break a tooth. *Motherfucker.* What did he do to her? How bad had it gotten? It was becoming abundantly clear to me why Iris allowed people to treat her like garbage. Her parents had deserted her. Some asshole much older than her had victimized her. She'd lived alone for ten years. And what really haunted me was how wonderful she was. All anyone had to do was watch her with her pets. She had a heart of gold. And an adventurous spirit that I was starting to appreciate more and more each day. Knowing she was also smart only added to her appeal. Iris was a diamond living in the rough.

My beautiful dinner companion remained slumped in her chair.

"You were young, Iris. Whatever happened wasn't your fault." I felt bad that her mother was sick, but at the same time, I was angry with both of her parents. Who was looking out for their daughter? From what I could ascertain, no one. "Don't be so hard on yourself."

Okay, enough poking into her past. The end of our meal was drawing near, so I decided to change the subject. "I've got some cupcakes for dessert. Do you want to save them for later or have them now?"

"Now would be great." She sprang from her chair as though dying to remove herself from our conversation, which I understood since I was literally sweating over it. Taking our plates in her hands, she headed for the sink. "*I've* got the dishes this time."

I rose. "That sounds good. I won't argue. And if you don't mind, I think I'll also take a shower. Get the grill and the pond smell off me."

A small smile lifted the edges of her lips. "Yes, please. You stink!" She crinkled her face at me and then giggled.

If I had known her better, I would have flung her over my shoulder and tickled the shit out of her for that comment. And I almost did.

* * *

Lightning flashed in the distance, the smell of ozone ripe in the air as we sat on my back deck sipping more wine and watching the water. I had work to do, but that would have to wait. I was struggling to tie myself up in the stock market, something I had lived and breathed since college. My focus had changed, and the reason was sitting right next to me at my grandfather's cast aluminum bistro set.

"If you could do anything in the world for a living, what would it be?" I wasn't sure where that question came from, but I wasn't about to back down from it.

Iris turned in her chair and reached toward her dogs, who lay between us at our feet. She stroked Maggie's fur. "I've always wanted to be a veterinarian like Dennis. I'd love to open my own clinic. That was what I was going to study at Cornell. They have one of the best programs in the country."

I glanced over at her. "I could see that for you." And I could, just like I could also see myself getting a dog, something *else* I never thought I'd do. I took another sip of my wine, patting Lily's head.

"I've gotta pee. I'll be right back." Iris stood and dashed into the house with Maggie on her heels. Lily stayed by me.

As the wind started to pick up, I thought about this new schedule of mine. If you had told me I'd be *hanging out* like this weeks ago, I'd say you were crazy. Before this *situation* with Iris had landed in my lap, I'd been working whenever free time allowed, mostly when the market opened and closed, doing research late at night. I had several portfolios to manage globally. Between the investors and the exchange, it was a tumultuous line of work. The market never slept. I thrived on that. Well, I *used* to thrive on that. You never wanted to lose your client's money, and I'd had a few close calls over the years, enough that I'd started having heart palpitations at age twenty-nine. Being here, those worries seemed so distant, but I knew they weren't far off.

I had just finished getting caught up when I heard Warren and company tearing up Iris's lawn last night. I called it Iris's lawn, but was it? She might not even own it. Iris didn't work outside of the home. How did she pay her bills? Electricity, water, and heating oil, plus food for her and the dogs didn't come free. Someone was funding her existence out here.

Once again, I thought of her parents. But something told me it wasn't them. I suspected it was the scumbag who had abused her all those years ago. Nathan. Dentists made a lot of money. And they also knew a lot of people. I could see Iris going to see him as a patient, his intentions appearing honorable. Until they weren't.

Distracting me from my musings, Iris returned. "Much better." She sat back in her chair and exhaled.

My fingers found the crown of Lily's head again. I truly loved that dog. "Welcome back. What were we talking about?"

No rain yet, but lightning was growing brighter, rumbles of thunder closing in.

Iris opened her mouth to speak when another boom had the dogs up on all fours. Even *I* flinched.

"Hold that thought. Let's take this conversation inside."

Chapter Twelve

Iris

Jacob and I stayed up just past midnight talking, the storm outside performing a beautiful light show in front of us. We sat on the couch in his living room, watching through his picture window. I was still nursing the second glass of Riesling I had ever had as Jacob sat next to me, sipping from his beer. The way the veins of electricity shot across the night sky, it was as if the hand of God were reaching down from the heavens. I think I might have even *oohed*.

Lily and Maggie weren't quite so enamored. Both huddled on the floor together with troubled eyes. They were coping, and that was all I could ask for.

I was coping with them. After my dinner conversation with Jacob, which threatened to upheave my delicious baked riga-toni, I worried what he'd think of me, especially after I had confessed that I had been with a married man. One of two men I had ever been with sexually. My mother had grabbed her rosary beads and wouldn't leave her bedroom for hours. Neither of my parents ever looked at me the same after that. I expected Jacob to pull away emotionally as well, his eyes filled with disgust. That didn't happen. He sympathized. He even compared my mistakes to some he'd encountered through his high school friendships or his own.

It made me realize how out of touch I had become with people. I'd been alone for years. That didn't mean I enjoyed the solitude. It just made my life easier, less complicated.

Until three years ago, when Warren and his gang had shown up, and I hadn't felt safe since.

Unlike most of the so-called men around here, Jacob was hotter than anyone I had ever met. Not only that, but he was also kind, his olive-colored eyes emitting an undercurrent of patience and generosity. Plus pure sexiness. I'd met cute guys in high school. And I'd dated a few of them, slept with one. (It wasn't good.) The cliché, captain of the football team, and I was a cheerleader. Jacob surpassed every single one of them. The muscles rippling across his chest and along his bulging arms made it difficult *not* to swoon. And that was *with* a T-shirt on. I'd never seen him shirtless. The ridge of his nose, the cut of his jaw, and that adorable cleft centering his chin—made him the perfect man in my eyes. His light-brown hair, always slightly tousled, grew thick, the length extending longer than when I'd first met him. Most importantly, he made me feel connected again—and safe. *But what will you do when he leaves? How will you feel then?* I'd have to deal with that reality someday, but not tonight.

"Remember when I told you how your grandfather had talked about you all the time?"

"Yeah." Jacob kept his eyes fixed on the window in front of us.

Having a storm outside to focus on made the conversation easier for me. Of course, every time I stared into Jacob's beautiful and kind eyes, my mind went blank.

Back to the subject at hand.

"I can see why he was so proud of you, Jacob. You have a kind heart like his."

He turned his head toward me. "Thank you for saying that. You have a pretty kind heart yourself." The corner of his mouth quirked.

I grew bashful, my cheeks heating up. I flipped one hand in the air. "Oh, you don't know me all that well."

He stared with intent, making my stomach flutter. "I know that much. I've seen you with your dogs."

His compliment made me uncomfortable. I wasn't deserving of it. I took a breath. "Anyway, back to your grandfather. He told me about how you used to visit him a lot when you were younger, and how much that meant to him."

Jacob took another pull of his beer, his muscular legs stretched out in front of him, crossed at the ankles. The first time I'd seen him, he was wearing a designer polo with some sort of cotton performance shorts. Crisp. Tailored. But since then, he'd dressed more casually. After his shower, he came out in a pair of gray gym shorts and a white T-shirt. Simple. He smelled musky and clean, whatever cologne he wore pairing nicely with his natural scent. "Yeah, well, I wasn't around much later on." His voice wavered as he picked at the label on his beer bottle.

Interesting. Neither one of us liked compliments. I assumed Jacob was above insecurities.

"Yeah, but he said you lived several hours away, right?"

He nodded.

"And you were getting older. He said you were an excellent student and great at math." I took another sip of my wine, enjoying the citrus flavors coating my tongue. The alcohol also worked at loosening my inhibitions. "I think it was those times when you were younger that he cherished the most."

Jacob turned sideways on the sofa, his left knee bent to rest on the cushion.

I turned toward him, angling my legs in a similar position.

"I wish I had been there for him when I was older. He'd asked me to come here, but I was too busy . . . always too busy." He blew out a breath and rolled his eyes. "He left me a letter, you know."

I leaned closer, hoping to show my support. "He did? What did he say?" I placed my free hand on the sofa cushion.

"I haven't opened it yet."

"Why not?" My heart reached out to him. I could tell this bothered him a lot.

"I'm too ashamed. I wasn't there for him when he needed me." He rubbed at his jaw, his eyes going distant for a moment. "Especially after Gram died."

"You don't know that. One thing I learned about your grandfather was that he was a very capable man. And you can't blame yourself for having a life. He understood that. And he knew this was a crazy world we live in. He just wanted you to succeed in whatever you chose to do." I cleared my throat. " 'A man is not made for defeat. A man can be destroyed but not defeated.' " I set my wine glass down on a side table. "Your grandfather used to read—"

"*The Old Man and the Sea.*" Jacob stared at me as if in disbelief.

I could feel my own eyes widen. "Yes! Have you read it?" I could tell he had.

Jacob set the beer on his side table and sprang from the couch. He dashed across the room, through the kitchen on my right, and into the back bedroom where he slept.

What's he doing?

I received my answer when he returned with his wallet in his hands. He sat closer, opened his wallet, and pulled out a laminated piece of paper, which he handed over to me. There, staring up at me was the same quote I had just recited.

I couldn't believe it. "Wow! That's incredible."

He pointed at the words cradled in my hands. "I read that quote every day. And I remind myself—"

"To never give up." I touched my lips, astonished. "He gave me a copy of that book, you know. And after what had happened last fall, he told me to remember to never give up on myself."

"I remember him saying something similar to me once." This time we both stared off.

It was like we were living parallel lives.

A smirk spread across Jacob's face, his voice light and airy. "I see he got to you too." He returned the laminate to his wallet and placed it on the side table by his beer. "Was the book he gave you old?"

"Yes, it was."

He angled his head and rubbed his chin. "Hmm. I'd wondered where that copy went. He'd had that book since he'd met my grandmother. Well, not the particular copy he'd signed out from the library where she had worked, but Gram bought him a fresh book, which he kept ever since. She had said that the reason she'd bought it for him was because he had used that quote to impress her. That book was the *key to her heart*, she had told him."

How romantic.

Jacob was engaging himself fully with me. It was very cool. And kind of scary, but only because of how much I was enjoying myself.

"I didn't realize how special the book was. I can give it back to you." Knowing how much Callum meant to Jacob, I couldn't help but worry I had done something wrong by hanging onto it.

With friendly eyes, Jacob shook his head. "He wanted you

to have it." His warm hand found my shoulder, sending my focus in another direction. "He must've thought you were pretty special." His voice hitched, his eyes glowing with intensity. So much so, I had trouble maintaining eye contact. "*I* think you're pretty special too." His face moved inches away from mine, the hand holding my shoulder sliding up to cradle the side of my jaw.

He'd draped his arm around me before. He'd even hugged me to provide comfort. This was different. And I wanted him to touch me more. My heart pitter-pattered, an exciting storm riling up my insides, enough to compete with the one raging outside our window.

"I know you've been through a lot with men, and from what I've seen, I wouldn't blame you for not trusting—"

Before he could finish that sentence, I slammed my lips onto his, my fingers running through his soft hair with abandon. I knew I was coming on strong—maybe too strong for his taste—but I couldn't seem to help myself. If this connection—whatever was happening between us—was temporary, I wanted to capture it in the jar of my heart before his light went out forever.

He pulled back, and I braced myself for the I-think-you-may-have-gotten-the-wrong-idea speech. Although, if I recalled, he *had* said he thought I was beautiful—the most beautiful woman he'd ever seen. I'd never forget those words.

"I'm sorry." I lowered my chin, my lungs trying to catch up to the emotional rush I had just experienced.

A pair of fingers lifted my chin to meet Jacob's gaze. "Oh, please don't apologize. I have wanted to kiss you since the *second* time we met. I'd say the first, but you had a shotgun pointed at my head." His voice played with his words, his grin supporting the romantic moment.

I slapped him lightly on his bicep, which felt more like a rock. "I told you the gun wasn't loaded."

And then his face slackened, a more serious expression washing over his features. "That wasn't true anyway. That day, I saw you taking your clothes down off the line—*before* the gun —I was mesmerized by the sight of you." He ran his fingers down my jawline. "And I haven't been able to stop thinking about you ever since." His breath touched my face before his lips returned to mine.

This time, he opened his mouth, allowing his tongue to ride along my lower lip. It was so sexy, I had to return the gesture, only I parted my lips fully and stimulated my tongue against the soft velvety texture of his. The hops from the beer, along with the sweet buttercream frosting from our dessert, made me want to devour him all at once. His mouth was succulent, his breath so refreshing against my face. I loved feeling him this close to me.

My fingers continued to comb through his silky hair as my mind let go. There was no longer a past or a future. There was only this moment, and I clung to it as though the moment itself were saving my very life. I felt alive, my insides stimulated in all the right ways. I had cast the cobwebs out, my sexual needs awakening. I wanted more.

I became aware of every nuance, every shift of his hand up and down my back. When he coiled his arms around me, our bodies matted up against each other, his heart pounded against my breasts, my nipples hard and ready. A small sauna steamed between my legs. I felt him hard against my hip, and I was encouraged by it. He wanted me too. He hadn't touched me, but I was close to climaxing by the mere idea of it. I wanted him to take me, right there on the couch. My desires were desperate for a release. And then I moaned.

All at once, Maggie jumped onto my lap, distracting us

both. She yipped, Lily watching us from the floor, her eyes clouded with confusion. They weren't used to seeing me entangled with another human being. This had to be strange for them. And as much as I loved them both, I wished Jacob and I had this moment alone.

Jacob expelled several short breaths as he stared over at Lily. "Wow. That was . . ." He ran a hand down his face as his cell phone buzzed from the side table near him. It had been doing that often, but I wasn't bothered by it. Jacob was a businessman. And I was sure he had work to do. He reached over and took the call, stood, and walked out of the room, leaving me alone with my canine family and my body struggling to return to normal. *He sure ran out of here pretty quick.* That was . . . what? *Great? Unexpected? Too much?* What was he going to say?

I stroked Maggie's fur as Lily came over to get some of her own pampering. Thunder faded in the distance. The storm was moving on. I was sad about it. I wanted it all back—the passion and the intensity. The feeling that Jacob wanted me as much as I wanted him. Or was I grasping at straws—looking for things that weren't there? I had done that before, and it hadn't turned out well for me. *When will you learn?* When it came to a quest for true love, maybe never. I waited another fifteen minutes for Jacob to materialize. When he never showed, I sighed. "Okay, you two, time for bed."

I awoke with Maggie snuggled up next to Lily on the floor in her doggie bed. I had just brought one bed, figuring Maggie would sleep with me. This was unusual. But given that Laddie was gone and we were in another house, she must've wanted comfort from her big sister. It was adorable.

Careful not to awaken them, I rolled onto my back and stared up at a ceiling fan with a white domed light at its center, the wooden blades rotating lazily around. A picture of an old covered bridge took up one wall, a set of tarnished brass sconces taking up another, everything wallpapered with small flowers and ribbon. Was this a little girl's room at some point?

On my left, a closed window did little to muffle the sound of birds and crickets waking up for a new day. With the storm behind us, nature was perky and loud. I wished I were perky with them. *That kiss.* I touched my lips, remembering every second of it. I'd never think about thunderstorms the same way again. For me, it was magical.

With a moment to myself, I tried to imagine what it would be like to wake up next to Jacob, his strong arms wrapped around my body. His face so close I could kiss it . . . and I would, over and over again.

I'd never slept in a bed with a man. My sexual encounters included back seats and even a hotel room *far* away from town. I was ashamed of my behavior. How could I have ever fallen for someone who had a wife? The man I now called *the egomaniac* was handsome but nothing like Jacob.

The truth of the matter was that the egomaniac came along at a time when I was upset . . . angry at my parents for taking my dream of attending college away from me. As years passed, I realized how unfair I was being. Mom was sick. Dad had tried his best to keep food on the table. But I was young and selfish. When they left, I could see the heartache in their eyes. The fights we'd had; the awful things we had said to each other. It was all still there in my mind's eye. Some things I could never set right.

I should have known better. And I should have chosen better friends. Haley was swooning over Tom. He bought her things, and he lavished her with ideals about their future.

Feeling my college career slipping away, I allowed myself to get caught up in something that brought me nothing but pain. The egomaniac had made promises. *I'll help you go to college.* It was all a ruse. He just wanted sex from a seventeen-year-old girl. And when things turned bad, he ran for the hills.

I suspected Jacob would never do that. He was a good man. Although, even good men had their limit. If Jacob ever found out the truth about me, he'd surely take off running for the hills as well. And who could blame him? This successful and gorgeous man from the city wasn't interested in a long-term relationship, especially one with a recluse who had major *issues*.

My adorable little Maggie jumped onto the bed and came over to me. She licked my face and then gave me *the look*.

"You need to go out?" As soon as I said those words, Lily was up and at the door.

Chapter Thirteen

JC

I awoke to the aroma of something delicious encircling my bed, dishes and pans clanking in the distance. Iris must've found my stash of breakfast foods. I'd filled the fridge with them. It reminded me of waking up at my grandparents' house. Gram always had something cooking on the stove. Blueberry pancakes were my favorite. My sisters liked scrambled eggs with ham. Living in the city, I chose healthier options, but I wasn't in the city, now was I? *When in Rome.*

Expelling a long breath and rubbing my eyes, I turned over and gazed at my cell, which I grabbed and stared at in disbelief. "Holy shit! Ten-thirty?" I sprang up and rushed into the bathroom to brush my teeth and splash some water on my face. Since when did I sleep until ten-thirty? Then again, I'd stayed up well past three to get more work done. I had a client who was considering a merger and in need of extra coddling. When deals included large dollar signs, this was common practice. I was used to that. What I wasn't used to was a woman turning my world upside down with one kiss. Maybe it was those dreams. *Keep telling yourself that, asshole.*

I had rushed out of the living room last night to answer a call and to hide the raging hard-on, trying its best to push through the fabric of my gym shorts. *Again.* Not a good way to end the kiss of all kisses, but what else was I supposed to do? I hadn't had this lack of self-control since I was in middle school. I had learned to handle myself around beautiful women. What was happening to me now?

Iris had a past. Nathan had hurt her. That was obvious. Was the dude friends with Tom at the time? Did the two of them hunt underage chicks for thrills? Tom abused Haley. Nathan abused Iris. Fucking losers.

I also wondered if Brody was pulling the same shit back then. No doubt, he was a helpless flirt. Everybody's friend, especially of the female sort. He practically drooled over his female waitstaff. And although Brody might not have known Iris personally, his wife sure carried a grudge for her. Did Nicole understand that Iris was being bullied by those dickheads? And even if she did know, would she care?

The woman walked around the club with a stick permanently wedged up her tight ass. *I want to see those tables cleared off right away. . . . I saw smears on that window. . . . You've been on break long enough. Get back to work.* Hard to miss whenever I was enjoying a beer and some nachos with the guys. Nicole always made her way over to our table, batting her eyes at me and then rolling them at her husband.

Her smile was as fake as her tits. I'd been with enough women to know the difference. Nicole's shoulder-length blond hair was always ramrod straight, her skin the exact same shade of bronze, and her designer clothes a direct contrast to the Vermonter lifestyle, which I had come to learn was more laid back and casual.

Unlike Nicole, Iris embraced informality. The woman barely wore shoes. Unbeknownst to her, Iris had made those short shorts, simple tank tops, and one sheer sundress sexy as hell. I suspected she hadn't been inside a clothing store in years, maybe since high school. Her clothing was old and dated. *She* was young and vibrant.

Not Nicole, though, who lived for the spotlight, and it showed in the way she sauntered around the club, doling out orders and daring anyone to challenge her authority. There were a lot of *Nicoles* in the city, both male and female versions. People who sought power and prestige and would tear the next guy limb from limb to achieve it. From what Brody had told me out on the course, Nicole immersed herself in all aspects of his business, which explained how he was able to golf so much. He paid the bills. She called the shots. End of story. I avoided her type at all costs.

Knowing Iris's past, *I* planned to tread lightly where she was concerned. I wanted her to know she could trust me and that I wasn't here to climb into her pants and move on. And I *was* planning on moving on. Sleeping with her, however much I wanted to—obsessed about, really—wouldn't be fair to her. The kiss was fucking amazing. Like epic. It was maybe the best kiss I'd ever had. Touching those plump lips against mine and tasting her sweet breath, my hands *finally* allowed to roam over her body, albeit carefully, were not hard to take. And *she'd* made the first move. It couldn't get any sexier than that.

After I'd made my quick exit, I realized that things would have to stop there. I'd be leaving soon, returning to my life in the city with Iris in my rearview. I could help her out while I was here. I could be her friend.

I rinsed and wiped my mouth as I continued to rationalize my plan, even though I knew it was total bullshit. Who was I trying to fool? The real reason I didn't push things with Iris had more to do with an emotion I wasn't ready to face. Or accept. It was the reason I stuck around and why I wished I had never delivered those goddamn groceries to her door all those weeks ago.

When I wasn't paying attention, that woman had crawled inside my heart and made herself a home. For a brief moment, I let myself admit how desperate I was for her company. And how lonely I felt when she wasn't around. I'd known the woman for four days! This would not do. I intended to retire in ten years with enough money to set me up for life. I'd still be young enough to enjoy it. My parents also came to mind; two people who for years had finished most of their arguments with a reliable *Fuck off!* That was *not* for me.

More clanking from the kitchen distracted me from my thoughts. *I'd better get out there before she thinks I'm avoiding her.* I *was* avoiding her. And longing for her at the same time. Who was the nutcase now?

I threw on a fresh white T-shirt and a pair of cotton black gym shorts, combed my hair, and ventured into uncharted territory, otherwise known as my kitchen. When I arrived, Iris was buzzing around the room like she owned the place. Christ, I'd *give* her the whole damn thing if she would only release me from her spell.

"Good morning. Whatcha cookin'?" *Could you sound any dorkier?*

Dressed in pj shorts with a navy elephant print and a navy short-sleeved top, Iris had her hair pulled up into a curly ponytail, a few ringlets falling around her face. She stopped working and glanced over, a slight flush on her cheeks.

Christ, she looked good.

Should I go over there and kiss her? My cell phone ringing from my pocket offered another alternative. Brody's name flashed onto the screen. *Hmm. Ears ringing?*

I held the phone up. "I've gotta take this. I'll be right back. And then, you can put me to work."

"No problem." She smiled before she resumed cooking what appeared to be French toast, while I dashed out of the room.

I closed my office door to keep the clanking in the kitchen down and stared out the window at my SUV in the driveway. "Hey, Brody, what's up?" I opened the window to offer the room some fresh air.

"Hey, man. I haven't seen you around the club lately. Grown sick of us already?" He chuckled over the line.

"Nah, just been busy with work and getting a few things done around here."

"We'd love to have you join us for tomorrow's tournament."

I had to think. *Tomorrow is Friday. Oh, yeah.* I had blanked on the Summer Golf Tournament he had mentioned at his Fourth of July party last week. It included mostly local people. A few pros who had ties to the area. "Shit, Brody. I forgot all about it. I won't be able to play."

"Why not? I was counting on you, dude." His voice carried an edge.

"I know, man, but I've got a client who is wigging out about a deal. I need to work tomorrow and most of the week. I can't get out of it. Too much money on the line." I rubbed my eyes with my thumb and forefinger. "Can't Dennis or Tom play, or maybe Kurt?"

Brody huffed. "None of them are good enough. Come on, man. I've got a couple of skilled golfers on our team. We may actually win this one." He was really pouring it on, the sounds of movement in the background, telling me he was already at the club.

But the thought of running into Tom was enough to force me to stand my ground. "Sorry, man. It can't be helped. Listen, I got a call coming in." I didn't, but I was growing tired of his pleading. I'd also embellished the needy client. "Good luck tomorrow." I ended the call, and in doing so, I might have also ended our friendship. I was okay with that. Something was going on around here that left a bad taste in my mouth. And I wasn't sure how much Brody was involved. He was too close to Tom to be clueless about what had happened ten years ago. He might not have known Iris, but he definitely knew more than he was letting on.

What really confused me was Dennis. Why would he also hang around someone like Tom? Dennis was a good man. Tom was not. Had Tom helped him in some way? Or were they casual friends who golfed together and not much else? I rubbed my eyes some more. This place was taxing my brain. And given my profession, *that* was saying a lot.

When I returned to the kitchen, Iris was placing three pieces of French toast onto my plate at the table, the scent of cinnamon harmonizing the air.

Do I have cinnamon?

"Better eat before it gets cold." She put the frying pan back on the stove. "I brought a few things from home, including maple syrup."

Near my place setting, a quart-sized container with a diagram of a large maple leaf adorning the front sat ready to sweeten my breakfast.

"And cinnamon, I see." Sprinkles of the dark spice coated the bread.

"Yes." She poured me a cup of coffee, which was also next to my plate.

"Thank you, Iris." I took a seat. "You didn't have to do all this." My stomach rumbled with gratitude.

Having already filled her plate, she sat across from me. "I know. But you slept late, and I wanted to thank you for putting up with us." She glanced over at Lily and Maggie, who were lying on the same area rug near the back door.

I gazed down at a folded paper napkin with a knife and fork on top. She'd done the same thing for dinner last night. In a large glass of water, the Queen Anne's lace she'd picked, along with some white daisies, added a colorful dressing to the center of the Formica table. That was the thing about Iris, she wasn't just beautiful; she made everything around her beautiful.

And these assholes want to squash that out of her. I made a decision. I wasn't sure where she and I were headed, but I couldn't leave this place without her. We could find her parents, and she could live anywhere she chose, as long as it wasn't here. I could even help her get into college if she wanted.

I slathered on the syrup and wolfed down the French toast as Iris did the same. The sugary sweet goodness against the cinnamon had me savoring every bite. I was about to go for seconds when Iris cleared her throat, her coffee mug cradled in her hands.

"I'm sorry about last night, Jacob." Her eyes grew sheepish. "I didn't mean to come on so strong."

Strong? She had no idea what I was used to sexually. The thought made me laugh. Not the appropriate response, given her furrowed brow.

The legs of her chair scraped against the ceramic tile as she pushed back from the table and flew to her feet. "You think I'm a joke, don't you?" She crossed her arms tight over her chest. Then she exhaled through an open mouth and shook her head. "I think it's time we leave!"

Before I knew what I was doing, I hopped up and went to her. "No! You've got it all wrong, Iris. I don't think you're a joke. Far from it."

Not convinced, she continued to pull away, her face tense. She flung one arm out. "Then, why are you laughing at me?"

I grabbed her upper arms firmly. "I'm not laughing at you.

You are not a joke to me. I'm laughing at how absurd it is that you *think* I'm not interested. Do you have any idea how much self-control it takes for me not to rip your clothes off and take you right here on this kitchen floor? Do you know how many sex dreams I've had about you? I have never wanted a woman more. It's been torture for me. And last night, I did have to take that call, but I also didn't want you to see how hard you had made me from that kiss. It was the best kiss of my life, Iris, and that alone blows my fucking mind!"

A slow smile spread across her face.

"I want you to understand. I have sex. I *don't* have relationships. And just so you know, I am careful, and I get tested regularly. I don't take chances when it comes to my health. And I've been perfectly happy to keep my life the way it is." I let my hands fall away. "Until I met you. These past few days have screwed with my head. *You've* screwed with my head. I'm not blaming you for it, but it's the truth. And I can't offer you a long-term commitment. It would be unfair of me to promise you something I couldn't deliver." I was backtracking from my earlier confession, but at the same time, I needed to get this out. If she wanted something more from me that I couldn't give, this was the time to say so. We'd continue as friends.

Iris pivoted her body back and forth playfully, her eyes sparkling as she gazed up at me. She bit down on her index finger.

It was sexy as hell.

"I don't need a commitment, Jacob. That is the last thing I want. But I haven't been with or even thought about being with a man in ten years. Until *you* came along. Being around you is just as much torture for me. If you want to take me on this kitchen floor, say the word. I'll put the dogs in my bedroom, and you can have me anyway you want me. If this is my one chance"—she compressed her luscious lips—"to feel alive again.

I'm not going to shy away from it." She moved in closer and whispered against my skin. "Please, Jacob, give me something to think about after you've gone."

This mysterious and breathtaking woman was offering herself up to me. My dick was already hard. I pulled her into my body so she could feel me pulsing for her. "This is what you want, beautiful?" No more hiding.

"I haven't wanted anything this much in a very long time." She reached down and stroked my dick over my shorts.

Jesus! I slammed my lips hard against hers, my tongue eager to continue what we had started last night. The syrup on her tongue mixed with the bold flavor of coffee was the dessert to my meal. She smelled so damn good, apricot laced through her golden curls. I was aware of every aspect of her, including her full breasts mashed against my chest. My fingers were eager to explore.

But we were quickly interrupted when the dogs came over, trying to figure out what was happening with their humans. I could feel them staring, the makings of a bark rumbling in Maggie's throat.

Iris's index finger touched my lips. "Give me one minute."

She guided Maggie and Lily into her bedroom, cooing them with her soft voice. "You two can take a little rest on Lily's bed for a bit, okay?"

And then she returned to me. I'd never been more grateful.

This was happening. My entire body came alive, every inch of me stimulated by the mere thought of it. I flung her T-shirt off and then her bra. I couldn't wait another second to suckle those tits.

And when I did, she let her head fall back and moaned.

"Christ, your tits are so perfect." I fondled her nipples, knowing what it would do to her insides.

She moaned some more. "Oh, Jacob. I want you so much. Don't stop."

"I have no intention of stopping, gorgeous."

Her hands found my dick again. She stroked me over my shorts.

I pulled my head back. "You better stop that or I'm gonna explode all over myself." I took several measured breaths.

"Good. And then we can continue." She knelt down and pulled my shorts to my ankles, gazing at my dick. "Wow." She took me in her mouth, her tongue and full lips doing a great job of massaging me from shaft to tip. Her hands fondled my nuts, heightening the pleasure. Those lips. That tongue. This woman knew her way around my cock. It was too much too soon, and I lost it, my hands braced on the sides of her head. "Holy shit!" The sensations throbbing through my lower half made my legs weak and my heart about ready to pound through my ribcage.

She rose up and gazed into my eyes. "Thank you for letting me do that." She kissed my chin and quickly rinsed her mouth in the sink.

"I didn't mean to cum so soon." Now it was my turn to be embarrassed. I prided myself on being an exceptional lover. PE wasn't a problem for me.

With her shirt off, she just grinned at me. "I'll take that as a compliment. I love satisfying you." Her voice was low and seductive.

I took one of her perfect breasts in my hand. "Oh, yeah? Well, wait till you *feel* what I'm about to do to you." I suckled again, this time my other hand sliding down her stomach and between her legs. She was already wet and warm to the touch. "I'd like to take you into my bed, but we did say the kitchen floor, didn't we?"

I stepped out of my shorts and grabbed a small rug by the

sink. Not ideal, but it would have to do. And then, I lowered her onto the floor. My dick was already gearing up for more action.

She stared up at me, her long fingers combing through my hair, and I lost my ability to breathe. I wasn't sure where to begin. Part of me wanted to savor this moment of anticipation. We would never be here again. Our first time. I wanted to appreciate this moment, but primal urges had other intentions. I started at her neck, kissing and licking her salty skin, my hand returning to her center. I couldn't wait to taste her. *Patience.* That was something I didn't have at the moment. But I would do my best.

The sound of gravel crushing under tires reached my ears. *Oh, shit! Damn it, not now!* Maybe I had imagined it?

Scratching came from the door to the guest room. And then a bark. *The dogs heard it too.*

Chapter Fourteen

JC

Iris sat up, her eyes bugged and her cheeks feverishly red. "Someone's here!" She jumped to her feet and grabbed her pj's shirt and bra, putting them both on in record time. Then she disappeared into my office, where an open window faced the driveway. "It's Dennis." She paused. "No, wait. It's Vanessa." Her feet bounded through the kitchen and down the short hallway toward the bathroom, the dogs scratching and barking from the bedroom. "I've gotta brush my teeth and wash my face. Can you answer the door when she gets here? And let the dogs out!" Her instructions came out rapid fire.

Already on my feet, I grabbed my shorts and threw them on. "Copy that!" My mind and body struggled to come back to earth as I returned the small rug over by the sink. I was ready for something spectacular to happen. I'd anticipated nothing else for weeks. The blow job and the way she took control, although hot as well, were just a warm-up. But there wasn't much choice here, so I adapted, promising myself that when the moment came around again, I'd satisfy that woman like she'd never been satisfied before. I'd make her forget every man she'd ever known.

With the dogs by my side, I opened the door as Vanessa stepped up onto the porch. "Good morning, Vanessa. I didn't expect to see *you* here. Everything okay with Laddie?"

Looking pretty hot in a pair of black yoga pants, white sneakers on her feet, and a scoop-neck white top, Vanessa approached. "Good morning, JC. Yes, everything is fine. I'm sorry to drop by unannounced. I tried Iris's phone, but she didn't answer." She touched the wide headband that pulled her short curly black hair away from her face.

I hadn't even heard Iris's phone ring. I knew she'd had it on since she'd been worried about Laddie. It had to be in her bedroom.

"No problem. We were just sitting down to breakfast." *And a marathon session of body worshipping.* "I worked until late last night, so I slept in." I stood back to allow her entry, holding the dogs, who were bouncing all over the place. "Iris made French toast if you're hungry."

"No, but thanks, I already ate." She stepped over the threshold.

Iris came rushing over next. She'd changed into jean shorts and a light-green T-shirt with a large sunflower adorning the front. "Hey, Vanessa. Is Laddie okay?" A worried wrinkle slid across her forehead as she re-gathered her curly blond hair into the same high ponytail, her breath smelling of mint.

"Yes, Laddie is fine. Doing very well, in fact."

Iris exhaled, her shoulders lowering. "Oh, good."

Lily and Maggie swarmed at Vanessa's feet, causing her to bend over and pet them. "Well, hello, you two. You being good girls for your mommy?"

With Vanessa's attention averted, Iris caught my gaze and

winked at me, her smile one of utter contentment. A simple gesture with a monumental impact.

It was in that moment that I realized something: *I'm in love with this woman.* Goddamn it! There was no point in denying it any further. I had never been in love, which was how I knew it was real. And it wasn't as if coming to this conclusion had brought me any comfort. What was I going to do about it? The answer came to me as though Gramps had said it himself. *You will do whatever is best for Iris.* There *was* no other option.

"Okay, you two. Let's give Vanessa some breathing room." Iris ushered both dogs away from her. She guided them into the kitchen and over to their food bowls. The sound of dried food landing in their stainless-steel bowls came next. "Eat your food, so we can talk to Vanessa."

The lady of my house, *and* my heart *apparently*, returned a moment later. "What can we do for you, Vanessa?" Iris stood next to me, her hand touching my lower back again. Were we a couple? It sure felt like it. She'd said she didn't want a commitment. *That is the last thing I want.*

Why did her words bother me so much?

Vanessa seemed to hesitate for a moment. She glanced over at me and then looked at Iris.

Somehow, I got the message. "Why don't you two talk while I go watch the dogs. If they get restless, I'll take them down by the dock." I grabbed their leashes from where I had hung them on the hall tree and made my way toward the kitchen.

Vanessa and Iris stayed by the door, their voices a murmur.

What were they talking about?

I was dying to know what was happening out there. A few short minutes later, Iris appeared. "Would you mind if I went with Vanessa to see Laddie? She said they'd like to keep him for a bit longer." She chewed on her lower lip, indicating there was more.

"Everything okay?" I had been sitting at the breakfast table, watching the dogs eat. I rose.

"Absolutely. I just want to see him and make sure he's good." She glanced down and then up into my eyes. "She said she'd be willing to take all the dogs for a few days to give us some time together." With her head tilted, she studied me again.

As the dogs ate and drank, I took her hand in mine. "If you're asking me if I would like a few days alone with you, I obviously haven't made myself clear." I intensified my gaze. "The question is, do *you* want to be alone with *me*?"

She smirked, the color of her face changing. "Yes, I want that."

I leaned in and whispered in her delicate ear. "Are you sure? There's no telling what I may do to you." I nudged my shoulder into hers. "Don't worry, beautiful, I'll be gentle."

She pulled her head back. "Maybe I don't want gentle."

"A challenge?" I nodded and rubbed my chin. "Interesting. Well, we will see where things take us, won't we?"

The sound of Vanessa clearing her throat distracted us both. And it was a good thing. My dick was starting to react again.

Iris stepped away. "Okay, we won't be gone long." She turned toward Vanessa. "Once they finish eating, I'll pack them up. Are you sure about this, Vanessa?"

"Damn sure."

Wow, she'd answered with such gusto. It almost felt as if Dennis and his wife were encouraging this connection between Iris and me. I rather liked that.

We quickly cleaned up the kitchen and got everything ready to go.

Before they left with both dogs in tow, I had a thought. "Hey, babe?"

Iris turned, something registering in her eyes.

The nickname?

"Yeah?" She slid her adorable toes into those same faded yellow flip-flops.

There was no question, she'd rock a grain sack, but this girl still needed some new clothes. In the time I'd seen her, those same shorts, T-shirts, and one sundress were all she had worn. Coming from one of the four fashion capitals of the world, this would not do.

"Can I get a key to your barn? I'd like to see what condition your car is in. If we're gonna have a few days to ourselves, I'd like to teach you how to drive."

Her face beamed like I had never seen before. She even clapped her hands together. "Really?"

Vanessa smiled. "I'll get the dogs in the car. Come on, you two." She guided them out the door. "See you out there, Iris. And have a nice day, JC."

"You, too, Vanessa." I had to admit, Iris's enthusiasm was contagious. "So, about that key?"

"Sure. I mean, absolutely." She reached into her pale-pink heart-shaped purse with a chain strap, something a high school girl would use, and withdrew a set of keys. "This is for the house"—she held up a traditional flat key—"and this one is for the barn." It was a padlock key. "The barn door is a slider, and it's pretty huge. You just need to take the lock off and slide it open. Sometimes, it gets stuck. I open it just enough to get the mower out. Tell you what, I'll grab my cell phone, so if you have any trouble, I can try and help you." She spoke quickly, her voice exuberant. "If you pull it too hard, it may come off the track."

I took the keys from her hand, knowing I wouldn't need any additional help. "I'm all over it." *Just like I'll be all over you soon.*

I walked her to the door, my fingers brushing up against hers. "I'll go for a run, and then I'll check it out. I scouted out a few garages in case your car needs repair. One place inspects and has a flatbed for vehicles if the wheels are shot." Given the amount of time her car had sat idle, I suspected those tires were unsafe. "You'll need to renew your registration either online or at the DMV, but we can figure that all out later."

"Wow, thank you." She slung her purse over her shoulder. Newfound energy billowed off her.

So, this was what Iris looked like happy. I recalled that woman disguised in a big hat and long coat, a shotgun poised in her hands. And the woman grieving over her injured dog. I never wanted to see either of those people again. And I suspected, neither did Iris.

"No problem. Research is my thing." It would have to be in my line of work.

"Thank you, Jacob." She rode up on her tiptoes and kissed me. "See you soon."

I watched her walk away and then closed the door, feeling guilty about not being entirely honest with her.

After our first kiss and when I had finished with my business call, I was too wired to sleep. So I did some looking into local garages, as I had said. What I didn't divulge was that I also thought long and hard about a few tech people who could find out almost anything there was to know about a person. They had their ways—far beyond anything my mind could comprehend—and they were good at it. So I contacted one of them. Her name was Danny (short for Danielle). Danny had dated Zach for a while. They remained friends. I asked her to find out who owned Iris's house and who was paying the utilities. *Does Iris Flynn have a bank account?*

These were things I hoped to know soon. I could have asked Iris, but somehow, questions of this nature seemed more like prying than asking about her family. She would wonder why I wanted to know. And since I wasn't entirely sure myself, I decided to find out on my own.

I changed into my running gear, strapped the cell phone holder onto my arm—something I hadn't needed when Lily ran with me—and popped in my wireless earbuds, finding high-energy music to keep me pumped. And then I headed out the door. Given the morning's events, I had a lot to think about on this run. Iris would be back soon without her dogs. We'd be truly alone. The thought of it both excited and spooked me.

These past few days, I found myself clinging to the edges of my former life, my metaphorical knuckles white, and I was slipping . . . into a world unknown. A wiser man would have packed up his shit and hightailed it out of there.

Unfortunately for me, I wasn't a wiser man.

* * *

I made four laps, all while missing my running companion. Every now and then, the sun poked its head out to warm the air as a traffic jam of clouds fought against its efforts. My app said the temperature had reached the high sixties, which was perfect running weather. A light breeze refreshed my tacky skin.

After much thought, I also came to the conclusion that being with Iris romantically wasn't a bad thing . . . for her. I'd been crystal clear about my intentions, or lack thereof. No promises came from my lips. Or hers, for that matter. We were attracted to each other. Being intimate might just set my mind right again. I had thought I was in love with her. Now I wasn't so sure. But this was me, doing everything in my power to deny the undeniable.

When I was satisfied with my workout, I veered off to Iris's place. It was weird being there when she wasn't, this woman who had wasted herself away in this house for so long. Everything appeared normal, a thick layer of straw encasing the field in seed. I examined the broken-down fence and the cockeyed shutters. I could fix those. A project for another day.

The red barn wasn't as large as most. It was attached to the house but didn't appear to offer entry from that direction. I'd noticed as much when I had been indoors. A quick trip around the building told me the slider out front was the only way inside. Clusters of weeds surrounded the structure, a small window covered in grime off to the right of the sliding door.

A large padlock gleamed in the morning sun as I approached. Wasting no time, I unlocked and removed the padlock and began pulling the door open. Iris wasn't kidding. This thing was stuck, partially anyway. Only the top track allowed the door movement. The bottom of the door met gravel, which appeared to rise up halfway across the span of the opening. With more than enough room to enter, I went inside, planning to find a shovel or a hoe to knock that ground out from beneath the door. I figured that would remedy the blockage problem and allow it to function properly. For now, the small opening would do.

The room smelled of old wood, dust, and decomposed grass. Small slivers of sunlight peeked through some of the cracks in the walls. With the aid of the open door and the dirty window, I was able to see just fine. At least it didn't smell like dead animal, which happened one summer at my grandfather's barn. Man, did *that* reek until he'd found the partially rotted carcass of a rabbit. We assumed his dog, Rex, had gotten to it before we could.

I gazed around at my surroundings. Just like with my Gramps's shed/garage, various tools leaned against this wall or that. A push lawn mower that Iris must've used to mow her sanctuary and the small area out front sat idle, a gas can waiting next to it. *Who brought her the gas?* Rolling Creek Grocery? It had to be. The space wasn't as organized as my garage or as clean, but Gramps had always kept everything he owned in order. I followed that same ritual.

The car Iris spoke of happened to be a cranberry-colored compact that required most of the room. Dust coated every inch, the tires indicating flat spots from nonuse. I suspected the engine was also probably shot. Leaving a car like this for so many years would most certainly promote battery discharge and fluid degradation. Given the tractors, haying equipment, and hauling vehicles at my Gramps's place, I'd overheard a thing or two.

I opened the driver's side door, confronted by more dust and mildew. The keys sat in the ignition, for all the good that would do. "This car is a piece of shit." I walked around the front and opened the passenger side door to access the glovebox. I pulled out the registration, dated ten years ago, which included the name Edward Flynn, with a different address than the one here. Iris had said her parents had moved away, so I was pretty sure the address on the form wasn't where they lived now. It also confirmed that this house was not where Iris had grown up. I had suspected as much. If her parents hadn't had a lot of discretionary income at the time, how was their daughter able to afford living here for ten years? *Nathan.* It had to be him.

Moving forward. A quick check under the hood told me this car wasn't going anywhere. I wasn't even sure a skilled mechanic could save it, but I'd give it my best effort. Or Ralph from Ralph's Towing and Repairs would, who I called next.

* * *

While I waited for Ralph Jr. to arrive with his flatbed, I went inside Iris's house to get a glass of water. I stood by the back door as I sipped my second glass, gazing out at her mowed circle of grass, which lengthened each day. Given the frequent rain, the grass everywhere in this region grew rampant. I'd resorted to mowing the yard at my place every five days, weather permitting.

Ralph Jr. quoted me forty-five minutes over the phone, ample enough time to clean up the yard for Iris. I had noticed some areas out front also needed attention. She'd had a lot on her plate. I could do this for her. And so I got busy, cutting all the areas I could see she had kept short. I finished with her sanctuary and then put the mower away, making sure to clean the new grass out from beneath the carriage with my hands. Having completed that task, I found a small shovel to clear the blockage under the door. Since the ground was mostly soft, it didn't take me long. And then the door slid all the way open. Mission accomplished.

The combination of the run plus the lawn and barn work had left me soaked with sweat. Although, a stiff breeze kept me from overheating too badly. I returned to the house for another glass of water. Given my sweaty ass, I chose not to sit on any of her furniture. The bench out back would suit me fine.

Several tall oaks and maple trees encroached on Iris's house, but the field remained open, allowing me a full vantage

191

point of Old Oak Road without much effort. I took a break and checked my cell. A text message from my tech friend Danny appeared on the small screen.

> Hey, JC. Got your email. I'm on a retreat for the next two days. Only way I can stay sane from computer screens. 😊 I'll check into that information you requested and get back to you. Should be easy enough.

> Thanks, Danny. I owe you.

A lull in energy set into my muscles and my mind. I tipped my head back to fully embrace the fresh air, my arms stretched over the back of the bench, and my empty glass lying in the grass by my feet. When I lifted my head, the sun came out again, casting a soft glow over Iris's boulder. Something scratched into the center of the rock drew my attention—a word—but I couldn't make out what it said. The only person who could have done that would be Iris. She had said she'd dragged that rock here from the woods. Other than a few trees here and there, the only woods within a reasonable distance remained on the other side of Old Oak Road, which had to be 300 yards away. That must've taken her some effort.

I knelt closer to get a better view. The word *Jade* appeared before me. "Who the hell is Jade?" I said to no one in particular. Was it one of Iris's pets that had died? Was this a monument? And then, Iris's words came back to me. *I may not have murdered anyone, but that doesn't mean I wasn't responsible for someone's death.*

She'd said *someone.* That didn't sound like a pet, and neither did the name Jade. Was Iris's sanctuary a place where she paid homage to someone named Jade? If that were true, then Jade must've died. Did that have anything to do with why those greasy assholes were harassing her? An even crazier thought came to mind. Did this death have anything to do with the reason they called her a witch?

An uneasy feeling crept through my chest, interrupted by the sound of a flatbed truck off in the distance.

I stood and headed toward the barn.

Chapter Fifteen

JC

After Ralph Jr. had loaded up the car, I slid the barn door closed, locked it, along with the house, and headed home. I walked this time, hoping to loosen a few muscles and cool down properly. I thought about texting Iris with an update, but decided to wait and tell her in person. If she was checking on Laddie and trying to get Lily and Maggie situated, she didn't need me interrupting her.

My phone buzzed, which I was now carrying. Brody's name flashed onto the screen.

"Hello?"

"Did I do something to piss you off?" I turned the corner toward my house.

"No, why?"

"You haven't been to the club lately, and now you don't want to play in the tournament."

"I was just there last week, dude. And it's only Thursday." Was Brody one of those possessive friends who needed constant contact? I hated those types.

His voice wavered. "Yeah, I know, but you're only here for another week, right? Not even."

"Right." I had told Iris I would stay longer, but in my mind, what I chose to do was none of Brody or anyone else's business.

"I was hoping we could get into the zone tomorrow. Show a few people up. Know what I mean? I'll buy the scotch afterward."

I swiped a hand across my forehead as my house came into view. "Yeah, I get it, dude, but I already told you, I've got too much work to do."

"Are you sure that's the real reason?"

I stopped walking. "What is *that* supposed to mean?" How much did Brody know about me and Iris? Again, none of his goddamn business.

"You got a lady holed up there with you from the city?" He chuckled. "I'm just messing with you, dude. But seriously, I can hook you up if you're in need, if you know what I mean."

I resumed walking. "Yeah, I know what you mean, and I'm good. Look, work has been nonstop. Can't be helped. I wish I could join tomorrow, but it's not possible." I was getting annoyed at this point. How many times did I need to beat this dead horse?

"Okay, I get it. Just make sure you save one last day of golf before you go. I still need my chance to kick your butt on the course."

"I'll try. See ya." I ended the call.

If I understood how to read Brody, I might have asked him a few things about Iris and maybe even Tom, but I didn't become successful in my career by underestimating people. I hadn't known Brody long enough to take that leap. Tom and Brody were close. And that offered some unpleasant possibilities. Dennis was another story. I trusted him right away.

I stepped onto the porch and made my way inside. After a nice long shower, I was good as new. *So, now what?* I decided to do a little work while I waited for Iris to return. I wasn't as swamped as I had told Brody, but there was always work to do, so I got on it.

Three hours passed, and I started to worry. I knew Iris was with good people; that wasn't what concerned me. Given the amount of time it took me to run, mow her lawn, and supervise getting the car onto the flatbed, she'd been gone for nearly five hours already. I just hoped Laddie hadn't had some sort of complication. Or that the other dogs weren't having separation anxiety. This makeshift family had been inseparable for years. It made me wonder how Iris would cope. However things went down, I'd be supportive, even if it meant putting off our *fun*. I changed the sheets regardless and straightened up my room. I liked things in order, and that meant a clean house.

I could have gone out on the boat, but I decided on a few minutes of shuteye instead. When I awoke, my cell phone flashed 5:15 p.m. at me. No text messages from Iris either. *Hmm.* Whatever she was doing, it had gone far beyond checking on Laddie and dropping off her dogs. Once again, I considered texting her. *Don't be a Brody-type.*

I made dinner instead. Since there were ample amounts of casserole left over from last night, I warmed it up, refreshed the salad, and opened a bottle of Riesling to let it breathe. In a cupboard underneath the bookcase in the living room, I scored two white tapers with glass holders, a perfect addition to the small vase of wildflowers in the center of the table. I straightened the placemats and set the place settings, Iris-style.

Six o'clock rolled around, and I decided to text.

> Everything okay? I've got dinner ready for you. 😄

I figured the smiley face would imply my mood. *Not being possessive.* I shook my head. "Man, who are you, dude?"

The sound of tires rolling up had me springing from my seat at the table and approaching the front door. This time, Vanessa stayed in her sedan, talking with Iris before the two women hugged, and Iris climbed out of the passenger seat, no dogs accompanying her. She opened the door to the back and pulled out several bags with store labels on them. *She went shopping?* "Nice one, Vanessa. This girl needed clothes."

I opened the front door and waved to Vanessa as she backed her car up next to Gramps's pickup truck and drove out.

"I see you've been busy today." I kissed Iris and then took the majority of her bags into the house. "I was starting to worry." *What the hell, dude?* Don't be saying shit like that.

"Oh, I'm sorry. We just lost track of time. Plus, I wanted to stay a while with the dogs to make sure they were comfortable." Iris slid her purse off her shoulder and hung it on a hook attached to the hall tree. "It smells good in here." She took the bags I had just placed on the bench. "Do you mind if I drop these off before dinner?"

"Of course."

"I'd like to take a shower, too, if you don't mind." She smiled at me, but it didn't quite reach her sapphire eyes. If it hadn't been for that, I might have asked if I could join her.

"Take all the time you need. Dinner is sitting warm in the oven, table is set, and salad is ready to go. I also opened a bottle of Riesling for us. I'll be out back having a beer. Come out whenever you're ready."

Half an hour passed, and I returned inside. Showers didn't take this long. As I approached the hall bathroom, I heard it— Iris crying. And my heart sank. I was right; this was a lot for her. I knocked lightly on the door. "Iris, you okay, babe?"

No answer.

And then, "Yeah, I'll be out in a minute." She sniffled as my ears picked up movement in the room.

"Iris. Can you open the door? Please?"

The sound of the lock turning on the other side preempted the knob turning. Slowly, Iris opened the door, her eyes bloodshot and her face blotchy with emotion.

I didn't say a word. I just took her in my arms and held her, her apricot scent fresh. "It's okay. I know this must be hard for you. And if you want, we can go get the dogs right now." I moved her back so I could stare into her eyes. "You've all been together for a very long time. It's normal for you to feel separation anxiety."

She sniffled some more and wiped her eyes and nose as best she could.

With nothing else at my disposal, I unrolled a sheet of TP and gave it to her, which she used to properly wipe her cheeks dry.

"No, I want to get through this. It's not just that." Her breathing shuddered as she placed her hand on my chest. "Let's have some dinner and wine. I'll be okay."

If I'd had any inkling of asking her about who Jade was, I had to put that question aside. *Fragile* was the word that came to mind as I watched Iris hang up her towel on the towel bar and follow me out. Something else occurred to me that had me in awe of this woman. I got the sense that as painful as this moment was for her, she was trying her best to move past it for me. For us, really. With the exception of my grandparents and my younger sisters, no one had ever made a sacrifice so great. And I had offered her nothing. No commitment. No promises of any sort. I had never felt shallower and more selfish in my life.

During dinner, we sipped wine while Iris picked at her food.

"Cheers." I clanked my wine glass against hers. "I want you to celebrate getting out today. How long has it been?"

She sipped her wine and then placed the glass onto the table. "Ten years."

I knew this, but hearing her acknowledge these things pulled heavily on my heart. "Well then, we really do have something to celebrate. I'm so proud of you, Iris. That must've been difficult *and* stressful. But you got through it." I finished my wine and poured another glass. "So, I see you went shopping. Are you planning on modeling anything for me?" I wiggled my eyebrows.

That brought a smile to her pouty lips. "I'd love to." She actually blushed.

What I would do to keep that smile on her face.

"Okay then. Let's finish up here, and then you can give me a fashion show." Did I dare to hope she'd bought something sexy and see-through? No harm in wishing.

With dishes behind us and a fresh glass of wine poured, Iris disappeared into the bedroom while I sat on the couch, anticipating her next appearance.

The first thing she came out wearing was a small red dress with tiny white daisies all over it. Although the bodice formed well to her shape, the skirt portion was flowing, reaching halfway down her thighs. Three small spaghetti straps rode over each of her delicate shoulders. "Beautiful. I love it!"

She twirled, the skirt flashing her upper thighs at me. I was quickly a fan.

The next outfit was a teal-colored romper with a coral palm leaf pattern. The shorts allowed her long legs the respect they deserved, the top wrapped around her thin waist by a tie, creating a V-neck and a little bit of cleavage. "Gorgeous. I love that one too." I sipped my wine and smiled.

A pair of distressed jean shorts and sheer white tank came out next. "Oh, that's my favorite." I stood and approached, my gaze locking on her nipples that poked through the fabric. She wasn't wearing a bra, and this shirt required one. Did I dare take this as a sign?

"I thought you would." There went that index finger between her teeth.

This woman was driving me mad. "That material looks so soft." I ran one hand down her chest, stopping at one of her full breasts. "Oh, yeah. That's soft alright." I kissed her. "How about I make it hard?"

Her eyes dilated; Iris met my gaze. "I would like that."

My fingers went to work, massaging her nipples until she was moaning and starting to sway. I scooped her up in my arms. "I know we had said the kitchen floor, but I'd much rather put you in my bed." My lips landed on hers as my tongue sampled her luscious mouth. "That okay with you?"

Something flashed across her face, enough to make me pause on my route toward my bedroom. "Everything okay? We don't have to—"

"No, it's okay. I mean, I'm okay."

She wasn't quite, but she was trying to be.

"Do you have birth control? I started taking some today, but the doctor said it takes seven days to be effective." Her gaze drifted away from mine.

I carried her into my room and placed her on my bed. "You went to the doctor today? That's where you were?" I perched myself next to her, placing my hand on her thigh.

She nodded. "That was just one place Vanessa took me. But, yes. Does that bother you?"

I made a face and blew out a heavy breath. "Bother me? Not at all. I'm just impressed. You were thinking ahead."

Her chin fell, right along with her gaze.

Once again, I lifted her chin to look at me. "Oh, Iris. You are a mystery to me. I know there are a lot of things holding your heart hostage, but if you let me, I would like nothing more than to make you forget all of those bad things right now. I have condoms. Good ones. I can pull out, too, if you want. I'll make sure you are safe." I touched the tip of her nose. "What I can't promise you is that I won't ravage every inch of your hot body and make you cum like you've never cum before." I touched her breast over her shirt, my thumb running over her nipple. "All you have to do is say the word."

Her voice dipped low and seductive. "What word would that be?"

"Yes!"

She let her head drift back. "Yes, Jacob. Make me forget." And then the rest of her body fell back onto my mattress.

"Let this be all about you right now," I whispered as I hovered over her. "I have never wanted to satisfy a woman more than I do you right now, Iris." I kissed her lips, my tongue eager to return to her warm mouth. "You are so gorgeous. I think about you all the time." I kissed her again, my tongue moving to her neck. "You want to know what *specifically* I think about?"

A throaty *yes* answered me.

I cupped her breast, my fingers resuming their massage. "I think about how much I want to suck those tits and bury my face in them."

At first, she kept her eyes closed tight as though trying to block out something . . . or someone. *Nathan?* But the more I encouraged her to let go with my touch and my words, the more I could see her body relaxing from my efforts.

Her eyes opened, meeting my gaze. "I would love that."

I pulled her shirt over her head and admired breasts that were natural and suited for my mouth and hands. I suckled; I massaged. "I can't wait to feel that warm pussy. And taste you. Would you like that?"

She eased her legs apart, inviting me in. Her hands roamed my back, her fingernails adding just enough stimulation to my skin.

And then, she said it. "Please don't make me wait any longer."

Music to my ears *and* my dick.

I slid off the bed and unbuttoned her jean shorts, sliding them off those long legs. To my surprise, no panties. She *was* ready for this. "You have the sexiest legs I've ever seen, Iris. And when I taste you, I want you to wrap those legs around my shoulders, so I can feel them." I spread her legs more and took in the most alluring woman I had ever seen. All those past experiences paled. I never thought such a thing was possible. My dick was throbbing at the sight of her. But my needs would have to wait.

Iris lifted one of her legs to rest against my shoulder. And when she did so, I caressed her outer calf and thigh, kissing my way down to her sweet center. She tasted as good as I had imagined she would. Wet. Warm. And needy. I licked her clit, knowing just where to apply pressure and to stimulate all those nerve endings. This was a body part I knew well. I took my time, savoring her essence.

Soon, Iris was arching her back and grabbing for handfuls of sheet. Her lungs screamed for joy. "Oh, Jacob, don't stop. . . . Oh, god!" It was the best sound I had ever heard. When the screams subsided, I expected her to need a minute. And I was prepared to give her one. It had been a long time for her. To my surprise, she urged me onto my back, her eyes dilated with erotic thirst. I grabbed a condom as quickly as I could.

Hair wild, Iris climbed on top of me and rode me with everything she had. She ran her hands down over her breasts as they moved with her body's rhythm, my dick celebrating every second of it. I held her hips and watched her eyes unfocused—lost in a cloud of carnal ecstasy—and her head rolling back.

Sweet Jesus! I was in awe. It was a show I never wanted to see end.

Chapter Sixteen

Iris

I had wondered what it would feel like to wake up wrapped in Jacob's big, strong arms, and now I knew. It was wonderful. My body still tingled from the hours of lovemaking. No one had ever done to me the things Jacob had. My first time was with a football player named Theo who had put zero effort into foreplay. Thinking back, he probably didn't know what he was doing. We'd only hooked up twice before he was onto someone else. It was fine by me.

My second experience was with the egomaniac, who wooed me into thinking he was the answer to my prayers. What a mistake. Making love to him never felt right. He was always in a hurry or wanting to try something he'd seen in one of his porns. Honestly, he made me feel cheap and worthless as though I was a vessel, not a person with wants and needs of her own.

Jacob knew about him, and he still wanted me. If he ever found out what really happened, I wondered if he would feel the same.

I had to remind myself that Jacob had sex. He didn't have

relationships. And yet, he still made me feel more valued and appreciated than anyone had before him. If Jacob ever did fall in love, I couldn't imagine what that would feel like as a woman. And I would never know. I was okay with that. *Not true.* I had accepted that. He'd given me this. And I'd bask in it for the rest of my life. He would be the flower I would press into a book and keep for as long as I could. If only I could spend the rest of my life with someone like Jacob. I wanted that more than I had ever thought possible. My happy ending. Some things weren't meant to be.

But I had to face the truth. And the truth was, I was running out of options. I'd lost everyone close to me. And some-day, I'd lose the house too. I could feel the tides turning. Warren and his gang were coming around more often. Were they doing this on their own behalf? Or had someone sent them? Callum had stopped them last fall. Jacob had stopped them this time. What would happen when I was alone again?

I needed a plan. I could apply to college again, but I had little money or housing, and what would I do with the dogs? I couldn't ask my parents to take care of them. Not after the way we had left each other. I knew they loved me, but we'd not communicated in ten years. How was Mom? Was she even still alive? She was on the mend when they left to pursue a job my father had landed at a regional trucking company in Harris-burg, Pennsylvania. He'd have better health benefits and a raise, enough that Mom wouldn't have to work as she recov-ered. He'd chosen Harrisburg because that was where his brother and cousins lived. It was also where he had met my mother. Home.

For better or worse, this was *my* home. Laddie, Lily, and Maggie were *my* family.

Daddy left me the car, a few hundred dollars, and a disap-pointed look in his eyes. He expected more from me. They both did. Why didn't I expect more for myself? If things got any worse, I'd have to turn to Dennis and Vanessa to care for the dogs, which was my ulterior motive when asking them to take care of them now. After what Warren had already done to Laddie, I couldn't put them in danger again.

Jacob's breath warmed the back of my neck, acquainting me with better things to think about. We had three days to be together. Three days for me to pretend what being in love was really like. And he was going to teach me to drive. I even had a few dollars I could use to repay him. The rest, I'd figure out later.

I ran my hand down his forearm, tanned by the sun, as it remained wrapped around my waist. And I basked in the warmth of his muscular body spooning mine. I wanted to wake up next to him every morning for eternity. It was everything I had imagined. A gorgeous man who wanted nothing more than to please me. How many times had he made me orgasm? I'd lost count, each encounter different from the last. But it was when he was inside me that I cherished the most. We were one, our bodies connected like I'd never experienced before. I was in love with Jacob, but I would never tell him that. *He didn't have relationships. He had sex.*

"Good morning, beautiful."

I smiled. "Good morning."

As Jacob fell onto his back, I turned over to face him. I covered my mouth with my hand. "I need to brush my teeth." I slipped off the bed and into the bathroom to freshen my mouth.

Jacob came right up behind me, doing the same. Then he scooped me up in his arms, making me squeal, and brought me right back to bed. "We need some cuddle time before we get up."

I thought he wanted to make love again, but he didn't. We faced each other, our hands clasped together.

His eyes, two pools of the most perfect olive color, shone back at me, the sheet barely covering his broad shoulders and robust chest. Holding my hand in his, he kissed my knuckles. "You were amazing last night."

"*I* was amazing?" I tried not to scoff. "I think I may have blacked out at one point. *You* were incredible, Jacob. I don't recall doing much to show my appreciation." I wasn't lying. It was as if he were a sex savant, and I was his student. If there was a spot on my body that could evoke a new sensation, Jacob had found it—before I was jelly in his hands.

He chuckled. "You *let* me do all those things to you. And that was appreciation enough." He reached out and brushed some curls away from my face. "You are the most beautiful woman I have ever been with. You know that?"

I refrained from rolling my eyes. He had to be lying. There was no way that statement could be true. He worked and lived in New York City. I found myself looking away from him.

He moved so that the upper half of his body lifted over mine. "You don't believe me, do you?" His face drew near, his eyes trying to fasten mine in place.

"No. I don't, but it is kind of you to say." I ran my fingers through his thick brown hair. "Your hair is getting longer. Want me to cut it for you?"

"You cut hair?" He quirked a brow.

"I cut my own hair. And I have clippers for Maggie."

A bright smile spread across his handsome face. "You want to use dog clippers on my hair?" His fingers reached down and tickled my waist.

I yelped and giggled. "No. I would use my scissors on your hair. But if you want me to shave you, I can do that too." I spoke through pants.

More tickling. More yelping from me.

Jacob's eyes filled with mischief. "If I'm a good boy, will you give me some treats?"

I lifted my leg around his hip and used my body to tip this muscle-bound man over onto his back. And then I flipped my hair over so it would slide down his chest and stomach as I worked my kisses toward an erection already waiting for me. "How about I give you my treat now?"

* * *

We showered and then had breakfast on the back deck, the sky unusually clear this morning. I decided on my new red dress with white daisies all over it, a pair of strappy sandals I had also bought. I even put on a little bit of makeup, surprised that time hadn't spoiled it yet.

The birds sang all around us, the wildlife near the pond croaking and chirping. A fish splashed in front of my eyes. It was so tranquil. Jacob made scrambled eggs with fresh basil and tomato for us. He also brewed us a pot of coffee, professing I had exhausted him, and he needed the caffeine boost.

We sat at the small bistro table, enjoying our food. I'd brought out the makeshift vase (which was really a large glass) of flowers and the placemats to dress up the table. As I ate, I appreciated the burst of basil and tomato on my tongue. They were a great addition to the eggs and a healthier choice than bacon. I'd have to remember that for future meals.

"I looked into it, and it's pretty easy to get a learner's permit." Having finished his eggs, Jacob sat back in his chair. "You can use one of my laptops to take the online test and pay the fee. And then they issue you a temporary permit that's valid for ninety days. So we can get started right away."

I put my fork down and wiped my mouth with my paper napkin. "Yes, I did know that. Well, I sort of knew that. I used to have a learner's permit, but it expired. They're only good for like five years. I don't have a computer, or else I would have checked. Thank you for looking into that for me."

Jacob sat forward and leaned his forearms onto the table. "Do you need to study? I'm sure we can pull up—"

"Nah." I waved him off. "I remember the rules. I've always been good at remembering facts. That's why I was such a good student. I didn't have to study as hard as my friends to get good grades."

The sun warmed my arms as it rose higher in the sky, its rays reflecting off the water's surface, offering a sparkly effect.

The corners of Jacob's lovely lips curved upward. "Oh, so you're a smarty pants, are you?" His eyes smiled as he spoke. "I suspected as much."

I shook my head and made a noise in my throat. "I never said *that*." I tossed my balled-up paper napkin at him. And then I stood. "And I've got some cash I can give you for the permit fee. I believe I need to pay it online. I don't have a credit card." I took his plate and mine and then gazed down at him. "Is that okay? I can find another way—"

"Of course it's okay. It's cheap. And when you do the test, we need to schedule the vision and hearing test at the DMV. Are you okay with that?"

"Wow, you really checked into everything. Yes. I'm good with it, and thank you, Jacob. Once I pass, I can take the driver's test right away since I'm over eighteen. So, I'll schedule the vision and hearing test right away, and then I'll also schedule the driving test for the same day." I suddenly realized I had no idea how long Jacob would be here. The Fourth of July had come and gone, with the middle of the month fast approaching. "Passing the written driver's test will be easy. But I need driving experience. If I work really hard on it, I could see myself being ready in a week, maybe less." I was thinking out loud, hoping Jacob would offer some indication of how long he planned to stay.

But he didn't respond. He just sipped his coffee and listened to me. Until I stopped talking. And then, he seemed to focus.

"Sorry, what? I was just listening to you. A week sounds great. We can practice all you want. And with the dogs gone, we should have plenty of time." He gazed up at me. "Why are you looking at me like that?"

"I just. I, um." *Speak.* "I guess I wasn't sure how long you plan to stay."

Since my hands were busy holding our plates, he touched my forearm, his warmth sending a message of comfort to my troubled heart. "I'll be here at least that long. No worries."

Helpful but not decisive. Somehow, his answer caused a pit to form in my stomach. I didn't want to ask him how long he *was* planning on staying. Knowing such information would only make me stress over that dreaded moment when he'd be gone. And I wasn't ready to face that. Not yet.

I don't have relationships.

I leaned over and kissed his amazing lips. "You stay out here and finish your coffee, and I'll take care of the dishes."

I passed the learner's permit exam in no time, then took the driver's test online, which I also passed with flying colors. With that behind me, I scheduled the vision and hearing test for Monday at 8:30 a.m. at the DMV. I also scheduled the *actual* driver's test for 10:00 a.m., with the proviso that my hearing and vision were up to snuff, which I knew they were. I let Jacob know all of this.

"That works. Since the DMV is in Montpelier, I'll bring my laptop and find a place to do business."

"The public library is located on the same street. State Street, actually. And I'm sure they have Wi-Fi."

That made him smile. "Take all the time you need, then."

My mind went into processing mode. I needed to provide two forms of ID when I went to the DMV. I was sure I had my birth certificate somewhere in my house. The other form of ID would be tricky. Maybe my Social Security card was there as well. I also had many invoices from Rolling Creek Grocery that included my address. *Check.*

I rode with Jacob to a place in Barre where we printed off my temporary permit.

The race was on.

"Do you want to drive us home or wait until we get there to practice on Old Oak Road?"

We were approaching his expensive SUV in the parking lot when he asked this question.

I wagged my index finger in the air. "Written tests are a breeze, but I'd better wait for the actual driving when we get home." We climbed into our designated seats.

Until Jacob had brought me to Dennis's veterinary clinic, I hadn't even been inside a car in ten years. Other than my parked car in the barn. And only one time since then, with Vanessa. I was nervous about this. Especially with *his* car, which was top-of-the-line, having everything one could possibly need from the touch of a button or a voice command. I had never been in a vehicle like this. I wished *my* car were available. Driving into a ditch wouldn't worry me so much.

"Don't worry." Jacob's hand found my knee. "You'll do fine. It's not that hard. You'll be surprised. Learning on a dirt road covered in washboards and ruts will only make you a better driver." He chuckled.

I gazed over at him from the passenger seat. "How do you do that?"

He draped his arm over the steering wheel and eased us out of the parking lot. "Do what?" Bloomberg radio had been governing our airspace on the way into town. Jacob had said he wanted to listen for any market fluctuations. He turned the radio down.

"Read my mind. You always seem to sense when something is wrong. Like in the bathroom last night. How did you know I was upset?"

He waited before he answered me. "Truth be told, I have no idea. Last night, I sensed something was wrong, and then I heard you crying through the door. I make it my business to read people. Maybe that's it." He exhaled a long breath as though he was still trying to work it out himself.

When we reached Old Oak Road, he stopped the vehicle. "Okay, no more stalling. We're doing this." He shifted the car into park and exited, circling around the front toward my door.

I was already climbing out. "Okay, but I'm gonna take it slow."

"You mean, you don't want to race down this beautiful road?" His voice mocked as his hand fanned out toward our scenery. "I can't imagine why not."

Jacob spent the next several minutes going over the controls of the vehicle, which was a learning experience within itself. This Black Label Special Edition Luxe Navigator didn't just come equipped with touchscreens; it had a panoramic display and even an automatic air freshener. I felt like I was inside the cockpit of a commercial airliner (even though I'd never actually been inside one). Plush leather seats in light gray, and a sound system that fooled you into believing Bloomberg was right in the car with us, this thing made my compact look like a tin can. The outside was black, and, man, did it show dirt, the wheels thick with new tread. I was careful to avoid the larger potholes, and there were a lot of them. "Man, this road is in bad shape. I guess I never noticed it much when I was walking along it."

"Like I said, it will only make you a better driver." He gave me a side look. "Just don't tear my muffler off."

"I'll do my best." If only I were kidding.

Once we had driven back and forth several times—muffler still intact—Jacob suggested we try the main road. His hand returned to my knee. "You got this. And I'm right here. I'll coach you through it."

But will you always be here? I had to stop that thought process before it had a chance to take over my mind.

We drove back to the print shop in Barre. And then, we headed to Montpelier, where Jacob instructed me to take Main Street, turning left onto State Street. I knew all of these places well. And they hadn't changed much in the ten years I'd been MIA, which I had also noticed when Vanessa had brought me here earlier to buy clothes. She even tried to pay, but I refused to let her. I had a few bucks socked away that I had grabbed on our way out of town.

We passed by various shops and restaurants, most privately owned, and each one colorful and distinctive. I made sure to stop at every crosswalk, allowing passersby to continue on their way.

I pointed at a large light-gray granite building on my left. "That's the DMV." The sign out front confirmed it.

"Great." Jacob peered through my window. "Easy to find. And I see the library too."

Across the street, the massive gold dome of the capitol building gleamed with pride. The *crown jewel* of Montpelier. Out front, five robust pillars made of granite hoisted the iconic Doric portico, where a statue of Ethan Allen, founder of Vermont, awaited appreciative onlookers. I remembered coming here for the fireworks displays every summer and sitting on the grass, an outdoor blanket providing cushion for me and my parents. Sometimes I had friends with me. Sometimes I didn't. Later, I attended parties on the Fourth with some of my wilder friends—Haley being one of them—sneaking away with the egomaniac. My parents never had a clue. It was all so adventurous back then. There were no limits to my life. And no guardrails, either. I wanted to shake that girl and tell her to wise up. I had put my faith in someone who had only ever seen me as a possession. *How had I let my life become this?*

Not fully aware of what I was doing, I slowed to a near stop until a car behind me honked. And then, I proceeded forward.

"That's a nice-looking capitol building. I didn't realize it was so big. Did you used to come here?" Jacob glanced over.

I nodded. "I did. Many times."

"Do you want to stop? We can walk around if you want."

I thought about my limited time with him.

"No, that's okay." There was nothing here for me, anyway. These were buildings—albeit charming ones—not family, both human and canine.

My driving companion stared out the window as we rode along. Instead of obsessing over my past mistakes, I focused on crosswalks, stop signs, and stoplights, including the ones on yellow. I used my turn signals, didn't tailgate, and navigated each turn, making sure not to cross the middle line. I knew the rules well.

When we reached the edge of town, Jacob instructed me to turn around in a gas station parking lot and drive through the city again. We had just taken a right from State Street onto Main when Jacob pointed. "Turn left up there."

I did as he asked.

"Okay, turn up that small incline."

When he told me to turn left the next time, I gulped.

"Are you sure? That's a pretty steep incline." My stomach tightened. This was the hill where Vermont College resided. I had never liked the incline when I wasn't driving. It was steeper than steep. Like, no way could you ride a bicycle up it.

"Yes. You can do this. You'll need to do hill stop-and-start for your test. And we'll also have to practice parallel parking."

Needless to say, I had a few pitfalls along the way, but I managed to survive the day. And so did Jacob's Navigator, thank the lord. When I had completed my third parallel park in front of the statehouse, no less, I turned the ignition off and rested my head against my headrest. My shoulders were aching, and so was my neck.

"You want to quit for the day?"

I turned my head to face my instructor. "If you don't mind." I rubbed my neck and rolled my shoulders around.

Jacob shifted in his seat. "You did great. If I were your instructor, I'd pass you."

My enthusiasm lifted as well as my confidence.

"A couple more days, and I think you'll be ready for an actual test." His stomach growled loud enough that I could hear it.

Mine had been doing the same for the past hour.

"I noticed a restaurant along the river. It's off Main Street." He glanced at the clock on the right side of the dash, 5:14 flashing back. "An Italian place. We skipped lunch, so let me take you to dinner. We can celebrate with a bottle of wine."

I wasn't sure about that. I had been to two stores with Vanessa recently, and both were relatively empty. The doctor's office she had taken me to was the same. School was out, and I assumed people were on vacation. I was nervous, my eyes focused on every face, waiting for someone to recognize me. *There's the witch who lives out on Old Oak Road.* Ten years had passed, yet it all felt like yesterday when my scandalous behavior had been the talk of the town.

The restaurant Jacob had suggested was not only excellent, it was also one I knew well. I'd had a part-time job there. It was during the summer between my junior and senior year. And it didn't last long. The egomaniac needed me more. Being in a restaurant with people who might or might not remember me from high school made my empty stomach roil with acid. I wasn't prepared for this. The owner could recognize me. *He's had many employees over the years. Would he even care?*

I had to remember that Jacob would be gone soon, and my contact with the outside world could be gone with him. Unless I chose differently. I'd already made some huge changes in my life. What was one more? *Go for it.*

With my head reclined, I glanced over again. "Sure. But if I'm gonna have wine, you have to drive us home after."

Chapter Seventeen

JC

When we entered the restaurant near the river's edge, the scents of garlic and several other spices came at me all at once. I went from hungry to starving. And I was sure Iris felt the same. She'd done a great job driving. Better than I had expected, given my SUV wasn't the easiest vehicle to understand. But she had done it. The more I got to know Iris, the more faith I had in her ability to accomplish just about anything.

The walls, sponge painted in shades of gold and coffee, provided a suitable backdrop for various artwork, ornate mirrors, and wall sconces. The color scheme also blended well with a few hand-painted murals of archways and Italian landscapes. The lighting was soft and relaxed; the tables embellished with white linen. An acoustic guitar emanated from hidden speakers. Near the bar area, a tower of wine bottles displayed the restaurant's extensive selection.

"Welcome to Uliveto. Do you have a reservation?" the dude with round, dark-rimmed glasses and black hair asked. His white shirt was crisp, and the black bowtie with a black vest and pants lent it a stylish look.

"No, we don't."

He smiled. "It's still early. I'm sure we can accommodate you. Would you prefer the porch area over the water or a table in the dining room?"

I glanced over at my dinner companion to see what she preferred. With a furrowed brow, cheeks flushed, and a guarded stance, Iris did not look happy.

I somehow knew why. I had developed the ability to sense this woman's feelings as though I could read her mind. I had always been good at reading people, but not to this degree.

"We'll take the porch." I took her hand in mine as the host led us through the semi-crowded dining room and onto a porch with open windows and tables lined up single file. No one would be across from us.

I sat on the side facing the main portion of the porch, allowing Iris a more private view. Outside, the sun was still high and mighty, the temperatures climbing into the low 80s. It was a nice change from all that rain. Across the water, cars drove back and forth along another street I didn't know the name of, but that was off in the distance, leaving us to enjoy the river and the fresh air. At least one of us, anyway.

"You will find our extensive wine selection at the back of your menus." The host who led us here placed a hard-covered menu at each of our place settings. The table was also dressed in white linen, complemented by fine silverware and pedestal water glasses. "Enjoy your meal."

Before I opened my menu, I took Iris's hand. "It's okay. We're pretty much alone over here. I know it's been a while since you were in a restaurant. Does this place bring back memories?" I hadn't even thought of that aspect of things until now. I just knew she was trying to adapt to being around people again.

"Good evening. My name is Elena, and I will be serving you this evening. Have you dined with us before?" Dressed similarly to our host, Elena smiled at us. She'd pulled her black hair tight into a ponytail, her brown eyes large and welcoming.

Since Iris wasn't answering, I handled it. "No. We haven't."

The server went through her spiel about the menu and the specials. "Could I start you off with an appetizer or two or something besides water to drink?" Another young dude came up and filled our water glasses as she spoke.

"Yes." I opened my menu and slid my finger down the antipasti page, pointing to one with tenderloins sprinkled with parmesan cheese and capers. "We'll take this." My finger landed on another option: roasted red peppers with garlic sauce. "And this. Oh, and some bread and garlic oil, please. We'll also take the best Sauvignon Blanc you sell."

"Oh!" Elena seemed to like that request. Expensive bills meant big tips. And I was hungry, so if she served us well, she would surely benefit.

"I will get a bottle and an ice bucket for you right away."

When we were finally alone, I was able to take Iris's hand again. "Is this too much?"

She took a quick sip of her water. "No. It's just been a long time. I used to work here the summer between my junior and senior year, but the job didn't last long."

My eyes widened. "You did? Why didn't you say anything? We can go somewhere else."

She was already shaking her head. "No, it's fine. It was a long time ago. I used to come to Montpelier a lot when I was younger. Sometimes with my parents." She stared out the window at the river flowing by. "That's the Winooski River, you know." A sigh escaped from her lips. "Montpelier has fireworks here every year, and I used to watch them with my family and some of my friends. They also usually have a parade. It was a fun place to hang out."

I kept my grip on her hand, wishing I had known her on the Fourth. I could have done something. "You know, Iris, if you want to track down your parents, I'd be happy to help you do that. Do you know where they live now?"

She nodded. "Harrisburg, Pennsylvania. My father got a job there ten years ago. It had better benefits and pay than he was getting here. That's where both of my parents are originally from. We used to visit a lot when I was little. I guess my father's job brought them to Vermont."

"Have you heard anything from them since they left?"

"No. My dad sends me cash in the mail every Christmas. No note."

Jesus. It hadn't occurred to me that Iris had not only been alone for ten years, but she'd spent every holiday and birthday alone as well. Knowing this about her made me want to wrap her up in my arms and make it all better.

"Here we are." Elena began uncorking the bottle while the same young dude who had filled our waters placed a standing ice bucket next to our table and vanished.

"Would you like me to order for you?"

"Sure." Iris attempted to smile, the lines around her eyes showing strain. "I'm starving, so order a lot!" She unfolded her white linen napkin and placed it in her lap.

I quickly perused the menu, reciting our order to Elena. Angel hair pasta with fresh tomatoes, salmon with pesto, Mediterranean chicken, and a dish of Fettuccine Alfredo would satisfy our hungry appetites.

Order placed, I lifted my glass to Iris's. "Congratulations on learning how to drive. This was your first day, and you did an excellent job. You will have no trouble passing your test. I believe in you." I took a sip of my wine, enjoying the citrus flavors as they washed over my palate.

With her glass halfway to her mouth, Iris froze. It was as if her face had suddenly fallen. Her expression was one of either horror or shock. And then a tear ran down her cheek.

My heart ached over that tear. "Did I say something wrong?"

She wiped her cheek clean. "No, it's just that it's been a very long time since anyone believed in me."

Son of a bitch, Iris. You're tearing me apart.

On the ride home, Iris stayed quiet in her seat, the window halfway down, and a light breeze fluffing her golden curls. She gazed out the window with her hand on my thigh. It was crazy how much I liked having it there.

I turned onto Old Oak Road. "Do you want to stop at your house for anything?"

She glanced over. "Nope. Everything I need is here."

That was nice of her to say. Our connection was strong, no doubt, the immense burden of it making my head spin. I had a lot to think about. A career back in New York City. My luxury apartment. My friends and family. A life of my own. At times, I could feel panic setting in. *What are you doing with this woman? You know you will eventually let her down. Best to cut ties now.* All of it ran through my thoughts, cluttering my brain. She was like a drug for me. I didn't feel I had a choice. Was that good or bad? If I were asking Gramps that question, he'd say he never had a choice, either. And he had gone for it, never looking back.

I pulled up next to my old brown pickup—the one I had only driven once—and shifted the car into park.

Iris's tone took charge. "Don't get out yet."

I placed my fob in a pocket of the console. "Okay, everything alright?" Did she have something else she wanted to tell me?

Iris pulled off her panties and climbed over the console before bending down to push my seat back, something she had learned how to do when adjusting the driver's seat to her height. And then, she worked on the zipper of my tailored navy shorts, which she had undone within seconds.

"So, is this my reward for volunteering to be your driving instructor?" My heart was ramping up and so was my dick. I grabbed a condom from my console—a new supply for just such an occasion. Truth be told, I had them stored everywhere.

"Uh, huh," she said with determination dominating her pupils.

I lifted my hips so she could get my shorts and boxer briefs off, happy to oblige. A few strokes of her soft hands, and I was ready.

She straddled me, her knees braced on both sides of my hips. "Mmm," she said, her eyes rolling back, and my cock deep inside her. This was fast becoming my happy place.

She eased her hips up and down as I lifted her dress high enough to taste her nipples and excite her. We moved together for several minutes. And then she quickened her pace as an orgasm took hold of her. She cried out. A few seconds later, I went with her.

This woman is going to be the death of me.

* * *

We spent our time driving around the area, making love, and cooking together. She even fished. And not as a bystander. She hooked the bait and unhooked the fish, which she threw back. The tables had turned. I was now learning from her.

Iris also had a voracious appetite in and out of the bedroom. She was insatiable. And I wasn't about to complain about it.

I worked at night after she had gone to sleep, making sure I was available when the market opened and closed. I wasn't behind with my duties, but I could sense something shifting, and I needed to stay focused. As Jen had pointed out, *you're in one day and then you're out.* I did my best to keep my head on straight.

During last night's dinner, Iris opened up to me a little more, but not enough to tell me who the married man was or what terrible thing had happened that had ruined her life, right along with her parents' lives, according to her.

I felt she was being too hard on herself, which I told her repeatedly. "Iris, the whole point of being young is to make mistakes. It teaches us what to do when we become adults." Nothing seemed to sink in.

She had done something terrible. She was solely responsible for her mistake. And she was never going to forgive herself for it.

My job was to convince her otherwise.

On Saturday, her phone rang while we were about to go out for a drive, hoping to get one last practice session in before the dogs returned later in the day.

She took the call and walked around my house as she carried on a conversation with someone I assumed was either Dennis or Vanessa. They were the only people she knew. I waited in the passenger seat, checking my phone for any new emails or texts. I had a lot of both.

She came back a few minutes later. "Dennis said everyone is great. He offered to keep the dogs until Monday after my driver's test. He said he could come by at noon. I could see the conflict in her eyes. "I really miss them, but . . ."

I put my cell phone down. "We can do whatever works for you, babe. That's only an extra day-and-a-half. And we could practice some more." I winked. "And fuck some more too."

She patted the edge of my open window. "Yeah, that would be great." She leaned in and kissed me. "Be right back."

When the moon came out, we skinny-dipped for the first time. Then we made love in the shower. I had her thrust up against the wall as water cascaded down my back. Those long legs did a fine job, curling around my waist and keeping her upright. We drank wine—she even tried bourbon—and we stretched out on the sofa watching an old movie, our bodies entwined.

It's the closest thing to heaven any man or woman could ever find on earth, JC. Gramps had it right.

We waited at Iris's house on Sunday for her car to be delivered. It was now the day before the dogs would return home. After Ralph Jr. had driven off with his father, *Ralph Sr.*, Iris handed me two hundred dollars, which I refused to take.

"I don't want you paying for this," she'd said.

The bill for four new tires and a complete engine overhaul —I also asked them to detail the inside and out as well as inspect the vehicle and deliver it—far exceeded her cash offer, but that didn't bother me in the least.

"Look, babe. I got this." (I had already paid over the phone.) "And you can pay me back after you open your new animal clinic someday."

Her head flinched back. "What?"

"Why the hell not? It's what you want to do, isn't it? I'll help you get started." I rubbed her upper arms and kissed her. "Look. When I went to college, I was able to utilize a shit ton of grants and apply for all the financial aid I needed." It was true. I hadn't started out rich. Back then, I became an expert at finding money that was just sitting out there for the taking. Zach had called me the *money detector*. "I can help you do the same. It's not as hard as you think." I was making light of my offer for a reason. This was a lot for her to take in. And I *would* help her, regardless of how long we were together. That I could do. It wasn't as if I was offering her a free ride. She would have to do the work. But I also knew she was up for it.

Avoiding her wide eyes and mouth hanging open, my gaze found her car. "As far as the car goes, just drive over to the right, and you'll avoid some of those ruts." I quirked a brow. "We don't want you losing your muffler, now do we?"

She stood there speechless, her face slackened.

"When you've had a minute to think this through, we can talk more about it. Just let it sink in for the moment." I started to walk away. "Listen. Let's drive over to my place so I can change and take a quick shower (I had just gone for a run), and then we'll take *your* car out for a drive this time." The more vehicles she learned how to drive, the better.

Still quite dazed, Iris put her money back in her purse and agreed with a nod. As far as I was concerned, it was about time this woman lived again. She'd sailed through her driving test online. And she hadn't even studied. Iris was smart. And she was still young enough to pursue whatever dream she chose. Helping her get started was the right thing to do, regardless of my conflicted feelings about our future. And it wasn't locking me into anything. Not really.

Gramps would approve.

A quick shower and we were off again, this time in Iris's car. She was driving down Old Oak Road when a car approached in the other direction. It wasn't a big truck or a police cruiser this time, nor was it a landscaper's vehicle. From what I could make out in the distance, a black Mercedes-Benz S-Class was approaching.

How the hell did she drive that car down this goat path of a road? I'd gotten used to the washboards and ruts. *And* I had the vehicle for it. "What is Morgan doing here?" I leaned toward the windshield to optimize my view.

"Who?" Iris asked from the driver's seat.

"Uh. A friend of mine. Morgan. She's from the city. Can you pull over when we reach your driveway?" I unlatched my seatbelt.

Iris did as I asked. "Is everything okay, Jacob?"

I was so distracted, I barely answered. "Uh, yeah. Of course."

She put her hand on my knee, and like an idiot, I removed it. I couldn't believe Morgan was here. When Iris parked, I climbed out of her car. "Catch you later." What the fuck was I doing? *Being a real shithead, that's what!* I wasn't prepared for this.

Iris drove up her driveway, while I walked along the road, conflicted with my feelings, until Morgan pulled up. Why hadn't I just introduced them? Was I embarrassed by Iris? If I was, I hated myself for it.

The stark contrast between Morgan's luxury sedan and Iris's compact mirrored these women, except for when it came to one thing. They were both beautiful and quite remarkable in their own right. This felt like a test of my will. My former life challenging my new one.

Morgan was intelligent, aggressive at her job, and made no apologies when it came to getting what she wanted. She also never burdened herself with unimportant details such as who owed who a phone call or messy innuendos that she proclaimed did nothing but ruin a perfectly good fuck buddy. I loved that about her. But during our last conversation, I sensed something had changed. I was thirty years old, five years younger than she was. Morgan had broached the subject of us seeing each other again. Did that have anything to do with her age? *Internal clock and all that?*

"Hey, stranger. You may owe me a new muffler." Morgan's window slid down, her flowery perfume infusing the air between us. No dust or mold like Iris's car when I first saw it. "I had to visit a client in Albany and thought I'd pay you a visit."

Shiny lips, perfect makeup, and long black hair that gleamed under the sun's rays, Morgan's smile stretched wide. "I thought you were coming home this week, but then Jen said you're staying longer."

The sound of a car door shutting brought her gaze over to Iris's house across the field. "Does the reason have anything to do with that hot blond I just saw?" She wiggled her brow as I circled around the front of her car.

I slid into the passenger seat, the scent of fresh leather competing with her perfume, which I was sure had already attached itself to my clothing. I always smelled Morgan's signature scent on me long after she had left. "Nah. I've just been enjoying life away from the fast lane. It's been great."

"I see." Morgan shifted her car into drive, and within no time, we were at my place. Through the windshield, my modest abode presented itself, the natural wood siding, the Adirondack chairs sitting vacant on the covered porch, and the trees shading the front and blocking out an incredible view. "Hmm. Not what I expected." Judgment rolled off her tongue. "A far cry from your apartment, isn't? A bit rustic."

"Yeah. Definitely rustic. It's growing on me, though."

Another *hmm* barely reached past her lips. "And who is the blond?" This was unlike her. She never asked about the women in my life. And I never asked about the men in hers. It was how we did things.

"Just a friend. I'm teaching her how to drive." Hearing me diminish my relationship with Iris brought shame to my heart. I wasn't prepared to answer questions about us to Morgan, to Brody, or to anyone else. Somehow, that made everything feel fluid, as though I still had an out. Selfish but true. And even though I was only thirty, I was still an old dog when it came to love.

Blah, blah, blah. None of that bullshit did much to convince me. If I were being honest, I already missed Iris. My moment of doubt had already left me, almost as quickly as it had arrived. I also worried I had just fucked up with her. Rejected a woman who needed support and love.

But Morgan *had* come all this way, and for that reason alone, I'd give her a few minutes.

We made our way inside, where I showed Morgan around the place with the exception of my bedroom. Iris had stored a few of her things in there, and I didn't want to deal with more questions. The tightness in her face told me she wasn't impressed with any of my surroundings. The place was old, but it was clean. I'd made sure of it.

In the kitchen, I asked, "First of all, how did it go with your client in Albany? And second, would you like a glass of wine?"

Decked out in a gray skirt and matching jacket cut perfectly to her toned body, a white blouse layered underneath, and a pair of closed-toe black stilettos that elevated her height six inches, Morgan strolled over to me, touching my face. "Client was good. Your hair is getting so long." She brushed her fingers along my jawline. "And since when did you stop shaving?" She kissed me and smiled, her breath offering hints of fruity goodness. "I came to see you before you turned into a complete mountain of a man on me. Plus, given our phone calls, I thought you might be missing some of our extracurricular activities. We haven't spoken in a week." After she straightened my bangs, she stood back. "And I would love a glass of wine." Those big brown eyes surveyed me, the ones that were capable of swallowing most men whole.

I poured her a glass of cab, knowing her preference and making sure to allow myself a *generous* pour.

She eyed the glass. "Charming."

We clanked our glasses together. "Let me show you my favorite part of this place." I led her out onto the back deck where my small bistro set sat empty, the ghost of Iris and me having breakfast earlier still lingering.

Morgan examined the seat of the chair, her lip starting to curl. This place was definitely *not* for her.

I wasn't offended. Her outfit cost in the thousands. So did most of mine. Just not the ones I had been lounging in lately.

"It's clean. I wipe them down after every rain."

Morgan lowered herself onto the chair and took a stabilizing breath. "This is . . . nice." Her heels came off, and she moved her chair closer to me, resting her feet on my lap. This was something Morgan used to do a lot, and I'd reward her efforts with a nice foot rub.

"Not a fan, are you?" I rubbed her feet as best I could, my mind consumed by Iris. *What is she doing right now?* It was crazy how much I missed her. And I was rude to her earlier. Would she forgive me? I wasn't sure I would.

She held her glass up and examined it as she spoke. "Well, the country isn't really my thing. I like the city. And so do you, right?" She gazed over at me with a knowing look in her eyes. "When are you coming back, anyway?"

A fish splashed in the pond, capturing her focus for a moment.

"My month isn't up until Tuesday, you know."

Her eyebrows shot up. "Yes, I know. Your birthday. So when are we going to celebrate?"

"I'm not sure." I took a large sip of wine.

Keeping her attention on the pond, she nodded. "Does that answer have anything to do with the hot blond? Or are we going to pretend she doesn't exist?"

One thing I appreciated about Morgan was her ability to cut through the bullshit. I wanted to come clean. I'd known Morgan for years. We had a history. And even though I knew she'd survive the loss of me in her life, I took no pleasure in cutting our ties.

I exhaled, not sure how to put all of that into words. Admitting my feelings also made things too real. Part of me still preferred to hide behind them. But that would mean losing Iris. And a loss of that magnitude was not an option. Morgan would move on. I would never move on from Iris. Not fully.

"It's that bad, is it?" Her voice lightened. "I wondered why I hadn't heard from you over the past week. And she *is* pretty from what I could see through the windshield." She swirled her red wine around in her glass. "How serious is it?"

I was literally tongue-tied. This was new for me. Then again, everything was new when it came to Iris. "I'm not sure." Well aware that I had just said those words *twice* now, I took another large sip of wine, nearly emptying my glass.

Those brown eyes narrowed on me. "Since when are you so indecisive?" She stared me down, tapping her manicured finger against the surface of the table. "I think I see what's going on here. You're in love." She pulled her feet back and planted them on the deck. "You son of a bitch. You actually fell in love. I never thought I'd see the day." She smirked. "You went and fell in love before I had the chance, JC." She set her wine glass down and stood, running her hands along her skirt to flatten out the wrinkles. Her eyes worked on something for a moment. "Since I came all this way, would you like an early birthday present before I go?" She undid the top button of her blouse. "The blond can join us if you want."

Fuck. What was I supposed to say to that? If she'd asked me that question a week ago, I would have jumped at the chance. But what struck me now was how uninterested I was in exploring her offer.

"Hmm." She re-buttoned her shirt. "I figured." Her tone remained light and airy. "Can't blame a girl for trying. She must be something special." She tipped her head to one side.

I got to my feet. "I'm sorry, Morgan. I hate that you made the trip all the way here." I also wasn't entirely sure I didn't need a CAT scan.

She waved me off with her shiny red nails. "Oh, don't be so dramatic, handsome. I'm a big girl. I can handle it. Once I locate a car wash, I'll find a hotel on my way home." Carrying her heels in one hand, she stepped in front of me. "If things with the blond go south, you know where to find me." She kissed me on the cheek, her perfume lingering on my skin and clothes.

My past was gone a few minutes later.

I'd crossed a barrier with Morgan, which left me more determined than ever to see what this *thing* with Iris could actually be for us. That was if she didn't hate me right now. Temptation had shown up at my doorstep, and I had turned her down. That said something for a guy like me.

It was time to face the music, as they say.

But first, I had to wash Morgan's perfume off my skin. I headed for my second shower of the day.

Chapter Eighteen

Iris

I have sex. I don't have relationships.

"Got it." And I had. *Finally*. When Jacob removed my hand from his knee, he was sending me a message. I realized in that moment that I had taken liberties with our relationship. I had grown comfortable with his affection, fooling myself into believing we had a future together. The truth was, I warranted no say in his life. And the minute someone from his *real* life appeared, he tossed me aside. *Catch you later.*

I had to accept a stark reality. The brunette driving that fancy car was Jacob's equal. *That* was the type of woman he deserved. Not someone with enough baggage to fill a warehouse. He was kind. He was generous. He was gorgeous. *And* he was gone. I wondered if they were having sex right now. Reacquainting. The thought made my stomach churn. Who was I to him? I was the pathetic recluse he had lent his charitable heart.

At some point along the way, I stopped pretending. This was very real for me. I loved Jacob. More than I had ever loved any other man in my life. At the same time, I didn't even have the right to be angry. Jacob had never made any promises to me. He had been nothing but wonderful and kind. He'd given me everything I had asked for. He'd made me forget. Without realizing it, he'd also given me hope for a new life. I was devastated that it was over between us, but I *had* to be grateful.

The sound of a car reached my ears. Were they leaving together? That was fast.

I went to my room, where I gravitated over to my dresser. And that was where I let the tears fall. Why couldn't life be easier? I opened the top drawer of my dresser and pulled out a photo. It represented a time when I had hope for a new life—the last time I felt truly happy.

In that same drawer sat a stack of cards, a hallmark of the manipulation I had endured from the egomaniac ever since. Placing the photo down, I took the cards out and sat on the side of my bed, examining them. Ten to be precise. I flipped through each one, just as I had done so many times before, the edges thin and weathered by tears and touch. Those same messages stared back at me: *I love you, Iris. . . . Someday, we'll be together again. . . . You are always with me.* And one that haunted me the most: *Don't blame yourself.* No postmarks. No stamps. They were hand delivered every April 11th. The darkest day of my life.

I would watch from the house as he drove up, paused, and then drove away. At times, I wanted to run out to him and beg him to stay. *Don't blame yourself.* I was too ashamed. Days turned into months, and soon, I was facing a decade of isolation. All those winters when the snow fell thick, coating my road that was barely a road at all, in inches upon inches of frigid snow or ice. The times when Becky couldn't make it out here, and my food supply had run thin. Where was he then? Or when one of the dogs had eaten something they shouldn't have, and I worried for their health.

All I had were these cards—markers—much like notches on a prison cell wall. I used to pore over them, clinging to his every word. But I had changed. And I owed that change to time—alone with my thoughts—and to Jacob. These empty pieces of paper were nothing more than a pathetic attempt to keep me on a leash. The *reality* of what went down all those years ago was becoming clear. I think a part of me always knew the truth, but I was too busy blaming myself for my hand in what happened to allow the burden to lift. *Don't blame yourself* implied I *should* blame myself. That was what he wanted.

I took the stack of cards to the trash can and thrust them inside. I could almost hear the click from the invisible lock on my prison cell door. It had cracked open. I could feel it—a small victory with no one to share it with.

Now what?

This was where my future got all muddled. I wanted to leave here, start a new life, and be free. But that would mean leaving this place. My heart palpitated, my lungs straining for air. I hugged my waist for comfort.

Would Jacob honor his offer to help with college? Or was that all part of our alter reality where I was his and he was mine?

I placed the photo back in my dresser and made my way out back, sitting on the bench and soaking in my sanctuary. This was the one place in the world where I felt complete. But for how long?

Warren and his cronies would surely return. I knew this. Just like I knew who was *really* behind the attacks. It was becoming crystal clear to me who had held a grudge all these years. When they did return, I shuddered at the thought of what they would do next. It wasn't safe here for me or for my dogs. Realistically, it wasn't safe *not* being here either. The world was a big place, and even bigger for those who ventured into it alone. Before Jacob, I could accept my fate.

By giving me hope, he had changed my perspective. And when he contacted me to apologize for letting me down, I would accept his apology and move on, even if my heart didn't want to.

As the sun warmed my back, I considered my options. I could ask Dennis and Vanessa to keep the dogs for me. I would get my driver's license. I had a small stash of money hidden away. Would it be enough to start over? And where would I go?

I thought about my parents. I loved them. So much. But they had left me here. I had disgraced them, embarrassed them in front of their parish. And they were ashamed. I could see it in their eyes. It was all I could envision whenever I thought about them anymore. I suspected it was also the reason they chose to move so far away. *Out of sight, out of mind.*

I refused to go crawling back as the same loser they had remembered from a decade ago. Once I had made something of myself, I would contact them with my head held high. And not until.

Someone cleared their throat from behind me. My lungs froze. My stomach clenched.

I turned as Jacob approached, taking the seat next to mine. His hair was wet, his scent musky. He'd taken *another* shower.

"Whatchadoin?" he asked, all casual like, as though we were friends hanging out.

Trying to be as unobvious as possible, I wiped my cheeks again. "Just sitting here, enjoying the day." I refused to look at him. Not out of anger but more out of self-preservation. "How's your friend, Morgan?" It took everything in me to keep the jealousy out of my voice. "Did she drive up from the city?" I didn't wait for him to answer, my heart racing as I spoke. "It was nice of her to come all this way."

Is she waiting out front for you now to make your Dear Jane speech?

"Iris." He said my name as though he could read my thoughts—which sometimes I wondered if he could—and knew how broken my heart felt. "She's just a friend."

I mustered the courage to gaze over at him and his freshly washed hair. Where was Morgan? Was that the car I had heard? After Jacob had reclaimed his life, did he and Morgan decide to meet up in the city? She wasn't here long. Or was she coming back? My head started to ache.

"Jacob, I don't have a problem with your friend being here." I rose, and then I wondered what I was supposed to do with myself. I wished the dogs were here, providing me with an excuse to divert my attention. "If you're going back to the city, I can ask Vanessa to drive me to my test." I *had* to make that driver's test tomorrow. I'd drive illegally if I had to.

Jacob stood and fanned his hands out. "What? No. I'll drive you. Morgan and I—"

"Listen, I'm gonna take a couple more runs along Old Oak Road in my car. I can go alone." I gestured toward the road in the distance. "There's no one around who will notice, right?" Keeping my voice pleasant, I walked away, the sound of Jacob's loafers thumping on the ground behind me.

He grabbed my wrist. "Stop! You've got the wrong idea here."

I pulled my hand away. "No, I don't have the wrong idea. You've been completely honest with me from the beginning. You 'don't have relationships.' I'm not angry, Jacob. I'm grateful to you for everything you have done for me." I raised a palm. "Please don't drag this out. It's over. And you gave me some great memories to look back upon after you've gone. There is no anger in my heart." And there wasn't. Just a lot of hurt feelings and unresolved emotions. Story of my life. "I told you I didn't want a relationship either. And I meant it."

His eyes narrowed. "As I recall, you said a relationship was the 'last thing you wanted.' Is that still true?" The sun reflected off his striking olive-colored eyes.

I couldn't allow myself to stare. He was everything I ever wanted.

"Because if it's not—"

"Yes! Completely true." *Liar.*

He rubbed his jaw, his eyes going distant.

I could see him working something out. It was time I made things easy *for him* for a change. "Look, Jacob. I didn't mean to take things this far. I don't want to continue. It's better this way. You know, before we got too attached. I just didn't know how to tell you."

"Is that true, or are you just saying what you *think* I want to hear?" He crossed his arms, his jaw muscles flexing.

"I'm doing my best to be honest with you." I couldn't believe the rancid words spewing from my mouth. But I had to protect my heart, or what was left of it. If I lost Jacob now, I *might* recover. "Go back to the city. Return to your life there. You don't belong here. This isn't your home."

Finally, he let his hand drop, an unpleasant smirk compressing his lips. He gazed up at me with eyes drained of compassion. "Well, I guess I should be grateful that you didn't tell me to fuck off like my parents used to." With that, Jacob walked away.

It's better this way. I hugged my waist and silently cried.

* * *

Not sure who or what I would encounter, I walked to Jacob's house after the sun went down, the nighttime sky making me feel less obvious. If Morgan's car was back, I'd turn around and leave, but it wasn't.

Expression deadpan, Jacob opened his front door looking sexier than ever in a white T-shirt and a pair of navy cotton shorts.

"Hey, do you mind if I grab my things?" I didn't have a lot, so I couldn't let what I *did have* go to waste. Especially, those three new outfits I had purchased—plus a pair of strappy sandals—the first in ten years.

As I busied myself, Jacob followed me throughout the house, never saying a word. He kept running a hand over his mouth and chin. There were moments when I could almost feel him start to speak. What would he say? *I'm sorry? I didn't mean to hurt you? Thank you for making my job easier?*

He hadn't hurt me. I had hurt myself. I allowed my heart to open again. And now, I was paying the price. Once he was gone, I would heal. And then, I'd put a plan into action and start anew.

There would never be another Jacob for me. He was a miracle in my otherwise broken life. I would never feel for anyone the way he had made me feel. And for that, I owed him this release.

His slanted eyebrows and hunched shoulders told me he was angry. Maybe he wanted a little more time. But what good would that do? *He doesn't do relationships.*

When I had my shoulders weighed down with my overnight bag and one backpack, I stood by the door with my strappy sandals hanging from my fingers. "If you don't want to take me to my driver's test tomorrow, I can try calling—"

"I said I'd take you! And I'll take you! I'll be leaving for the city the next day." He glared down at me, his voice firm. "Is that all?"

Anger flushed his cheeks and narrowed his eyes, hands

braced on each hip. But why? I'd set him free. I'd avoided playing the jealousy card. He had his life back. He had Morgan.

"Yes, that's all. Thank you, Jacob."

"My name is JC!" He practically kicked me out of his house, and then he slammed the front door shut.

I didn't sleep a wink that night, conflicted by everything that was happening in my life. Should I have told Jacob I loved him with all my heart? That felt like a trap. And he hadn't exactly told me those words himself. He'd implied the opposite.

The dogs returned the following morning, Laddie looking even better than when I had seen him last.

Standing in the kitchen, I had thought the commotion at the door was Jacob, and I wasn't ready to leave yet. I was still in my pj's.

I opened my front door, confronted by three dogs hopping around and jumping up on my legs and waist. Laddie was less energetic than the rest.

"Hello, my lovelies." I kissed their heads and stroked their fur, especially Laddie's, who deserved some extra coddling.

But why were they here? Dennis had said he'd be by at noon.

The man in question walked up onto my porch. "I figured I'd watch the dogs here if that's okay. I think they missed being at home."

"Absolutely." I thought for a moment. "Are you sure it's not too much trouble? You and Vanessa have already been so kind to me."

He waved me off. "No problem at all." His bald head glinted against the morning sun. "Did you have a nice break?" His voice was different—lighter and more fun-loving. I was used to the Dennis who was worried and doing his best to save my life.

I straightened up as the dogs ran around my legs, too excited to stand still. I swiped a hand across my forehead. The rainy season had ended, leaving a hot-and-humid climate. I loved this time of year in Vermont, probably because it never lasted long. "Yeah, it was okay."

"Okay?" Dennis's smile wavered. "How are things with JC?"

"Good. He's going back to the city tomorrow."

His face fell. "Oh?"

The sad look in his brown eyes was too much for me to take after a sleepless night, so I changed the subject. "I've been practicing driving a lot. And I think I'm ready for the test! JC got my car fixed too. So, I'll be able to drive again." I beamed on the outside. I cried on the inside.

Dennis ran a hand over his head, a few beads of sweat gathering on his brow. "I'm glad to hear it, Iris. Will you be joining JC in the city?" I could tell he was still trying to work this out in his mind.

He wasn't the only one.

"Come on in." I moved out of the way for him and the dogs to enter my house and closed the door behind them. Answering his question, I shook my head as I loved on my canine family some more, fluffing heads and bestowing kisses. "No, I won't be joining him in the city. But once I get everything settled, I would like to talk with you and Vanessa about a few things. Not about JC. We've decided to part as friends." Another untruth. At this stage of the game, I wasn't even sure Jacob considered me an acquaintance.

"Well, we can all use a few more friends, can't we?" Dennis approached the feisty bunch, bending down to play with them.

It gave me a short reprieve. "Yes. And thank you again. I will be back by noon at the latest. I made some coffee, so help yourself. Mugs are stored on the upper cabinet. They're easy to find, and I have sugar on the counter and creamer in the fridge if you need them." I dashed off to quickly change.

At least I wasn't alone anymore. I took comfort in knowing I'd sleep better with my beautiful dogs around me.

Thirty minutes later, I opened the door to Jacob. *Stop calling him that!* "Good morning, JC."

No response.

He'd dressed more formally than I had grown accustomed to seeing. A button-down linen shirt in soft gold highlighted his olive-colored eyes, the cut stylishly loose from his broad shoulders. Burgundy shorts with a pleat down the front, secured by a thick brown belt, complemented the outfit, as did a pair of suede loafers and no socks. Designer sunglasses did an adequate job of obscuring his eyes. With his hair slicked back and his cologne just the right amount of musk, JC embodied a New York Stockbroker to a tee. And he'd shaved. In some ways, it felt as though he had already left.

Before he stepped over the threshold, the dogs descended upon him. He smiled and spoke softly to Laddie. "Looking good, buddy." He petted all of them at once. "I've been missing you on my runs, Lily." More head scratches. He took his sunglasses off and laced them in the top buttonhole of his shirt. He picked up Maggie and loved on her too. *This* was the Jacob I knew.

In the half hour since Dennis had arrived, I'd showered, too, choosing my new teal-colored romper with a coral leaf pattern, which worked perfectly with my strappy sandals. I used my old diffuser to fluff up my curls and added makeup to my eyes. If this was the last time I would see JC, I wanted him to remember me. I wasn't able to keep much food down, but my nervous stomach did allow two cups of very strong coffee.

Just as the dogs began to settle down and the awkwardness

between JC and me was starting to take form, Dennis spoke. "I see someone else has been missed."

Jacob put Maggie down, who toddled over to me.

"Hey, Dennis. You're early." JC pressed his lips into a fine line, his eyes discerning.

I wondered if he thought Dennis would be taking me to the DMV and not him.

"Yeah. I sensed they were missing home, so I told Iris I would watch them from here." His friendly gaze found me next. "Take your time, young lady. And don't be nervous. You'll do great." He ventured into my kitchen. "Come on, you three. Let's get you some breakfast." He shook my bag of dog food, and they hightailed it out of the room.

As JC slid his sunglasses into place, I took several stabilizing breaths. Twenty-four hours ago, Jacob would have tried to boost my confidence like Dennis had just done, maybe even more so.

JC didn't seem interested, who approached the door, not a word escaping from his lips.

I grabbed my purse off a small bench and stepped out into the warm and humid morning, JC's SUV blocking the driveway.

"I wasn't sure which car you preferred, so I brought mine. I need to gas it up before I leave for the city tomorrow, anyway." Not a spark of emotion influenced his words.

"Your car is fine. Thank you, Jacob . . . I mean, JC." I chewed on my lower lip as I headed for the driver's seat. "Do you mind if I drive us there to give me one last practice run?"

He flipped his hand in a nonchalant manner. "Suit yourself."

Was that sarcasm? Man, if he was trying to make me feel worse, he was doing a good job of it. I stopped and put a hand to my forehead, my nervous stomach getting the better of me, my rapid heartbeat not helping matters. "Listen, if you want, I can ask Dennis to drive me instead. The dogs will be fine indoors for a few hours. I don't want to put you out, JC." I didn't want him to leave like this. I didn't want him to leave at all. I was putting his needs first. Why couldn't he see that? And it was just about killing me to do so. That was what you did for the people you loved. It was what I had longed for someone to do for me. My eyes moistened, and I hated that about me. And then, my hands began to shake. *Damn it!*

He stopped and turned toward me, his sunglasses shrouding the daggers he was probably shooting from his eyes.

A tear came unbidden. Why couldn't I hold myself together? I wiped it quickly away.

JC didn't move. He just stood there watching me. Finally, he slid his sunglasses to the top of his head, his olive eyes much more compassionate than I had envisioned. He stepped toward me and took my hands. "I'm sorry, Iris." He shook his head and exhaled as though remorseful. "I *want* to drive you there. This is important to you. And believe it or not, it's just as important to me." His kind heart was reaching out to me again. I wanted to grab hold of it and never let go.

"But, JC—"

He gripped my hands tighter. "*Please* call me Jacob."

"But I thought you said—"

"I know what I said. But I didn't mean it. I was being a prick. That is the last thing you need right now. I'm sorry." He paused, letting his words wash over me. "I am and will always be, *your* Jacob. I wouldn't want it any other way." The edges of his mouth curled ever so slightly. "Once you finish *passing* your test, I'd like to talk to you about a few things if that's okay."

I was a flurry of emotions. Cold-hearted JC was easier to deal with on some level. *Jacob*, however, had the ability to shatter me into a million pieces. "Are you sure?" My heart was begging for his response.

He took a deep breath. "Oh, yeah. I'm sure."

And that was all we said to one another before I drove us into town.

* * *

"Well, you passed. Perfect score," the man with bright red hair and wide sideburns said as he finished making some notations on a sheet attached to his clipboard.

He'd introduced himself earlier as Winston McBride. Easy to remember since it reminded me of a name a country and western singer would use.

"Well done. When we get inside, we will issue you a temporary license for now. We will take your photo and send you the certified license in the mail, which usually takes no more than seven to ten business days. *Congratulations.*" Winston offered a nod of approval.

I texted Jacob, who said he would be in the library. Then I called Dennis to tell him the good news. He was thrilled.

After the photo and the formalities, I found Jacob waiting on a bench out front of the DMV and screamed, "I passed! Perfect score!" I waved my temporary license in the air.

He hopped off the bench and grabbed me around the waist, twirling me in the air. "I got your text. I knew you could do it."

"It was all because of you, my awesome driving instructor."

His lips found mine, and I let them, lavishing the taste of his essence. When the kiss ended, he took my hand and led me to the bench where he had just been seated, the briefcase holding his laptop waiting on the other end. "Listen, Iris. Nothing happened between Morgan and me." He looked down and then up, his eyes yearning for my understanding. "She didn't even stay long enough to finish a glass of wine."

I knew that was true. I had heard her car, all while *assuming* the worst. I'd gotten good at building walls around me. It was how I coped.

"She knew I was in love with you. And she was right. I'm sure you noticed my hair was wet." His eyes beamed. "Morgan tends to load on the perfume, and I didn't want you to get the wrong idea. She hugged me, and that was all." He made a face. "I realized later that my shower had probably made things worse."

So when he came to see me, it was to tell me this? And I had blocked his efforts. If I hadn't been sitting, my legs would surely have given out. *He's in love with me?* It was too good to be true. All those feelings I had thought belonged to only me, he'd reciprocated? "But you don't have—"

"Relationships. I know. I'm just as shocked as you are." His words came out all flabbergasted. "That was who I was when I arrived here." A beaming expression, along with his glowing cheeks, made me believe him. "You've changed all of that, Iris. I don't just love you; I am *madly* in love with you. The summer has been unbelievable for me. The best of my life. I've never met anybody like you. I know I was a major asshole last night *and* this morning. But when I saw what I was doing to you, I had to come clean. You have suffered at the hands of enough people who didn't deserve you." He swallowed, his Adam's apple bobbing up and down. "I hate to admit it, but I have been pretty cynical about relationships myself, mostly due to my parents, who showed my sisters and me nothing but anger and resentment. Their fucked-up marriage made me *never* want to be like them."

The sadness in his confession was palpable.

"I'm sorry for you, too, Jacob."

He brushed my compassion away and cradled my cheeks in his hands. "Never mind that. This isn't about me. I want you to know how I really feel. What I should have had the balls to tell you last night. And the truth is, I don't want to ever be without you again. What my parents had wasn't what we have. Leave here with me!" His face drew closer. "It doesn't have to be tomorrow. We can go whenever you are ready." He held my cheeks firmly, staring into my very soul. "Take a chance on me." His fingers brushed my hair away from my face. "I promise you that I will do everything in my power to make you happy. And this has nothing to do with pity or me trying to swoop up on my white horse. You are the one saving me. I just hope I'm not too late, and that you will give me a chance."

I struggled to form words, my heart racing and my lungs breathless. If I were being honest, I was downright dizzy over his words. "It's not just me, though, what about the dogs?"

The warmest eyes I had ever seen stared back at me. He touched my forehead to his, a silly grin spreading across his face. "I love those dogs. I'm not going anywhere without them." Jacob was bearing everything. And I knew I could trust what he said. The connection between us was something I never imagined I could *or would* ever find. I had given up on love. But it had found me, anyway, just the same.

My throat thickened, my eyes already spilling tears. "Are you sure?"

He wiped my tears away and kissed my lips. "I've never been *more* sure about anything in my life. The question is, are you sure?" He tilted his head.

I threw my arms around his neck. "Yes! I love you too. I just didn't want you to feel trapped. You have been so amazing and I—"

He pulled back and used his finger to halt my words. "That's all I need to hear. I have never felt less trapped in my life. Trapped was how I felt when I got here. You freed me from that life, Iris."

I freed him? How ironic.

His fingers grazed my face. "I promise you. I will never do to you what Nathan did," he said.

Faced with the raw honesty of his devotion, *my* truth bubbled up in my chest. It was time he knew everything. I took a breath. "Jacob, there is something I need to tell you—" *Wait. Who is Nathan?*

"JC? Is that you?"

My heart seized. Every muscle in my body went tight as a drum. The air drained from my lungs. I knew that voice. It had been years since I had heard it. And I hated the man who spoke.

Chapter Nineteen

Jacob

Fuck, Brody, you are really starting to get on my nerves.

What was Iris about to say to me? I sensed it was huge. But I loved her, so I could wait, even if I didn't want to. Patience had never been my virtue.

She loved me. Something inside me felt whole. Gramps was right about finding the love of your life. It *was* possible. And in the most unlikely of places. All I knew was that now that I'd found her, I never wanted to let her go. We'd build a life together. The thought of what used to turn my stomach was something I would die to protect now. I wanted to lavish her in all the special moments she had missed. And I would.

Unfortunately, I had Brody to deal with at the moment. Was he going to give me shit for not golfing in his tournament again? I hadn't been to the club since Warren had torn up Iris's yard. Man, had my life done a 180 in a very short time. That simple fact had freaked me out, but not anymore. When Morgan came to see me, I realized my wants and needs had changed.

"Hey, man, how ya been?" Dressed in tailored shorts and a

collared polo, both in pastel colors, Brody strolled up the sidewalk with Nicole, who was wearing a very short tennis skirt and top that matched her husband's color scheme to a T (pardon the pun).

Shit. Nicole. I wasn't used to seeing them together. And knowing how Nicole felt about Iris, I had nothing left for the woman. Iris was just protecting herself three years ago. Her gun wasn't even loaded.

I rose, offering Brody a reluctant handshake. "Good. Hey, Nicole." I could play nice if she could.

Normally, Nicole batted her eyes at me, but not today. As I had expected, she seemed to take particular notice of Iris, who was still sitting on the bench, bent over and searching frantically through her purse. *Stall tactic.* I wanted to grab her hand and run with her out of there. But I had never run from a fight before. Not even against Ernie who had beat the living shit out of me. I didn't want Iris to run, either. I wanted her to stand proud. They'd beaten her down enough. Led her to believe she was nothing. That ended today! And when I found Nathan— which I had every intention of doing—I'd make sure the asshole knew his reign was also over!

I did take Iris's hand, though, and shot her a look that said, *We've got this!*

Iris rose and stood by my side, her palm sweaty. She had been so excited about passing her test. We had declared our love for each other. And Nicole was ruining this moment for her. I could see it in Iris's red cheeks and crimped mouth.

"Listen, we have to go."

I turned to walk away.

"Iris." Brody said her name as though dumbstruck.

What I witnessed next confirmed everything I needed to know. Brody stared at Iris as though he had just witnessed a miracle. His mouth dropped open; his eyes filled with longing. I could sense his need for her. I knew that look. He was in love with Iris—or he thought he was.

Nathan wasn't the married man. Brody was.

That picture he had painted of Iris when we had gone to dinner was total bullshit. It was him all along. Everything made sense. Why Nicole hated Iris so much. It also might explain why her son was there. Maybe he was curious about who this woman was. He had to know about her. The whole town knew about it. He and Tom were in it together. Recruiting young women to fuck. The marriage that Brody claimed Iris had nearly broken up was his own.

She got around, he'd said. Was *wild and not in a good way. Best to let sleeping dogs lie.* Brody wasn't just isolating Iris; he was manipulating me as well. Keeping me away from her so I wouldn't discover for myself what a magnificent woman she was. He was controlling both of our lives.

I wanted to punch that dazed look right off his face. Knock the motherfucker right out. *Scumbag.*

Nicole crossed her arms over her sizable chest, her chin held high. "I see you're back at it, Iris. Sinking your claws into someone new. You sure know how to pick the rich ones, don't you? But your little plan didn't work on *us.*" Nicole's gaze shot over to me next. "She's nothing but a gold digger, JC. You have no idea what she is capable of. Don't let her trap you, and trust me . . . she will stop at *nothing!*"

I saw red. "Fuck off, Nicole. You don't know what the hell you're talking about."

Brody glared at his wife. "That's enough, Nicole!" His cheeks went from pale to flaming. "That was a long time ago. Let it go!"

Iris's cheeks were flaring too. "I never wanted Brody's money! That was the last thing I wanted!" She let go of my hand, planting hers on her hips. "I was seventeen. Your husband came after me!" Her hands flew this way and that as she spoke.

Nicole made a *pfft* sound through her dark-maroon-colored lips. "Yeah, right. You tried to take everything we had!" She turned toward her husband and began pointing. "And I will never let it go, Brody! Not until she is far away from here!" Wearing an expression that reminded me of the wicked witch of the west, Nicole leaned toward Iris, her finger pointing at her face. "Even your parents saw what a slut you were!"

"You are a cold-hearted bitch, Nicole!" My chest heated up, hands fisted. "You have no right to speak to her that way!"

Iris touched my arm, sending me a message. This time *she had this*. She stepped closer to Nicole and pointed back. "Leave my parents out of this! And, yeah, I know how much you want me gone, Nicole. I know every time you send Warren and his gang over to harass me."

What the fuck? These people were certifiable. I couldn't wait to get Iris out of this cesspool. "You have got to be fucking kidding me. *You* were the one responsible for what happened to Iris's dog?" I was about to explode, all over these two.

"Jesus Christ, Nicole!" Brody stood back and glared at his wife. "What is she talking about?" The veins in his forehead protruded. "What have you and Warren been up to this time?"

Nicole practically cackled at Iris.

Man, she really was the wicked witch.

"You're delusional. I have no idea what you're talking about." She crossed her arms and looked away, her head shaking with defiance as she continued to scoff.

Iris spoke before I could.

"Yeah, *I'm sure* you have no idea, Nicole. You know what, it doesn't matter." Iris shook her head, her gaze falling to the sidewalk before her. And then she looked up. "But I want you to know, I never went after Brody. He came after me!" Iris was hollering now, her entire body rigid. "I was young and stupid. He said he was leaving you. He made promises that were all lies."

People across the street were staring as they walked past the capitol. Even a few drivers gazed over as they drove by. It didn't matter. Iris needed to get this out. And I was behind her 100 percent. It took everything in me to keep my mouth shut. She needed this more than I did.

"The person you should be angry at is him." Iris pointed at Brody. "But that doesn't work for you, does it, Nicole? Divorcing Brody means you can't have it all, can you? I know where you grew up. That's why you never divorced him, and why you wanted to *solely* blame me. Who is the real gold digger?" This time, Iris scoffed.

I couldn't have been more proud.

And that was when Nicole lunged at her.

"What the hell are you doing?" Brody grabbed his wife, while I held Iris, who was about to rip that uptight bitch a new one. Part of me wanted to let her. If I weren't completely sure that Nicole wouldn't press charges, I would have even helped.

I urged Iris behind me, doing my best to shield her from these lunatics. "Enough! I wasn't around ten years ago, but it doesn't take a genius to figure out that having sex with a minor is seriously fucked up. He's lucky she wasn't under sixteen, like your own daughter's age! He'd go to jail. Who you should have a problem with, *Nicole*, is your husband, not Iris. He leers at your waitresses for Christ's sake. You have to know this!"

I practically snarled at Brody. "Don't know her, huh?" With my chest out, I moved right up in his face. All he had to do was land the first punch, and then, I'd take care of the rest. "Who the fuck is Nathan the dentist?"

"*My* Uncle Nathan, who just retired from his practice?

What is he talking about, Brody?" Nicole searched her husband's face for an answer.

"You are a fucking scumbag for what you did to this woman. If I had known you were capable of this, I never would have been friends with you." I turned my ire toward his bitch of a wife again. "And you lay one fucking hand on her or her dogs, I'll see to it that she sues your skinny ass for assault. I may do that anyway. I don't know who you people think you are, but this ends now!" I grabbed hold of Iris's hand and led her away, snatching my briefcase as I passed by. I kept our pace quick, not out of fear, but out of anger and aggression. Beating the living shit out of Brody might make *me* feel better, but it wouldn't help Iris, and she was my priority.

When we reached the parking lot behind the DMV, a text message came in on my cell. Iris climbed into the passenger seat, her eyes unfocused, as I read the message from Danny.

> Brody Larson owns the house and the surrounding land. He also pays the utilities. Need anything else?

I opened the back door to place my laptop on the back seat, then quickly typed my reply.

> No. Thanks. I appreciate the help.

I slammed the door shut and climbed into the driver's seat.

So tearing up the land wasn't just an assault on Iris, it was Nicole's way of saying *fuck you* to her husband? That also explained why everyone wanted to brush it under the rug. Only, Brody never knew anything about it. Tom did. But Tom also knew how Brody felt about Warren. And if Brody filed charges, Tom's son would be caught up in it. *Looking out for number one.* The entire lot of them took that statement to the extreme.

What I couldn't fathom was why Iris had stuck around all these years. Did she still love Brody? Why would a woman of her intelligence allow him to fund her life? I wanted to ask her this but was afraid it would come out hostile. I needed to calm down first.

We didn't speak the entire way home. Iris needed time to decompress, and she wasn't the only one.

I parked in front of her house, barely registering the drive there. "Listen, Iris, what happened wasn't your fault. Brody is a scumbag and a flirt. I knew that the day I met him. And I suspect he's cheated on Nicole with far more women than you. His wife is a controlling bitch, who clearly doesn't want to see who she's married to. And from what you said, she's just in it for herself, anyway. They deserve each other if you ask me. But *you* don't. You deserve better."

All three dogs came bounding around the side of the house, Dennis half jogging behind them. "Sorry, they heard the vehicle." He came up to my window, which sat open, his breathing labored. "Are we celebrating yet?"

Iris shook her head, her arms hugging her waist. She never said a word beyond that.

Dennis's smile faded away. "What's wrong? Isn't this good news?" His gaze pivoted between Iris and me for an explanation.

How much did Dennis know about what had happened ten years ago? He'd given Iris the dogs. And he clearly cared about her.

"Listen, Dennis, I know this is a lot to ask." I looked over at Iris, who nodded. It seemed I wasn't the only one who could read minds. "Iris and I have a lot to discuss. Would you mind taking the dogs for one more night?"

* * *

Having helped Dennis corral the dogs into his vehicle, Iris and I stood in her kitchen, both of us silent.

"I know that Brody owns this house and the property." I pivoted my body as I spoke. "He's been paying for all of this for the past ten years?"

Iris snapped her head up. "How do you know that?"

"It doesn't matter how I know. What I can't understand for the life of me, is why you would stay here alone all these years. Or *have* you been alone?" I wanted to ask her if she still loved Brody, but I wasn't confident my heart would survive her answer.

Her brow slanted toward irritation. "What do you mean, *have* I been alone?" She hugged her waist and then stood tall with her shoulders back. "No, I haven't been alone. In fact, I would like you to meet someone." With firm steps, she stomped into her bedroom. The sound of a dresser drawer reached my ears before she materialized and handed me what appeared to be a small black-and-white photograph. "I want you to meet my daughter, Jade."

In my hand, a sonogram photo of a fetus stared up at me. I had no words. I swear the room spun around me, my brain trying to play catch-up. "Your daughter?"

Iris took my hand and led me out back. She sat me down on the bench and stood by the boulder. "Yes, my daughter. I got pregnant. And it was Brody's. He promised me things, Jacob. And I was too young and naive. I found out I was pregnant in the fall of my senior year. By winter, I was starting to show. Brody convinced me to graduate early, so no one would know and blame me. I had the credits. I believed that he loved me. He said he wanted to leave Nicole. She made him miserable. And when I got pregnant, he kept saying those things. Even though he had promised to help me go to college, I had a baby to think about."

Still, words refused to land on my tongue. Nicole's husband not only had an affair, but he'd gotten the other *teenage* woman pregnant? That's why she thought Iris was after her money. *She will stop at nothing to get what she wants.* In Nicole's mind, Iris had gotten pregnant intentionally. Or maybe she just chose to believe that. It was easier that way.

I stared down at the sad photograph. "What happened to Jade, Iris?"

She bowed her head, hand placed on the top of the boulder. "She died. I was seven months pregnant. Brody had come by to say once again that he was planning on leaving Nicole. I was sick of hearing it. My hormones were all over the place." Her eyes flooded with tears, her voice unsteady. "We argued. We were standing on my front porch at the time. I wasn't watching where I was standing, and I . . . I fell down the front steps, right on my stomach." She placed both hands on her abdomen as though Jade was still there inside of her. "I-I don't remember much after that. It was all a blur. Dennis came, and so did Dr. Perry, the woman I saw the other day with Vanessa. They said I went into labor. They all worked frantically around me. And then I lost consciousness. When I awoke, Jade was gone." Her entire body quaked with sorrow as she bent over and cried.

"Holy shit!" Placing the photograph in my back pocket, I rushed to her. "I'm sorry, Iris. I had no idea." This was a lot more than I had imagined. I wanted to hold her and tell her it was all going to be okay, but I was in a state of shock myself. I never imagined this. But it also made sense. Sort of. The pieces of her mysterious life were finally floating to the surface. She hadn't stayed here all these years for Brody. Iris could have lived without him. She'd stayed here for Jade. That was something I didn't have an argument for.

I touched her arm. "What can I do?" I felt like a dumbass asking such a stupid question. My mind reeled.

"There is nothing that anyone can do, Jacob. I lost my daughter, and it was my fault. I shouldn't have been standing there."

"You don't know that. People fall down—"

"Don't." She raised a palm, tears dripping off her clenched jaw. "I know you mean well. But I need to be alone, Jacob. And I think you need some time to decide if this is too much for you." She laughed through her tears, lifting one hand and letting it fall, slapping against her thigh. "Hell, it's too much for me, even. I'm not sure if I can give you what you want. Too much has happened." She lowered her head. "I think it would be best if you left."

"Don't shut me out, Iris."

Those sapphire eyes that held so much pain lifted to catch my gaze. "Please go, Jacob."

Was she asking me to give her a minute, or was she asking me to leave her for good? Either way, I didn't feel I had the right to protest. What she'd been through was beyond anything I could make sense of. I tried one last time. "I love you, Iris. We can get through this together. Let me help."

"I can't right now. I'm sorry. I need to be alone. Please, give me this."

Not respecting her wishes seemed like a dick move. I had to do as she asked. As I walked away, I wrestled with conflicting emotions. Anger for meeting her so late? Frustration that she hadn't told me all of this sooner? Sorrow that I might never have another chance with her? I could live without women like Morgan. This wasn't that. Iris had changed my heart, but did she have the ability to trust me with hers? Could she trust *anyone*, for that matter? Those scars ran deep. I'm not sure *I* could. Either way, there was no going back for me.

I climbed into my Navigator and drove home, my brain overthinking everything. Inside the cottage, I called the one person I hoped could fill in some of the blanks.

"Hey, JC. Is everything okay?"

I pinched the bridge of my nose with my thumb and forefinger. "I'm not sure, Dennis. I'm hoping you can help me understand a few things." And then I relayed to him everything that had gone down in Montpelier.

Dennis didn't speak for a moment. "I'm sorry that happened. Poor Iris. That must've been devastating for her. Nicole has always blamed Iris for the affair."

I stepped out onto the back deck. "You and I both know that Iris isn't Brody's only *indiscretion,* right?"

"I suspect you're right, JC, but I've never seen him with another woman myself. I can't confirm that is true."

I was losing my patience. "Tell me what you *can* confirm, then, Dennis. I want to hear it all."

He took a breath. "Well, I moved here from New Hampshire about fifteen years ago, hoping to make a start with my clinic. I ran into some snags with the town council, and Brody helped smooth things over."

"What kind of snags?"

"The kind that involved one council member not liking Black people. *That* kind. Most of the people I have encountered were the opposite. A few even rallied for me, Brody being one of them."

"I see. Some people are just dicks. Go on." Normally, I'd offer more support and share my outrage. Now, though, I was too focused on Iris.

"I had a few hellions try to make trouble for me when Vanessa and I had first opened, but that was where Tom came to my aid. I was grateful for their help, and so, we became friends. I didn't even know Brody was seeing Iris until one night when he called me frantic, saying she had fallen. He had explained where he was and that she was seven months pregnant with his baby, and she was bleeding. He said she was on the ground, and he didn't dare move her."

"What did you do?"

"I told him to call an ambulance. But unfortunately, ambulances in your area are a bit harder to come by. Brody also begged me to keep this under wraps."

Of course, he did. I didn't think my opinion of Brody could have sank any lower, but it had.

"He asked if I could come help her. As luck would have it, I had recently saved a woman's dog who had fallen off a ledge. The woman happened to be Dr. Perry, who told me to call her if I ever needed a favor. This is the same woman who saw Iris the other day." His voice lightened. "I don't think she expected me to take her up on a favor of this magnitude, but I did, anyway. I had medical training for animals, not humans, and being that Iris was pregnant, I couldn't risk making a mistake."

I tried to imagine it all as he spoke, Iris on the ground clutching her belly, and Brody still trying to save his worthless ass.

"As it turned out, I'd made the right decision. Dr. Perry, Gloria, came with me. We brought IV bags and everything we could think of we'd need. She didn't understand why Brody didn't take Iris to the hospital, and I was at a loss to explain it myself since I didn't even know Iris existed. The population is small here, but it's also a very rural area. Folks go years without seeing each other. Some stories ride the wind. Others, they bury." He cleared his throat. "Anyway, when we arrived, Iris was lying on the ground in front of the house where she lives now."

I could guess that Iris was the same then as she was now, kind to everyone. She would have been so very young. And she put her faith in Brody, a man I suspected only wanted a cheap thrill.

"Brody kept saying that he didn't dare to move her. He said she fell down the steps right onto her stomach. Blood pooled between her legs, which Gloria pointed out. If I had taken a moment to assess what I was seeing, I might have questioned things."

"What things?"

"I don't know exactly. The position she was in on the ground. Why Brody hadn't at least rolled her over? Gloria was insisting we report it." He took a breath. "Until Tom showed up."

I could feel my insides quaking as a bad feeling festered in my gut. I was sure I was going to puke. But I pushed those feelings aside for the moment. "Why was Tom there?"

"Personally, I think he was there to support Brody. He was a deputy at the time. But he looked official enough. Whatever the reason, it seemed to satisfy Gloria's discomfort. And to be honest, there wasn't a lot of time to waste. We got her inside, all while Iris kept begging us to save her daughter, Jade."

Tom was there. Brody had caused all of this. Iris never had a chance. Tears drenched my cheeks, the scene playing out in my mind. Unable to stand through this, I sat at the bistro, trying to keep my shit together. I'd never felt such sadness in my life.

"As you know, we couldn't save Jade. Gloria had tried her best. She filled out the birth and also the death certificate. Tom had insisted she let him handle the filing. He said that Iris and Brody were too distraught. All I could think was that we were lucky we were able to save Iris. Not knowing her blood type, we were fearful of giving her a transfusion at first. But Gloria had brought a typing kit that night, and I was able to give her *my* blood. Still, for two days, it was touch and go, but Iris made it. *Physically.*"

I wiped a hand across my cheek, my lungs shuddering. "What do you mean physically?"

"Losing that child seemed to drain the life out of her. She stayed in bed for weeks. I kept checking on her. One night, I arrived during a thunderstorm. I found her in the backyard, soaking wet and sobbing. She had insisted that we bury Jade back there. Iris was covered in mud. I quickly got her up and inside. It was the only time she had gotten out of bed. Somehow, she had rolled or dragged that stone out of the woods to Jade's grave."

Even in her devastated and depleted state, Iris was determined to get her daughter a proper tombstone. The woman was a warrior. It only made me love her more.

"Where was Brody during all of this? And did you try to contact her parents?"

"Oh, Brody tried to console her, but nothing he could say seemed to help. Before long, he started coming less and less."

The asshole had broken her spirit and then stood back and let her stay broken. I had never hated anyone more in my life. My neck and shoulders felt as though someone had pummeled me with a two-by-four, my jaw shooting pain into my temples.

"I did call her parents and left messages. They never called me back. I learned from Gloria that Iris's mother had been ill with cancer, so I didn't push it. I have to tell you, JC, I'd seen animals that were beaten down that looked better than Iris did. She needed a reason to live. And so, I thought of one."

"A dog."

"That's right. I had just gotten Laddie, who was a rescue from a woman who was too old to take care of him. He was malnourished and neglected. I brought Laddie to Iris and asked her to take care of him for me. She didn't want to, but something in Laddie's lost eyes seemed to resonate with her. It got her out of bed, if for no other reason than to care for him.

Two years later, I brought her Lily, and five years ago, Maggie."

Iris had lost her human family, so Dennis had brought her another option. "And that's where she's been ever since." I didn't ask this. I just confirmed it.

"Unfortunately. Yes, JC."

I ended the call with Dennis. But not before thanking him for saving Iris's life and giving her a reason to live again. As I had suspected, Dennis was a good man, which made me think of another good man I had put off for far too long.

It wasn't just that. I was vulnerable and needed my Gramps. A childish reaction, no doubt, but he always gave me strength. And something told me, I'd need it to survive this ordeal. Not just survive, rally. For Iris. The damage was done. A few more minutes wouldn't change that.

Inside the packet for the house, I found the sealed envelope from Gramps. As I sat on the couch, I wiped my cheeks dry and opened it, pulling out the piece of paper I had been dreading.

Dear JC,

If you are reading this letter, it is because I have passed on. The doctors had told me my ticker wasn't going to last much longer, so it is no surprise to me. Now, don't go stewing over whether or not I could have done something to fix it. I've lived a full life, JC, but when my Evie died, I lost my way. Living year after year by that woman's side, raising a family, and dancing around our farmhouse was the reason I got out of bed every morning. My soulmate, if you believe in such things. I only wish your father had found that kind of love for himself. And maybe he will someday.

But that is not what I wanted to say in this letter to you.

Thank you, JC, for being the best grandson any old geezer could ever hope for. I can't tell you how much it meant to me to have you working alongside me on the farm all those years when you were a boy. The fishing was my favorite! I suspect it was yours as well. You gave me those memories, and I will take them with me wherever I go. You never said so, but I also knew Ernie Parker was causing you grief. I did speak to the boy, but you had stopped coming by then. I want you to know I understood why you didn't tell me, even though I would have tried to help. You were proud, and you wanted to work things out on your own. I would have done the same.

We are cut from the same cloth, JC. And I am proud beyond words of the man you have matured into. What worries me now is that life will pass you by. The small step between becoming a young man and looking back with a lifetime of years behind you is shorter than you think. A blink of an eye. And so I have left you a gift to try and show you another way.

It is a house in a beautiful place called Buckingham, Vermont. You might not want this house, and I expect you might even sell it. That is your choice. But if you do decide to keep it, I hope it becomes a place where you can visit and unwind, take the boat out, and enjoy nature and all she has to offer. Don't work your life away, son. Stop and smell the roses. Find a good *woman who will stick by you and share in your life's joy. Going it alone isn't everything it's cracked up to be. I suspect your father knows this as well.*

Do me a favor. Take Evie out on the water and catch a fish for me. It's the closest thing to heaven any man or woman could ever find on earth, JC.

Love, Gramps.

PS Don't ever forget. "But man is not made for defeat . . . A man can be destroyed but not defeated." And that applies to women as well.

Speaking of which, there is a woman up the road named Iris. If you are lucky enough to meet her, tell her Callum said hello. And I enjoyed our walks together. She is young and quite spectacular if you take a moment to notice, and she is surrounded by people who are no good. Keep an eye on her place for me, will you? And don't forget to pet the dogs!

"You got it, Gramps." I lowered my head and let the tears fall where they chose, my shirt soaking up my anguish. I sobbed like I had never sobbed before.

This trip was more than just a getaway or a chance to honor my grandfather. It was transformative. I might have come here JC, a person who was naive and selfish when it came to love, but JC no longer existed. Jacob had taken his place. And it was about time for *Jacob* to go convince the love of his life that she couldn't live without him.

Chapter Twenty

Iris

As the sun continued to bake my little part of the world, I sat up from my resting spot in the grass and wiped my face yet again. The engine of a car reached my ears. Was it Jacob? Was he leaving for good? If only I could leave with him.

But Jade. I lowered my head, fresh tears stinging my eyes. My parents had deserted me. I could never do that to her. This was an impossible situation. "What a mess I've made of things." I gazed over at the monument. "I'm sorry, Jade. I wish I could go back and stop the bad thing from happening to you. You deserved a full life. I can't tell you how much I wanted to be your mom. I imagined brushing your hair and shopping with you for that perfect prom dress. I wanted to be the one you turned to when life got you down. And if I had been more careful, we would have had all those things. As soon as I knew I was pregnant, I should have left here and kept you safe." *Should have.* Two words that refused to allow a second chance. "I want so badly to have that life with you again."

A voice startled me. "Iris?"

I hopped to my feet as Brody approached, wiping my face some more and smoothing out my romper.

"What are you doing here?"

"I came to check on you. I'm sorry about Nicole. She never should have spoken to you like that. I had no idea what she was up to, either."

And there he stood, the *man* who was anything but. He was a coward and a cheat. My chest burning with disgust, I shook my head. "And yet, you've stayed married to her all these years. I'll ask you again. What are you doing here, Brody?" Standing across from him, I struggled to recall what I had ever seen in this man so long ago. I hated everything about him, from his curly black hair to his lying blue eyes. The only emotion that remained was revulsion and maybe pity.

"I came to see you." His gaze landed on the boulder standing ground directly behind me. "And Jade."

My hands balled into fists. "Don't you dare say her name! She is *not* yours!" I wagged my fist at him. Rage boiled in my chest. My insides were in complete meltdown.

He stepped closer, offering a deep sigh. "She was ours, Iris. What happened was an accident. I miss her too. That's why I brought you a card on her birthday every year. April 11th. To show you I still cared."

His somber tone and weepy eyes infuriated me. None of it was genuine.

"If you had really cared, you would have driven up my driveway and faced me. You left those cards for one reason: to keep me stuck. Keep me hoping you'd come back. The truth of the matter is, you *stole* Jade from me."

"I did nothing of the sort. Why are you saying this? What happened was an accident."

It wasn't an accident. He knew it, and I knew it. I just let him believe that I didn't remember the truth. And there might have even been a time that I believed the lie myself. Those cards were his attempt to gaslight and trap me. *Don't blame yourself.* I was distraught and trying to cope. And I had blamed myself for being in a situation I never should have allowed. But it wasn't me who had hurt our baby. It was him! And I hated him for it. He took everything from me and left me here to rot in my sorrow. If it hadn't been for Dennis, I'd be with Jade right now.

For years, I could feel my heart giving up. But Jacob had breathed new life into my soul, and I could see things clearly now. Mostly, what a monster Brody and his wife were. Jacob was right. They deserved each other. He *never* deserved me.

"I don't want you here!" I stomped one foot. "Get out!" Where was my gun? *Jacob has it.* He had brought it to his place when they were landscaping. And here I was, caught unprotected. *Again!*

Brody reached one hand toward me, his eyes shining with fake tears. "Please, Iris. Just give me a chance to explain," he pleaded.

I wanted to laugh at him, but I was too angry. "Explain? What are you talking about?"

"Why I stayed with Nicole. I knew you wanted me to leave her. She threatened to take my kids away from me. You don't understand the pressure I was under. Three years ago, Warren told her you were living here. She thought I had bought the house to rent it out. She never knew it was you living here. Until Warren *and* Dylan told her. That's why she sent Warren. She's spiteful. I don't love her. I haven't loved her for years. Because I love you!"

I couldn't believe my ears. I was dumbfounded. It amazed even me how out of touch Brody was with reality. "First of all, the pressure *you* were under?" I grit my teeth. "The pressure *you* were under? Do you have any idea what it was like for me?" I slapped my chest as I spoke. "Did you have a child growing inside of you at seventeen? Did your parents up and leave *you*? I trusted you, and you betrayed my trust. You were never going to be there for me. It was all a bunch of lies. You groomed me. And I was young and stupid to believe everything you said!" He was worse than a monster. He was the devil.

Unwilling to listen, he huffed at me, the lightness in his aura turning dark. This was the real Brody, the man who refused to take no for an answer. The man who had everything but always wanted more. "You don't know what you are saying."

"I know exactly what I'm saying." This was how it went ten years ago. We were right here again—the same argument. "And I want you off my property! Get out of here!"

His shoulders ratcheted back, his chin lifting. "This isn't *your* property. It's mine, Iris." He pointed at the ground. "I kept it for you all these years. I did that for you because I love you. Provided you a home to keep you close to our daughter."

Not ours. Mine. My dead daughter.

"I helped Tom file the death certificate, so she could be buried here. Tom also kept the death out of the papers. To protect us. Would a man who didn't love you do all that?"

He was insane. I had suffered at the hands of a man who couldn't see what he really was. This was how he used to be. So sure of himself, convincing me that he was the giver, and I was the one lucky enough to receive his gifts. A complete narcissist. Of course, I fell for it. I was too young and uncertain of myself to protest. And then, when I did finally take a stand . . .

What I struggled most with was the notion that he was capable of such atrocities. He'd grabbed me, and he'd even pushed me before. I should have known. He was dominating me at every turn.

"To protect us? Or to protect you?"

He hesitated.

"Was your name even on the birth certificate?"

This time, he looked away.

"Yeah, that's what I thought. You have always only looked out for one person. Yourself." I shook my head and stared off. "You said you bought me this house? You imprisoned me here is more like it. Don't stand there and tell me you love me." I walked up and pushed him. "I don't want your pathetic love. I hate you!" I pushed him again.

He grabbed my shoulders, fingers boring into my skin. "Just calm down."

Calm down.

Those were the last words he had said to me before I turned to walk away from him ten years ago. We stood on my front porch. I was leaving him. He had tried to fill my head with more lies, and I was done believing him. From behind me, he took hold of my shoulders and shook me. *Calm down*, he'd said. And then, he'd thrust my body forward. I remember the exact moment when I left his hands, nothing to stop me from falling. Panic rose in my chest. *The baby*! All Brody did was stand there and watch me fall. I had blamed myself, but it wasn't my fault. It was always his.

I yanked my shoulders away from his grasp and stood back. "It wasn't an accident. You pushed me!"

Brody shook his head, his nostrils flaring. "No! You fell. We were arguing, and you lost your balance. I didn't push you. I would never do that!"

"Yes. You. Did." I pointed, my anger cresting. "We argued because you kept making promises to me you never intended to honor. You said you'd help me go to college. You said you were unhappy with Nicole. You said you wanted us to be a family. It was all lies! And when I called you out on it—when I told you I was leaving you—you pushed me." I lost my breath for a moment. "You said you loved me, but you never loved me. You only loved yourself."

His tone changed yet again. "That's not true. I did love you. I still do. Seeing you today brought it all back. I've been miserable without you. I confronted Nicole about Warren. You have to believe that I didn't know what was going on. We can still be together. I'm finally leaving her! I'll get a good lawyer." He stared at me as though I would believe him. Or care.

I was astounded by his arrogance. "What? Are you insane? I could never be with you again. I was young and stupid when you lured me in. I'm neither of those things anymore. You repulse me!"

He moved closer. "I don't believe you. Look me in the eye and tell me you don't still love me!"

"I don't love you." I didn't hesitate. If there was a word worse than hate, that was what I felt for him.

His mouth twisted. "You're lying! Don't forget. I know you. This isn't what you want!"

A pathetic giggle gurgled up from my throat. "You love me?"

"Yes, more than anything." He was practically panting, his eyes trying so hard to convince me he wasn't the man I knew him to be. I would never make that mistake again.

"You'd do anything for me?" I crossed my arms over my chest.

He nodded and fanned his hands out. "Anything."

"Then, let me go." My entire body was overheating, beads of sweat gathering on my upper lip and forehead.

He sighed. "That, I can't do. I love you too much. And it's not what you really want."

Once again, I chuckled. "You don't know what love is. I'm leaving here. You have kept me prisoner long enough! It's time I lived again."

His face reddened as he bared his teeth. "How can you say that? How can you leave Jade?" The contempt in his eyes was a clear indication of his bloated ego.

My shoulders rose, a fire brewing behind my eyes. "I will *never* leave Jade. I will find a way to take her with me."

He placed his hands on his hips and looked away, his jaw working. "You mean, you're leaving with *him?*" Once again, his eyes grew cold, the veins in his forehead and neck thick and threatening. "I won't let you go. I love you too much. We belong together. And I am not leaving here until you understand that!" His brow furrowed over the eyes of a predator. It was the same expression he'd had ten years ago. I knew what was coming next as he came toward me.

A voice reached out in the distance. "You *will* let her go because she doesn't belong to you!"

Jacob?

Brody stopped and spun around. "This is none of your business, JC."

"Oh, it is absolutely *my* business, you son of a bitch! She's right. You've kept her prisoner here all these years, believing what happened to Jade was her fault. You *let* her think that! You are nothing but a piece of garbage!" Jacob advanced on Brody, steps measured. "She doesn't belong to you. She's not your property. What you have done to this woman is reprehensible *and* illegal. You should be locked up!"

Knowing Jacob was here gave me strength. I had never felt more certain of my feelings for these two *very different* men.

"*Why?* Because she belongs to *you* now?" Brody spoke with disgust. Fisted hands dangled by his sides.

Jacob glanced over at me and then at Brody. "She doesn't belong to anyone but herself. *She* will choose who she wants to be with and what *she* wants to do."

I had never loved anyone more. This was the man I was

destined to be with. He was my one true love. And I couldn't wait to spend our lives together. Brody was nothing. A speck of dirt on the bottom of my shoe.

Jacob flattened his lips, rage burning his cheeks. Even his eyes were hard and unforgiving. With his hands braced on his hips, Jacob took a measured breath. "I will only say this once. You need to get the fuck out of here as fast as you can. You can have your house and your fucked-up marriage. The days of you controlling this woman are over."

Jacob shook his head as though struggling to comprehend the direness of the situation. "You murdered your unborn daughter, and you nearly murdered Iris in the process. There is no forgiveness for you or making amends. If you or your wife *and her cronies* ever so much as look her way again, I will make sure it is the *last* thing you ever fucking do!" He leaned into his words, his arms bulging and his hands now clenched. "Go . . . *now* while you still have the ability to walk."

For a moment, I wasn't sure how Brody would react. He rubbed his jaw as he stood there. Jacob was strong. And I sensed Brody was sizing him up. Then, he dropped his hand. "She wasn't worth it anyway—"

Crack! Jacob's fist slammed into Brody's jaw.

Brody stumbled backward.

With lightning speed, Jacob hit him again, landing Brody on his back in the grass. He grabbed Brody's shirt collar and pulled his fist back, his eyes enraged. "Don't say I didn't warn you, asshole." Another punch to the head.

Jacob was prepared to keep punching and never stop. I could see it. I dashed over and covered his hand with mine as he pulled it back, ready to fire once again. "*He's* not worth it. He doesn't matter anymore. Please, Jacob." I touched his fiery cheeks. "Let him go, so we can start *our* life together."

It took a few seconds, but he released Brody. "You see that, scumbag, even after all you have done to her; she still came to your aid. Now get your sorry ass out of here before I change my mind." Jacob paced, trying to calm down.

Brody scrambled to his feet. He wiped blood from his mouth. When he glanced over at me, Jacob motioned like he was going to hit Brody again, but he didn't. It was a scare tactic. And it worked. Brody ran off, the engine of whatever vehicle he had arrived in, grinding to life a moment later.

I flung myself into Jacob's arms. I could feel his heart pounding against mine. "I love you. I'm so sorry." I kissed him over and over, my heart desperate for his love. "I didn't mean to push you away."

"You have nothing to be sorry for." He draped my hair back away from my shoulders. "You've spent too much time already being sorry, babe. I don't know what our next move will be, but if you'll have me, we'll make it together."

"If I'll have you?" I knocked lightly on his head. "I'm already yours, silly." We kissed, our mouths hungry and our bodies mashed together. He was sweaty and warm, and I savored all of it.

Tears ran down my face. Happy tears this time. And then, I pulled away and took his hand. "I want you to meet someone." I guided him over to my makeshift monument.

"Jade, this is Jacob. And he is the love of my life."

Jacob pulled the black-and-white photo from his back pocket. "This belongs to you. And it's so nice to meet you, Jade. You have one courageous mother. And I bet you are proud of her every day." He touched my cheek. "I know I am."

We stayed there for several minutes, staring down at the stone, neither one of us saying a word. It was as if we were both caught up in a stupor of sorts, our minds and bodies returning to a sense of normalcy.

Together, we walked to Jacob's house, hand in hand.

"Did you know that in many cultures, jade symbolizes good fortune, protection, and harmony? Do you think Jade is up there right now watching us?" I gazed up at the summer sky in wonder.

With his arm already draped around my waist, Jacob rubbed my back. "If Jade is anything like her mother, I have no doubt she is watching over us all."

We stretched out on his bed for the next several hours, holding each other and dozing in and out of consciousness. I was exhausted by the day's emotion, and I sensed Jacob was too.

Jacob shook me some time later, the room starting to darken. "Wake up, sleepy head. I made you some dinner."

I sat up and rubbed my eyes. "How long have you been up?"

He perched himself on the edge of his bed and brushed his fingers along my groggy cheek. "Not long. I figured you would be hungry. We haven't eaten all day."

Our dinner was quiet, but in a tranquil sort of way. Our emotions had trudged through some dark waters.

After dinner, we settled on the couch. A letter sat open on the side table. "Is that the letter you had told me about from your grandfather?"

Jacob's warm hand caressed my arm. "It sure is. I finally opened it."

I snuggled in closer, my arms around his waist. "I'm so proud of you."

He leaned his head onto mine. "He mentioned you in it, you know."

I lifted my head, surprised. "He did?" I was honored.

"Yup. He said to tell you hello and how much he enjoyed your walks. He also told me to keep an eye on things." Jacob pulled me back to rest against his side. "His advice was to slow down and appreciate life more. You know, stop and smell the roses."

I moved to the edge of the seat cushion.

"Your grandfather was a wise man. 'Stop and smell the roses.' I think that is good advice for us both, don't you?"

Jacob planted a tender kiss on the side of my head. "I do, too, only I prefer Irises to roses, thank you very much." He reached over and touched his cell phone, activating the home screen. "Huh," he said.

"What?" I glanced at his phone and then over at him.

"It's five minutes past midnight."

Still confused, I said, "Oh? Is there some significance to that?"

"There is. Today is a month since I arrived here. Give or take. It was the day I had *planned* to leave."

I held him closer. "I'm so glad we get to leave together now."

"Me, too, babe. There is something else important about today, though."

I sat up straight again to see him better. "Okay, I'll bite. What is so important about today?"

"It's my birthday."

What? My first thought was *I haven't gotten you anything.* And then, I realized I had. What I had to offer Jacob was more than I thought I would ever offer anyone. *Me.*

"How old are you?" I brushed my fingers through his soft hair.

"Thirty-one."

He tilted his head. "When is *your* birthday, by the way?" He took my hand that had just combed through his hair.

"September fourth." Every year, I celebrated with Lily, Maggie, and Laddie. Cupcakes for me and doggie treats for them.

Jacob blinked with sad eyes. "You've missed ten years of birthdays and holidays." He kissed my knuckles. "You just wait, woman, you're gonna have a lot of celebrating to do *this* year."

My chest filled with joy. My gift for him came to mind. "I look forward to that." I nodded. "Well, I hope you like what I got *you*." I stood before him and untied the wraparound waist of my romper, wiggling it off my shoulders, and letting it fall to the floor. Wearing a bra and panties, I stepped out of it slowly, kicking it away. "How about sixty years of this?" I swept my hand down in front of me.

I had never been so bold, but Jacob wasn't just a man to me. He was my life partner. I trusted him with my heart, something *else* I never thought possible. When you'd been alone as long as I had, unable to imagine a future or a reason to continue past tomorrow, you didn't take anything for granted. I was his for as long as he would have me.

His eyes dilated as his gaze undressed the rest of me. "I can't think of *anything* I would want more." He ran his fingers up my inner thigh, making me shiver. "This is the best gift you could ever give me."

I leaned over him and pressed my lips against his. "Happy birthday, Jacob."

Epilogue

Jacob

"Where are you taking me?"

With her eyes shrouded by a blindfold—her fingers touching the fabric—I guided Iris up the street and across a vacant parking lot.

"Just a little bit farther, babe." I kept my hands on her upper arms, making sure she didn't stumble. And when I had her in the right position, I undid the blindfold and stood back. My heart was racing with anticipation.

"Surprise!" came from a crowd of family and friends who cluttered the opening to a large white party tent with a high peak at its center, balloons flowing in the May breeze, and side-walls of faux floor-to-ceiling windows framing the party within. Tables and chairs covered in white fabric, a buffet from a local Italian place, and music, along with ample amounts of spirits and champagne, would keep everyone entertained for the afternoon.

I motioned for everyone to stay put for the moment, which I had already discussed with them prior.

Iris's mouth dropped open, which she quickly covered with both her hands. "Oh my god! Jacob, what is this?" Her eyes were about ready to pop out of her head as she stared over at me.

"We're celebrating your admission into the vet program."

"What? But I have five more years still."

"Yeah, but you're in. And *I* wanted to celebrate it." I flashed her a smile. We'd done a lot of *celebrating* over the past two years: birthdays she'd missed, holidays (Christmas in July), and even the two anniversaries of the day we had met, but this was a biggie. Not only had Iris gotten into Cornell as she had hoped, but she'd also done so well that they'd accepted her into their seven-year BS/DVM program. Only highly qualified students were allowed to apply for early acceptance during their sophomore year, and Iris was one of them. She'd have her degree in seven years, not eight. She'd still have to pass the North American Veterinary Licensing Examination (NAVLE) plus fulfill state requirements and obtain her licensure, but in my mind, those were semantics she'd conquer down the road. Getting into the right school was a biggie. She'd kicked ass, and I couldn't have been prouder.

So, by the time she had finished her exams for the year, I had already organized this party. But that wasn't all I had planned for this extraordinary woman.

"Where are we?" She gazed around in wonder.

I understood her confusion. The lot wasn't anything special. Other than the party tent, an old abandoned building stood off to the left—that we'd soon tear down—and a parking lot filled with cracks for weeds to poke through (I'd had everyone park up the street), along with a small field of over-grown brush.

"I bought the lot, babe. It's just over an acre. I'll show you the boundaries later. We have the next five years to design and build your new clinic."

That lot hadn't come cheap. I'd financed some of it and paid for the rest, but it was worth it, the location optimal for her needs.

The tears began to flow, all the way down Iris's gorgeous cheeks. And there were plenty of them. I had done well. *Yes!* I hugged Iris and rubbed her back. Her tender heart always pulled at my own.

"How?" she whispered in my ear. "And so close to home."

That's right. The city boy in me was now embracing suburbia. We lived only eight miles away in Rumson, New Jersey. A house meant for many—five bedrooms to be precise, with a large four-car garage for my *toys*. I hired an architect to help me remodel our spacious house with a sizable yard. We had to include room for Lily and Maggie to run around.

Unfortunately, we'd lost Laddie last year to old age, and that just about broke Iris's heart, but I reminded her that Laddie would be well taken care of by my awesome grandparents and especially Jade. (We kept her daughter's ashes in a special urn in our living room.)

"Oh, Jacob." This is . . ."

I waved my hand, cueing my sisters to unroll a large banner, revealing the name of her future clinic: "Jersey Animal Doctor & Emergency." My gaze stayed glued to her face, waiting for a reaction. I'd been excited before, but this topped the scales. "What do you think? We can change the name if you'd like."

She was speechless. I loved it when words failed her. Tears, however, had no trouble glistening her eyes. "It's perfect." She sobbed against my chest. "I never thought . . . this is a dream come true."

Feeling pretty fucking proud of myself, I pointed. "Do you notice the acronym?" I knew she had, but I wasn't quite done patting myself on the back yet.

With her voice filled with joy and exuberance, she stood back and faced the tent. "I did. It spells out Jade." She bit down on her lower lip.

My sisters stood on chairs to hang the sign on two hooks residing over the tent's doorway as the rest of the crew descended upon Iris with hugs and words of encouragement. Lily and Maggie trotted over on their leashes, led by Dennis and Vanessa, their honorary grandparents. *My* parents were there as well as Iris's. She'd extended an olive branch to her family over a year ago. We even made the trip to Harrisburg, PA, to see them. They weren't bad people, just more reserved and, as she'd said, very religious. My heart struggled to open to them, knowing how they had abandoned their daughter, but I put on a good face, making it abundantly clear how smart and successful their daughter was and continued to be. *You should be proud.* Were they? It was hard to say. But for an occasion such as this one, I felt they should be invited.

My parents weren't fixtures in our lives either. Iris and I had decided that it was all fine with us. We had each other, plus a few close family members and friends. We had Lily and Maggie. And someday, our family would grow. She might have five more years of higher education, but that didn't mean she couldn't get married and enjoy life to its fullest within that timeframe. As far as I was concerned, she'd wasted too much time being sad already.

"Okay, everyone. Now, go get something to eat and drink, and I'll bring our guest of honor in a minute."

When we were alone again, Iris cradled my face in her soft hands. "Jacob, how did you do all this without me knowing about it? Was the land expensive? Can we afford it?"

I kissed her long and hard. "I've got it covered. Need I remind you of my extensive talents? You have quite a catch for a boyfriend, you know." I feigned arrogance.

She shook her head vehemently. "No need to remind me. I'm abundantly aware. Thank you. I am so happy, I feel like I need to pinch myself."

"Well, don't pinch yourself too hard. Cause it's all real, babe. And soon, it will be all yours. You earned it. Scott is going to help us design the clinic." Scott was the one who had helped with our house remodel.

I put my elbow out for her to take. "Shall we join the party? I hope you're hungry. I also bought champagne for a toast." What I didn't tell her was that after the festivities came to an end, I had a violinist arriving, along with an entire crew from one of our favorite restaurants in the city, to transform the party tent into an elegant dining experience. Since Vanessa and Dennis were staying with us, they agreed to take the dogs off our hands. The forecast promised a clear sky, with nighttime temperatures remaining in the low 70s. Mother Nature was cooperating on this springtime night in late May.

And that would be where I would propose to this woman, offering her my heart and my life for all eternity. The custom ring I had chosen for her wasn't made with one big stone, but many. A double band in platinum loaded with diamonds and intermixed with sapphires to match her beautiful eyes, an imperial jade at its center to honor her precious daughter. We'd have our own kids someday, and I relished the thought.

After we left Vermont, Nicole and Brody finally called it quits. Nicole was so angry at Brody that she burned the house Iris had lived in to the ground, with the help of Warren, whom she was apparently sleeping with to coerce into doing her bidding. It seemed they both liked them young.

Brody pressed charges against Nicole and Warren for

arson, and the two of them went at each other's throats, their lawyers growing richer by the day. While that was going on, I bullied Brody into selling *me* the land. All of it. I reminded him of the shit I had on him, making sure to highlight that there was no statute of limitations on murder. Whether Brody intended to kill Jade and severely injure Iris, we would never know, but it didn't really matter when it came to my argument. He would sell me the land or risk spending his life in prison. I realized that he had Tom on his side as a witness. But I had Dennis, who had cut ties with both of those losers. Even if Brody won, his reputation in the community would be permanently tarnished.

If Iris had said the word, I would have done everything in my power to bring his sorry ass to justice, regardless of the land. But as Iris had pointed out, things ran a bit differently in that neck of the woods. Not only that, but she also wanted to stop dwelling on the past. It was time to focus on *our* future.

A demolition crew did a great job tearing down what was left of the old house, which was replaced by fields of undeveloped land. Iris was part of the entire process. It was cathartic for her, she'd said. The ending of a life gone wrong and the start of one that would bring her nothing but joy.

I hung on to Gramps's place by the pond, the boulder making the short trip to its new digs. The cottage became our retreat for when the demands of life dragged us down. I owned all the land surrounding it now, which flourished with wildflowers in the summer months.

I also paved that goddamn road!

Someday, we planned to build an addition when our family expanded, but for now, it was our *heaven on earth.*

Life was a funny thing. I was so trapped in a way of existing from day to day that I couldn't see the possibilities around me.

Not anymore. I was given a second chance at a future with a woman who took my breath away every time she walked into a room.

And not a day has passed since, when I couldn't say I had *never* been happier.

Tell me what you think ...

I'd love to know how you felt about this book. And I would be grateful for an honest review on Amazon and Goodreads. A few words are plenty and can make all the difference in how I plan my next novel.

Acknowledgments

I had to check the calendar the other day to see how many years I have been publishing books. I had guessed four years, but upon further inspection, I realized it has only been three. *Let Me Go* is the seventh book in my collection, and I am excited to share it with you. This story started off a bit slow, but gained momentum as Jacob and Iris came to life on the page. Their strength and passion for each other continues to inspire me.

One fact that has never changed over the course of three years, is my appreciation for my editor, Melissa Shelton Harrison, who has become more of a right hand to my work. Melissa understands where I want to take my books and meets me there every time. Her skills as an editor, proofreader, and overall friend are beyond anything I could ever hope for. I am grateful for Melissa every day!

My proofreaders Hattie and Ryan LaRochelle are not only family, but they are gifted at finding blemishes in the work to the nth degree. They are also my support system and always there when I need them. I look forward to the bottle of celebratory wine and inspirational card from Hattie every launch!

Another growing tradition is sending Laurie Geraci a copy of my book before everyone else. I do this because Laurie is a champion reader and book blogger. She is also a huge supporter of my work. A launch wouldn't be the same without her input and support. As a bonus, she is also a sweetheart of a person.

There are so many aspects to publishing that have little to

do with editing. Maddee and Riley at Xuni.com for website work as well as Amy and Lauren from Indie Penn PR present my books to the world in a thorough and professional manner. They make me look good, and I am grateful to them for the many hours involved to make it so.

I'm always in awe of you book bloggers, Laurie from Reading in the Red Room, and Reading by Deb—among many others. You continue to rock my world.

A big thank you to my wonderful hubby, Bob, who has been there since this idea of publishing spawned. He celebrates the wins and consoles the losses. And I am truly grateful that he is with me on this exciting journey.

And no acknowledgement page would be complete without thanking my readers, subscribers, and friends who have stuck with me. Terry M, Anna P, Cheri G, Dawn M, Robyn X, Mary and Jess T, Marta M, Michael B, and Craig H (Craig writes the best book reviews on the planet), thank you all for being on my team. And to everyone else who I haven't mentioned here, but I keep warm in my heart. You all honor me with your presence in my life.

About the Author

Tricia T. LaRochelle is the award-winning author of the Sara Browne Series, a gripping romantic suspense along with *Sun in My Heart* and *A Collision with Love*, her stand-alone romances with a twist. (Her next stand-alone, *Let Me Go*, launches in June 2025.) Gut-wrenching romances with unforeseen plot twists are where she thrives. Her apologies ahead of time for the tears. 😊

Coming from a background and education in Marketing, Tricia has spent the past eleven years pursuing her author endeavors. She now lives in Virginia with her husband and new pup, Daisy, who keeps her on her toes. She enjoys long walks with her hubby, time with her two grown sons and DILs, and board games that bring out the silly.

Subscribe to her newsletter at TriciaLaRochelle.com, where you can receive updates on her work, announcements, and giveaways, or follow her on social media.

Also by Tricia T. LaRochelle

Sara Browne Series Romantic Suspense:

Flickering Heart - Book 1 (Available on Audible)

Revive - Book 2 (Available on Audible)

Handfast - Book 3

Bleeding Heart - A Holiday Romance - Book 4

Stand-alone Contemporary Romances:

Sun in My Heart (Available on Audible)

A Collision with Love

Let Me Go

A new stand-alone coming soon!

9 798990 910751